SAVING

CRAFTER

Books by Mark Cheverton

The Gameknight999 Series
Invasion of the Overworld
Battle for the Nether
Confronting the Dragon

The Mystery of Herobrine Series:
A Gameknight999 Adventure
Trouble in Zombie-town
The Jungle Temple Oracle
Last Stand on the Ocean Shore

Herobrine Reborn Series:
A Gameknight999 Adventure
Saving Crafter
The Destruction of the Overworld
(Coming soon!)
Gameknight999 vs. Herobrine
(Coming soon!)

a Gameknight999 adv

SAVING
CRAFTER

HEROBRINE REBORN
BOOK ONE

MARK CHEVERTON

SIMON AND SCHUSTER

First published in Great Britain in 2015
by Simon & Schuster UK Ltd
A CBS COMPANY

Originally published in the USA in 2015 by Sky Pony Press

3 5 7 9 10 8 6 4 2

Simon & Schuster UK Ltd
1st Floor
222 Gray's Inn Road
London WC1X 8HB

www.simonandschuster.co.uk

Simon & Schuster Australia, Sydney
Simon & Schuster India, New Delhi

A CIP catalogue record for this book is available from the British Library

Saving Crafter is an original work of fan fiction that is not
associated with Minecraft or MojangAB. It is not sanctioned
nor has it been approved by the makers of Minecraft.

PB ISBN: 978-1-4711-4495-0
Ebook ISBN: 978-1-4711-4496-7

Printed an

Simon &
that is made from
Stewardship Coun
Our books dis

est
on.

Falkirk Council		
Askews & Holts	2016	
JF JF	£5.99	

ACKNOWLEDGMENTS

I'd like to thank my family for putting up with my long hours writing, for waking them up at 4:00 a.m., writing, and spending the weekends writing, and generally spending every free second writing. I couldn't have written all these books without their support.

I'd also like to thank the readers—without all your kind words sent to me through my website, www.markcheverton.com, I would have likely lost the strength to continue when I was exhausted, but your support and encouragement has kept me writing. Thank you for all your support!

"As a child, we crave to be treated like a big kid; at the end of adolescence, we want the respect of adulthood. But both of these transitions require the shouldering of responsibility and the desire to reach farther than we can reach and become more than we were yesterday."

—Monkeypants271

CHAPTER 1

CRAFTER

Looking down on the battlefield, Crafter watched as the last of the zombie horde disappeared into the woods, their fallen comrades leaving behind glowing balls of XP and the occasional sword. Piles of zombie flesh floated about across the grassy plain.

"They almost made it to the village gates that time," Stitcher said.

She paced nervously along the battlement, her eyes probing the forest for any sign they might return.

Crafter grunted his agreement.

"If they didn't have all those leather caps, they'd be forced to attack at night," Digger said. "Then at least we'd know when to expect them."

"The zombie king is driving them harder and harder," Hunter added as she put away her bow and wiped her square forehead with a green sleeve. "Did you hear the zombies during the battle? They blame us for the defeat of their king's master, Herobrine."

"Yes, I heard them," Crafter snapped. "Everybody heard them. The zombie commander screamed it loud enough for all of Minecraft to hear him."

"We need to do something. We need ... you know ... *him*," Hunter said.

"He's done enough for us," Crafter said as he walked across the top of the wall and took the stairs down to the ground level. "We need to learn to defeat these monsters on our own."

He stopped at the foot of the stairs and looked back up at Hunter. The noon sun shown down on her curly red hair, causing it to glow with a crimson aura.

"Besides, the decision by the Council of Crafters still holds; we cannot interact with users for any reason—no matter what," Crafter explained. "Would you be asking him to risk his life again and come back *into* Minecraft? Are we that desperate?"

"Well ... I don't think ..." she stammered.

"We will let Gameknight999 live his life in the physical world while we live ours in the digital world," Crafter explained. "Is that understood?"

Hunter nodded her head as she moved down the stairway, her curls bouncing like little scarlet springs.

Crafter gave her a smile, then moved out through the iron doors to examine the battlefield closer. The lanky form of Herder followed close behind.

"Baker, collect all that XP," Crafter ordered one of the NPCs. "Give it to Smithy; we need some more enchanted armor. Gather it quickly before it disappears. Digger, we need some archer towers on either side of the bridge that crosses the moat. When Xa-Tul returns with a bigger zombie army, he'll be able to cross the bridge and reach the iron doors. With that huge golden sword of his, he'd smash them to bits within seconds and open the village to his horde. We have to protect it."

Digger nodded.

"Herder," Crafter continued, "we need your wolves to . . ."

Stopping in mid-sentence, the young NPC looked at the grassy plain before him, his bright blue eyes open wide with surprise. Zigzagging across the grassy plain was what looked like a dark, shadowy bolt of lightning. No, not a lightning bolt—the shadow of a lightning bolt, for it was all black, a diseased stain on the surface of the Overworld. It moved erratically, zipped forward in one direction, then abruptly turned and moved in another. Like a hound sniffing after a wild rabbit, the jagged shadow shot about the plain, stalking something. In a second, it had reached Baker and touched his foot. Instantly, the NPC yelled out in pain as black shafts of . . . something . . . stabbed at his foot.

"Baker, are you alright?" Crafter asked.

The dark stain seemed to hear Crafter's voice. It moved away from Baker and headed toward the young NPC. Herder stepped in front of his friend and looked down at the shadowy presence. When it touched the tip of the lanky boy's foot, he jumped into the air like he'd stepped on burning coals. Suddenly, the jagged stain turned when it had found the scent of its prey and shot straight for Crafter. As he took a step back, Crafter felt an evil presence emanate from the jagged shadow; hateful spite rose from it like steam from a boiling pot. Turning to run away, Crafter took a single step, but the shadowy form had found its target. It jolted forward with lightning speed, enveloping the ground under the young NPC's feet.

Crafter screamed out in agony as the shadow of evil attacked him from the ground. Dark shapes shot from the diseased patch like shadowy jagged blades. They stabbed at Crafter over and over again, causing his body to flash red, signifying the consumption of his HP. Hunter ran to Crafter's side and shot an arrow into the shadowy stain, but the barbed projectile just sank into the sandy ground, having done nothing.

Crafter moaned as he fell to the ground. Dropping her bow, Hunter caught the young boy. She held him above the ground and away from the darkness. It tried to reach Crafter, slicing the air with slivers of darkness, but could not. Hunter jumped from here to there, playing a deadly game of keep-away. As she held her friend high over her head, the shadow of evil evaporated, leaving behind a scarred patch of ground where it had killed the grass and flowers. Eventually, satisfied the threat was gone, she slowly lowered him to the ground.

"Crafter, are you alright?" she said softly.

NPCs ran out of the village gates to help their leader. A group of horsemen rode quickly across the bridge that spanned the moat and streaked past their fallen leader. Taking up defensive position, the cavalry readied themselves for battle in case the zombies were preparing an attack.

"Hun . . . ter," Crafter said weakly.

She looked down at him and could see that his skin was pale. He was cold to the touch. His normally bright blue eyes were dim and faded, as if the life had been sucked out of them. A worried look came across her face.

"Crafter, are you OK?"

He shook his head slightly, then tried to speak, but he was too weak to be heard.

"What was that?" she asked in a low voice.

He shook his head again. Leaning down, Hunter brought her ear to Crafter's lips.

His voice was so weak. Terrified thoughts of Crafter dying shot through her mind and chilled her to the bone.

Taking a strained breath, Crafter tried to speak again. "Bring Gameknight99—"

And then he fell unconscious, his breathing labored

"What did he say?" Digger asked.

Looking up, Hunter was surprised. She hadn't noticed the big NPC next to her.

"He said to bring . . . *him*," she said. "It must be serious."

Standing, she scooped the young NPC into her arms and handed him to Digger.

"Take him to Healer," she said. "I will handle the rest."

"You should take others with you," Digger said, motioning for the cavalry to approach.

"No, I can move faster alone," she said and asked for two of the warriors to dismount. Jumping into the saddle, she took the lead to the second horse. Turning, she looked down at Digger. "Take care of him. I'll be back as quickly as I can."

"We will do what is needed."

"I know you will." She then turned her horse, pointed toward the dark forest, and patted the horse on the neck. "I need every ounce of speed you can give me, horse, for we ride to save Crafter."

Sprinting away, she disappeared into the woods.

But where will I find Gameknight999? she thought as she galloped across the Overworld.

CHAPTER 2

GAMEKNIGHT999

Gameknight999 swung his sword at his adversary's head, stopping just short of actually striking a blow.

"You're supposed to block," he sighed. "I told you—don't just focus on attack; block as well."

"I don't see what this has to do with playing Minecraft," his opponent complained.

"There are monsters out there who will try to kill you," Gameknight explained. "You have to know how to defend yourself or you'll just die right away. Now come on, Dad, concentrate!"

Bringing up his wooden sword, Gameknight pointed it at his father.

"Are you ready?" he asked.

His father, Monkeypants271, nodded his head. His appearance was that of a monkey dressed in a Superman outfit, complete with red boots and a large "S" painted on his chest.

Gameknight looked at his father and just shook his head.

"Why did you have to choose that ridiculous skin?" he asked his father.

"All the other skins looked like warriors or ninjas or monsters," Monkeypants explained. "I wanted something that would stand out and people would remember."

"Well, if that was your goal, you nailed it." Gameknight said.

Monkeypants grinned.

"And what about that name? Really, Monkeypants?"

"I like it, don't you?" his father asked.

Gameknight shook his head, embarrassed.

A ridiculous name and a ridiculous skin, Gameknight thought. *What was I thinking, trying to teach my dad how to play Minecraft?*

At least his father was home instead of away on one of his many trips. Gameknight was glad his dad was back, though having to teach him how to play Minecraft wasn't what he had planned for their time together. He wanted him here, at home, just not down here in the basement or in Minecraft ... in *Gameknight's* domain. What could he say? His father knew how rough it was on the family when he was gone. But was this how he was trying to make up for it, all in one day? By playing Minecraft?

"Come on, let's try this PnP thing again," Monkeypants said, raising his own wooden sword, ready for battle.

Gameknight sighed.

"I told you a hundred times, *Monkeypants*. It's not PnP, it's PvP."

"Oh yeah," his father answered. "PnP is a transistor junction in computer chips, me bad."

"Not me bad, *my* bad!" Gameknight shouted, exasperated.

"There's a difference?"

Gameknight shook his head again, frustration boiling just beneath the surface. Looking past his father, he could see a tall outcropping that stood some twenty blocks in the air, a long stream of water falling from its height and flowing into a deep underground chamber. That was their next destination: the underground tunnels where zombies would be lurking. But first he had to teach his father how to fight or it would be a quick trip.

Sighing, he readied another lame attack to demonstrate fighting in Minecraft.

Why is he doing this? Gameknight thought. *Why is he pretending that he wants to learn how to fight? I know he hates this. All he ever wants to do is build and invent ... and the funny thing is, that's all I want to do with him. Why doesn't he realize that?*

Gameknight could remember the countless hours he'd spent with his father, building invention after invention in their basement. He loved those times, but his father was never home anymore and those invention sessions had happened so long ago.

It's unfair. Jenny has her art, that's her

thing. But my thing is helping my dad build new creations, and I can't do that when he's always gone. Gameknight was getting angry. *He's never home, and now that he is, we're wasting time in Minecraft!*

Gripping his wooden sword firmly, he danced from foot to foot as he allowed his anger to slowly dissolve, then sprang forward, his blade streaking through the air. As he neared, Monkeypants just dropped his sword and stared over his son's shoulder. Gameknight stopped the attack and started to yell at his father, but Monkeypants raised a hand and pointed to the edge of the basin where they were practicing.

Looking in the direction his father was pointing, Gameknight999 was surprised to see Hunter approaching on horseback, a riderless horse trailing behind. She rode to the edge of the falling water, then dismounted right where Gameknight had battled that spider on his first day trapped inside Minecraft. As soon as her feet hit the ground, her hands slid into her sleeves, arms linked across her chest.

Gameknight signed.

"The Council of Crafters has decided that users and NPCs must stay separate?" Gameknight asked.

Hunter nodded her head, her red hair appearing to be painted to the side of her head rather than the flowing curls that Gameknight had become accustomed to seeing. He wasn't *in* the game now, as he had been before.

In the past, Gameknight had used his father's invention, the digitizer, to actually enter the game and live it for real. While he was *in* Minecraft, everything looked so vivid, with more detail than he'd ever seen on the screen. But right now, everything was flat and just looked painted on the surface—like Hunter's curls. Gameknight and Monkeypants weren't really *in* the game, they were just playing it; a pair of users practicing their PvP skills.

Hunter glanced above Gameknight's head, then looked back down at him. He figured she was looking at the shining white server thread that stretched up from his head and high into the sky, connecting him to the servers. Only NPCs could see the server threads; that was how they knew who was a user and who was an NPC. Well, that and the letters that floated above his head.

"Why are you here?" Gameknight asked.

She did not respond. Instead, she glanced at the horses, leaning her square face toward him and then toward the horse.

"I think she wants you to go with her," Monkeypants said.

Gameknight looked at his father. Monkeypants stepped forward as he put away his wooden sword and moved to his son's side. Turning back to Hunter, Gameknight saw that she had mounted her horse again. The rider-less mount leaned its head down into the pool of water and took a drink.

"What's wrong? Is everyone alright?" Gameknight asked.

She shook her head.

"Is it Stitcher?" he asked.

She shook her head again.

"Herder? Digger?"

She said no.

"Crafter?"

She nodded.

"Oh no, not Crafter! What's wrong?"

Hunter looked at the riderless horse and looked back down at Gameknight.

"I understand," he replied.

After he leapt up onto the horse, Gameknight999 turned and looked back at his dad.

"Oh, no you don't," his father complained. "I'm going with you."

Monkeypants ran toward the horse and leapt up into the saddle behind his son.

"Let's go," Gameknight said as he turned to face Hunter, but she was already riding away toward the village.

Urging the horse to a gallop, he followed his friend toward the village that lay hidden behind the horizon. Glancing at the sun overhead, Gameknight knew it would only be up for a few more hours; they would barely make it to the village before sundown, and only if there were no delays.

"Monkeypants, take out your bow and get ready to use it," Gameknight said as they galloped across the landscape. "There will be more monsters as it gets closer to sundown, and we can't afford to let any of them slow us down. If you see any monsters, shoot them. Don't wait for an invitation. Do you understand?"

"That seems pretty ... violent," Monkeypants said. "You know, sometimes there's a better way other than the sword."

"Yeah? You tell the monsters that when they attack," Gameknight replied.

"Son, you will have to make choices in life when faced with challenges," his father lectured. "You will have to decide if you're going to do the *right* thing that will help the most people, or take the easy path and do the wrong thing. Violence is almost always the wrong path, for it just leads to more violence. Maybe we need to think of another way."

"Dad, you still don't understand Minecraft. Any monster you see will want to attack you over and over until all of your HP is gone. For us right now, we'd just respawn back near our hidey-hole, but for the NPCs, it means death. So we have to look out for them and make sure that they're safe, and the only way we can do that is if we're alive ... you understand?"

"Well ... yeah, I guess so," Monkeypants answered.

"So if you see a monster, like that spider over there," Gameknight said, pointing to the top of an oak tree. "You attack it before it can attack you.That's how you stay alive in Minecraft."

Monkeypants nodded his head, but

Gameknight999 could tell that he still didn't get it.

Hunter veered to the right; she'd seen the monster hiding in the tree branches. As they skirted around it, Gameknight kept a watchful eye on the creature. The spider sat atop the leafy canopy, glaring at them with its multiple red eyes, a look of anger in those tiny glowing orbs. Monkeypants drew an arrow back and aimed it at the monster but did not fire. Instead, he only watched it as they passed.

Spurring his horse forward, Gameknight followed Hunter's stead, moving from a trot to a gallop. As he rode, his thoughts went to his friend in trouble. *I won't let anything happen to you, Crafter,* he thought. *I'll take care of everything.*

He tried to make his thoughts sound confident and strong, but he knew that things must be dire to warrant Hunter looking for him. Driving his horse even faster, he thought about all of his friends while his soul filled with dread.

CHAPTER 3

THE VILLAGE

The trio rode across the landscape in silence, pushing the horses as fast as they could go. Glancing nervously at the square sun overhead, Gameknight followed its progress as it slowly crept down toward the horizon. They had to make it to the village before sundown or they were in trouble; in Minecraft, nighttime was monster-time.

Shifting his eyes from left to right, Gameknight was on high alert. He could hear the clicking of spiders echoing across the land, but he didn't see any of the fearsome creatures.

"What is that sound?" Monkeypants asked.

"Giant spiders," Gameknight answered.

"I'm sorry I asked. Where are they?"

"They're hiding. Usually they would attack anyone found on the surface of the Overworld, but that was before."

"Before what?" Monkeypants asked.

Gameknight brought his horse up next to

Hunter's and looked at his friend. She turned her head and gave him a knowing smile, then turned and looked forward.

"Before we killed their queen, Shaikulud," Gameknight said proudly.

"You killed their queen?" his father asked. "Why?"

"Well, she was trying to kill all of us," Gameknight999 explained. "The spider queen was leading a massive army against everyone in Crafter's village. I did what I had to so that my friends would be safe."

Monkeypants nodded his head and said nothing. Gameknight couldn't see the look of pride on his father's face.

"So what do you think is going on now?" Monkeypants asked.

"I don't know. Hunter said it was something about Crafter," Gameknight said as he turned his head so that he could look at his father over his shoulder. "He's my best friend, Dad, not just in Minecraft, but . . . in the whole world. I have to help him."

"Well, I guess we will found out soon," Monkeypants said as he pointed a stubby square finger forward.

Gameknight turned and could see the village in the distance. A tall cobblestone wall ringed the collection of wooden buildings, a watery moat surrounding the fortification. A narrow wooden bridge spanned the moat, stretching across to the iron gates embedded in the barricade. The orange light from the setting sun reflected off the metallic doors, making them appear to glow as though heated from within. It was beautiful. Tall archer towers loomed high up in the air, positioned near the bridge to give the warriors a clear field of fire upon those foolish enough to cross the walkway uninvited.

"We have to hurry," Gameknight said as the sky darkened, the bright orange slowly blushing to red.

As they approached the village, they could hear the sad growling moans of zombies in the nearby forest. Glancing at the dark collection of trees, Gameknight could see the decaying creatures gathering near the tree line. Those with leather caps stood out in the sunlight, their head-covering keeping them safe from the burning rays of the sun. Those without were hiding in the ever-darkening shade.

"Are those real zombies?" Monkeypants asked, his voice filled with excitement.

"Yes."

"Let's go closer. I want to see them."

"This isn't a game for these villagers, Dad. The zombies are going to try to break into the village and destroy everything. We need to do what we can to help them, and that means getting inside the village as quickly as we can."

Spurring their horses into a sprint, they headed straight for the wooden bridge that led into the village. When they neared, Gameknight jumped off and landed gracefully on the ground.

"Monkeypants, go into the village!" Gameknight shouted as he ran toward the zombie mob. "I'll be there in a few minutes."

"But what about—"

"Just trust me and follow Hunter. I'll be right behind you."

Not waiting to see if his father listened, Gameknight ran straight toward the tree line. Looking up, he smiled as the sparkling faces of stars emerged on the darkening sky. He stopped at a place he knew was still within range of the archer towers and pulled out blocks of TNT. He placed them on the ground in plain sight and spread them out across the battlefield. Running toward the bridge, he placed more of the striped blocks on the ground. As he crossed the wooden overpass, he placed four explosive blocks right in the middle and then ran for the iron doors. When he passed through the entrance, he looked for the person who he knew would be nearby—Stitcher. He found her on the top of the cobblestone wall. Her bow was likely tucked away in her inventory, her arms linked across her chest.

"Stitcher, shoot the TNT if you need to drive the zombies back," he yelled to her. "Destroy the bridge if you must. It would be better to rebuild it rather than let the monsters reach the doors."

He knew she wouldn't respond, so he turned and sprinted for the cobblestone tower that stood at the center of the village. He found Hunter standing near the entrance,

Monkeypants at her side. As soon as she saw him, she walked through the open doorway and moved into the building.

"Come on, Monkeypants," Gameknight said as he streaked past his father.

Moving to the far side of the room, he pulled out his pickaxe and dug into the corner block. After three strong blows, the cobblestone shattered, revealing a dark vertical shaft, a ladder clinging to one wall. Without waiting, Hunter stepped onto the ladder and disappeared into the darkness.

"Follow me," Gameknight explained. "We're heading for the crafting chamber. That must be where Crafter is."

Gameknight stepped onto the ladder and began his climb down. He could hear the footsteps of his father above him, though he could see little in the darkness of the tunnel. As he descended, Gameknight looked down and could see a faint circle of light in the distance—a torch marking the end of the vertical descent. Slowly, the tunnel grew brighter as he drew near the end. Jumping off the ladder, he found Hunter waiting for him, a look of annoyed impatience on her face. Gesturing him to follow, she sprinted down the horizontal passage. After running a dozen blocks, she stopped and placed blocks of stone in front of her, closing off the tunnel ahead. She then turned and closed off the passage behind them, enclosing her and Gameknight in darkness and blocking out his father. Pulling out a torch, she placed it into the wall, then turned and faced her friend.

"We need to talk quick," she said in a low voice.

Gameknight could hear the confused shouts of his father from the other side of the stone blocks, but ignored him.

"What's happening?" Gameknight asked.

"As you have already guessed, the Council of Crafters have instituted the rule about users again," Hunter explained. "NPCs cannot talk to users or use their hands when a user is around."

Gameknight nodded his head.

"That's not why we are here, is it?" he asked.

"No. Crafter is sick . . . he's dying."

"What?!" Gameknight exclaimed.

"Something is attacking him, consuming his HP and slowly killing him. We're able to keep him alive, but just barely. If the attacks continue, we fear he may not survive."

"What is it? Cave spider? The zombie-king?"

"We don't know," she answered. "We've been calling it a shadow of evil. It moves across the surface of Minecraft like a dark shadow. When it finds Crafter, it attacks with mysterious jagged things that are shaped like swords, but appear to be made only of shadows . . . and evil. This thing has come back twice, and each time it has been able to find Crafter and take more of his HP. At first, healing potions helped him recover, but after the last attack, the potions seem to have less effect." A worried look came over his friend's face. "We can't stop this thing and there seems to be no defense."

"Where is he? I have to go to him."

"He's down in the crafting chamber," she explained, "but I have to warn you, he's very weak and barely conscious. I don't know if he can talk, but just after the first attack, his last words were to bring you to him."

"Then what are we waiting for?"

Pulling out his pickaxe, Gameknight broke the blocks filling the passage.

"What's going on? That was kind of rude closing off the tunnel right in front of me!" Monkeypants said.

"Sorry," Gameknight replied as he put away his pick, "but Hunter needed to tell me what is going on, and the NPCs aren't allowed to talk with users or use their hands. If she were seen by anyone else, she would be kicked out of the village. NPCs that are expelled from their village and have to live out in the wild don't last very long ... It's a death sentence."

"So what *is* going on?" Monkeypants asked.

"Crafter is sick and something in Minecraft is attacking him," Gameknight explained as he turned and headed down the passage. "They don't know what it is. It's not a monster; it's something within the fabric of Minecraft."

"That sounds serious," his father said.

"Everything in Minecraft is serious for NPCs," Gameknight said as they reached the end of the passage and entered a large chamber, an iron door on the opposite wall.

This was where Gameknight999 had met Crafter on his first adventure into Minecraft. He could still remember how his friend had looked back then, his old wrinkled face framed with long gray hair, a look of ancient wisdom within his bright blue eyes. After that first fateful battle with the monsters of the Overworld, Crafter and Gameknight had stopped the horde at the cost of their own lives. When Gameknight respawned on the next server, he'd kept his same appearance, but Crafter's had changed from a body bent with age to that of a young boy, the same timeless wisdom still showing in his bright blue eyes.

He'd been through many adventures with Crafter since then, the pair of them defeating monstrous hordes to save Minecraft again and again. Gameknight just couldn't believe that his friend might be dying.

What would I do without Crafter? he thought.

"You OK?" Monkeypants asked.

Gameknight looked up at his father and could see concern in his eyes.

"Yeah . . . I'm just scared for my friend. What if he dies? What if I can't stop this thing that is attacking him? What if—"

"Focus on *the now*," his father interrupted, "not on the *what if*."

"You're right."

Gameknight looked at his father and gave him a nervous smile, then turned and stood in front of the iron door. Drawing his diamond sword, he banged on the door with the hilt. The sound resonated like gigantic gongs, filling the room. Slowly, the doors swung open, revealing Herder on the other side. The young boy looked at Gameknight with worry in his eyes, his long black hair painted to the side of his blocky face.

Reaching out, Gameknight placed a hand on the boy's shoulder and stepped through the doors and into the crafting chamber. Instead of being greeted by the sounds of fifty NPCs crafting everything Minecraft needed, as he would usually hear, he heard thunderous silence. All of the NPCs in the crafting chamber were looking up at him, the same worried look that Herder had in his eyes was visible on every square face. These villagers were terrified for Crafter and expected Gameknight999 to save him . . .

But what if I can't?

Pushing away his doubts, he headed down the steps and into the crafting chamber.

CHAPTER 4

CRAFTER'S FATE

NPCs stood throughout the large room, a crafting bench in front of each, but they could not craft while a user was amongst them. Each had their arms linked across their chests, but Gameknight could see the same fear he was feeling within the rectangular eyes of the NPCs. They were all scared for Crafter.

As he sprinted down the steps, Gameknight could hear his father and Hunter following close behind. As they descended, Monkeypants fired question after question about the purpose of the chamber. He asked about all the minecart tracks that wove past the crafting benches, each disappearing into a dark tunnel. They could see weapons lying in minecarts as well as armor and arrows. Monkeypants asked if the NPCs were still preparing for war, but Gameknight's only concern right then was Crafter.

He ignored the questions, looking straight

ahead toward the small room that had been carved into the stone wall of the chamber. A bed was placed in the room, with a chest and table nearby. Crafter lay motionless on the bright red sheets with Digger standing at his side. As he approached the room, Gameknight could hear the rumbling of TNT detonating far overhead; the zombies must be attacking.

That wasn't important right now—all that mattered was Crafter.

He stepped into the room and looked down at his friend and was shocked at how pale his skin appeared. It was almost as white as a ghast. Reaching out, Gameknight tried to feel his head for a fever, but of course he couldn't feel anything. He wasn't *in* the game; he was just playing it as a user.

"What's wrong with him?" Monkeypants asked.

"I don't know." Gameknight answered. "Do you think—"

Before he could finish his question, Digger moved away from Crafter and gently pushed Monkeypants out of the room, leaving only Gameknight999 and Crafter. Quickly, some-one filled in the entrance with cobblestone blocks, sealing Gameknight in the room with his infirmed companion. On the table, he noticed a bottle with a reddish liquid in it—a healing potion. Gameknight picked up the bottle, pulled out the stopper, and moved to Crafter's side. He carefully lifted Crafter's head and poured the liquid into his friend's mouth.

Instantly, the color of Crafter's skin changed, fading from bone white to something closer to normal, but still pallid and sickly.

Crafter coughed and slowly opened his eyes. Gameknight sat on the side of the bed and carefully placed his friend's head in his lap. He looked down into his now dull blue eyes and knew that his face showed the fear that filled every fiber of his being.

"Crafter, what's going on?" Gameknight asked. "Nothing personal, but you look terrible."

"If it's any consolation, I feel much worse than I look," he said in a weak voice.

Crafter managed to show a faint smile, then groaned as a shadow seemed to pass over him. When the dark stain touched Gameknight's leg, he flashed red as he took damage, but he felt no pain. He wasn't *in* the game, he was just an observer, a user out for fun. But this wasn't true for Crafter, who was overcome with agony as the shadowy thing stabbed at him with dark, jagged shades of evil.

Drawing his sword, Gameknight hacked at the dark stain, but his sword just bounced off the stone, doing little but chipping the ground and damaging his weapon. Casting his blade aside, Gameknight reached down and picked up his friend, holding his limp body high over his head. The evil darkness slashed at Gameknight as it tried to reach his friend, his own HP decreasing, but he didn't care. He had to help his friend. When it realized it couldn't hurt Crafter, the shadow of evil stopped its attack and moved to one corner of the enclosure. Gameknight felt sure the thing was examining him, inspecting its next prey, but then it slowly evaporated into nothing, the diseased evil blemish leaving behind untouched stone.

Carefully, Gameknight set Crafter on the bed. The young NPC's brow was creased in pain. Leaning down, Gameknight opened the chest and was glad to find it filled with healing potions. He pulled one out, then brought the glass bottle to Crafter's lips and poured. The magenta liquid flowed into his mouth, and instantly, Gameknight could see his friend start to breathe easier.

"They come about once every other day now," Crafter mumbled, his voice weak. "But sometimes they are more frequent."

"Crafter, what's they? What was that?"

"It's Herobrine."

"What?!"

Crafter nodded his head.

"I can tell by the feel of it," Crafter explained. "Herobrine has somehow managed to let his evil hatred leak into the fabric of Minecraft. And now his evil can move like that shadow across the landscape to strike out at people." He coughed, then took a strained breath. "They are calling that thing a shadow of evil, because that is what it feels like to all the NPCs. None of the other villagers believe me, but I *know* that it's Herobrine."

"But after the Last Battle, we trapped him in the body of a pig. He's still trapped, right?"

Crafter nodded his head.

"The NPCs built a gigantic monument over the spot," Crafter explained. "Tons of stone and dirt have been piled up on top of the cell that Digger made to trap the Herobrine-pig. You can be certain he is still trapped, but that tiny pig-body must not be strong enough to hold all the evil the fills Herobrine's soul."

Crafter struggled to sit up. Reaching out, Gameknight helped his friend so he could sit on the edge of the bed. The effort nearly sapped the last ounce of the NPC's strength.

"The evil is leaking out ... and getting stronger." Crafter said, his voice weak. "If we don't do something, permanently, then Herobrine's evil will destroy the land."

"But how can we destroy him?" Gameknight asked. "If anyone kills that pig, they'll be infected by Herobrine's XP and then he will be loose again. It's not as easy as just killing him."

Crafter took a deep and strained breath, then laid back down.

"Regardless ... we need a more permanent solution to our problem," Crafter explained, his voice now just a whisper. "There is only one location where Herobrine could be put. It is a terrible place, filled with danger, but it is the only spot where this monster can no longer hurt anyone or anything in Minecraft."

"Where, Crafter ... where?"

His friend closed his eyes for a moment and

took another pained breath, then opened them again. He turned his dull blue eyes toward Gameknight999 and sighed.

"I'm sorry to ask this of you, but we need the User-that-is-not-a-user. The villagers cannot do this alone without it being a suicide mission. I know there are those in the village who would gladly give their lives for me and for Minecraft, but I fear that their success without the User-that-is-not-a-user would be unlikely."

Gameknight moved closer to his friend.

"You know that I would do anything for you," Gameknight999 said in a low voice.

Crafter tried to smile, but all he ended up with was a sneer.

"It must be a small group of warriors, for a large group would draw the attention of the monster kings created by Herobrine," Crafter explained. "When they realize that Herobrine is still alive, the monsters of the Overworld will stop at nothing to rescue their Maker."

"I understand, but tell me, where can we take him so that Herobrine will be destroyed?"

Crafter took another strained breath, then spoke, his voice even fainter. "You must take him to . . . to . . ."

And then he passed out.

"Crafter . . . CRAFTER!"

Gameknight placed his head on his chest to check if he still had a heart beat, but then he realized that he didn't even know if NPCs had hearts. Standing, he looked down on his friend. Crafter's skin had faded back to the sickly bone white. Glancing to the chest next to the bed, Gameknight considered giving him another potion of healing, but he was afraid that the potions might overtax his body. Maybe he just needed sleep.

"You rest for now, Crafter," Gameknight said. "Don't worry, the User-that-is-not-a-user will take care of you."

Pulling out his pickaxe, Gameknight dug through the cobblestone wall that separated him from the rest of the crafting chamber. When he had finished, he found Hunter, Stitcher, and Digger standing next to his father. They all had scared looks on their boxy faces. But now, Gameknight was no longer afraid; he was angry, enraged. Herobrine was hurting his friend and he would stop at nothing to keep him safe.

"Dad, we have to go," Gameknight said, his voice filled with confidence and strength.

"What?" Monkeypants said, confused. "We just got here."

"Things have changed, and it's time to stop playing this as a game," he said. "Please disconnect. I'll talk with you shortly."

His father shrugged his shoulders and paused for a moment. Suddenly, his body disappeared, streaking up his server thread, yanked from the digital universe by the sparkling beam of light.

Gameknight faced his NPC friends.

"I'll be back soon," Gameknight said. "Get prepared, we're going for a little trip. The only problem is that I don't know where we have to go."

Hunter looked at Gameknight, then rolled her rectangular eyes and smiled.

"We're going to need weapons, armor, food, horses, lots of healing potions, and of course lots and lots of TNT."

Digger nodded his head and then spun and moved toward the NPCs in the crafting chamber.

"We must hurry, for I don't know how long Crafter can last. Do you understand?"

They all nodded their square heads.

"Look for me at the village gates," he said, but before they could even move, he disappeared, streaking up his own server thread, his Minecraft game disconnected.

CHAPTER 5

THE DECISION

Tommy took his headphones off and turned to face his father.

"What just happened?" his father asked as he pushed back from his keyboard and stood.

Standing next to the tall lamp in the corner, his father's gray curly hair almost glowed silver. His salt and pepper beard, mostly salt, framed his face and gave him a look of ancient wisdom.

"Why did we need to quit Minecraft so quickly?" he asked his son.

"Dad, they're in trouble and they need help," Tommy explained.

He glanced at the digitizer that stood in the corner of the basement and brought his eyes back to his father.

"Oh, no. You aren't doing that again."

"You saw how sick Crafter was. He's going to die!" Tommy exclaimed.

"Crafter's going to die?" said a voice from the basement stairs.

Glancing toward the entrance, Tommy saw his sister, Jenny, was coming down the stairs. Her long brown hair, tied in a ponytail, bounced around her shoulders as she hopped from one stair to the next. When she reached the bottom, she bolted toward her brother.

"What's wrong with Crafter? Is he OK? How are Stitcher and Hunter?" she asked.

"Hold on," Tommy said, raising his hand up to stop the barrage of questions. "They are all OK except for Crafter. He's really sick."

"Sick ... I didn't know that NPCs get sick," Jenny said.

"They don't," he answered and turned to face his father. "You see, the last time we were in the game, we kinda fought a war."

"A war?" their father asked.

"It was an awesome war, Daddy," Jenny said. "You should have seen it. There were spiders and zombies and skeletons and—"

"Jenny, you aren't helping," Tommy interrupted. "Just let me finish explaining to Dad."

His sister grew quiet and sat in one of the chairs next to the desk.

"So, I was saying ... We fought a war because there is a virus in the game that has come alive, just like all the NPCs," Gameknight explained.

"They aren't alive; they're just programs," his father said.

"They used to be programs, but something

happened and they all became sentient," Gameknight said. "They know they're alive. They have hopes and fears ... They love their children and want them to grow up big and strong, just like you and Mom. No one really knows what happened, but the fact is, they're alive and they're my friends."

Tommy stopped and waited for his words to sink in before continuing.

"But there's a virus trapped in the servers named Herobrine. He wants to escape Minecraft and destroy everything on the Internet. Jenny and I defeated him in the Last Battle and imprisoned him, but his evil is leaking into the fabric of Minecraft and slowly poisoning it. And the first target of his poison is Crafter."

"Crafter?" Jenny said, her face filled with concern.

Tommy nodded.

"Dad, if we don't help him, Crafter is going to die," Gameknight explained. "And then Herobrine's evil will spread until he kills all the NPCs in Minecraft. I have to go. If I don't, then they're all going to die."

His father considered Tommy's words, then crossed the cluttered basement floor to the digitizer. He looked down at his invention, then back to his son.

"I didn't invent the digitizer so that you could go risking your life in Minecraft," his father said.

"I know," Tommy answered. "But if you

hadn't invented the digitizer, you would have never met living creatures within Minecraft."

"I still don't believe that they are *alive*," his father said. "Just because they move like they are alive doesn't mean they are actually alive. They could be programmed for these motions . . . It could mean nothing. They're just software; they aren't alive."

"They are, Dad," Jenny added. "My best friend is Stitcher. She's Hunter's sister. She and I . . ."

"I know who she is," her father said. "I met her briefly."

"You didn't *really* meet her," Jenny added. "You were a user, so she couldn't talk to you. If you were in the game, then you'd really know who she was and learn that she is alive like you and me."

"I still don't believe it," their dad said. "Programs can be made to mimic human emotions and reactions. That doesn't mean that those programs are alive."

"You're right, but the NPCs in Minecraft can feel, see, smell, taste, and hear. They are self-aware and know they exist, but also know that they can cease to exist. They understand death and are afraid of it, but are also willing to sacrifice themselves for ideals like freedom or right versus wrong. These NPCs are every bit as alive as you and I and deserve that same right that we have . . . to live.

"You taught me something about life when we read Arthur C. Clarke's book, *2010:*

Odyssey Two. The book said, 'Whether we are based on carbon or silicon makes no fundamental difference. We should each be treated with appropriate respect.' You taught me that the book was about respecting life, even if it looks different than you. Well, here's life that is different than you. It's digital instead of physical and it lives within computer chips instead of in houses. But it's life nonetheless, and it deserves respect and the chance to live.

"You told me that we should do the right thing, no matter how hard it is." He took a step closer to his dad, Jenny at his side. She reached out and took his hand, their fingers intertwined. He looked down at his sister and smiled and then looked up at their father. "This is the right thing to do, even though it's hard." He paused as he moved his head close to his father's ear, then whispered, "Do you really mean what you teach us, or is it just a bunch of words?"

Their father looked down at his two children and Tommy could see a wry smile peek out from behind his gray beard.

"If we're going to do this, then we're going to do it right," his father said.

"What do you mean *we?*"

"You aren't going in there alone . . . I'm going with you."

"But Dad, you don't know anything about Minecraft," Tommy complained.

"Then you'll have to teach me really quick, won't you?"

Tommy sighed and rolled his eyes.

"This is the right thing to do, son," his father said, "but you aren't going in there without me. So if it's too hard to have me with you, then you can forget it and just quit."

"Never!"

"Then let's get ready," his father said. "We need to eat some food and put on some warm clothes. It gets cold in the basement and we have to keep our bodies protected."

"I'll go get my favorite Minecraft sweatshirt," Jenny said as she hopped up and down, unable to contain her excitement.

"Hold on, Jenny," her father said. "You aren't going into the game."

"I'm not?"

She was instantly visibly disappointed.

"No, you're going to stay here and watch over the digitizer," their father explained. "We might need your help, so you need to be here in the basement keeping an eye on us."

"But . . ."

"Jenny, last time we had Shawny watching over us, remember?" Tommy said.

His sister nodded her head.

"Well, we need you here at the computer watching out for us. You can warn us of traps or put things in our chest for us if we need something," Tommy explained. "Dad and I are counting on you to keep us safe. It's a big responsibility. Are you sure you can do it?"

Hearing that it was important, Jenny smiled as her eyes brightened.

"Yeah . . . yeah, I can do it!" she replied.

"And don't worry, Jenny," her brother said. "I'll tell Stitcher that you couldn't come with us this time. I'm sure she'll understand."

"OK . . ." she conceded. "But make sure you tell her."

"I will," Tommy replied. "I promise—now let's get ready."

He turned and stared at the digitizer, and a familiar feeling of dread filled his body. He didn't really *want* to go back into Minecraft and face off against zombies and skeletons for real, but he couldn't let his friends down.

"Don't worry, Crafter, I'm coming for you, and I won't let you down . . . not now and not ever!"

He headed upstairs to prepare.

CHAPTER 6
XA-TUL

The king of the zombies, Xa-Tul, stormed about through zombie-town, anger and rage filling his mind. His chainmail clicked and jingled as he walked, filling the air with delicate sounds that were almost beautiful, except for the growling moans of the nearby monsters. The huge zombie's generals surrounded and followed their liege, but at a safe distance. When Xa-Tul was enraged, it was never a good idea to be within arm's reach, and these days he was always enraged.

"It is still unbelievable that the Maker, Herobrine, was destroyed by that pathetic User-that-is-not-a-user, Gameknight999." He growled, then balled his clawed hand into a fist and punched the dirt wall of a zombie house. The block shattered, throwing small cubes of dirt in all directions. "The greatest insult was to capture the Maker in that tiny little pig body first. Xa-Tul is certain that the NPCs have destroyed Herobrine by now and he is gone forever."

He growled again and let out a sorrowful wail that echoed throughout the massive cavern that housed this zombie-town.

"But the Maker will still be avenged, is that not right, generals?" The big zombie stopped and turned to face his commanders. "What news is there?"

Most of the generals stepped back, all except for the newest of the leaders, who foolishly stood his ground. Xa-Tul's glowing red eyes fell on this zombie, then took a step closer.

"Su-Kil, tell me ... what has been learned about the NPCs responsible for the death of the Maker?" Xa-tul asked.

"Scouts have recently reported that their village has been found," Su-Kil said proudly. "My warriors are harassing the village."

The other generals cringed and took another step back.

"What did Su-Kil say?" Xa-Tul asked, his anger bubbling near the surface.

"Ahh ... Su-Kil meant to say *Xa-Tul's* forces are near the village and are attacking in the name of the king of the zombies." Su-Kil quickly directed his eyes to the ground and hoped that Xa-Tul would be merciful.

Xa-Tul looked down on the smaller zombie. He could see countless scars across Su-Kil's arms and face; they were from his battle training when he was younger. Zombies took pride in their scars, for it showed others how much pain they could take and what they could endure for their zombie-town. This one had a long scar that ran across his forehead and down along the right side of his face, the jagged scar going across his eye. Its appearance was fearsome, and Su-Kil was proud of it.

Xa-Tul nodded his massive head, took a quick step forward, and slapped his clawed hand on the commander's shoulder.

"Su-Kil did well," Xa-Tul said in his grumbly voice. "A promotion is deserved. From now on, Su-Kil will be addressed as Ur-Kil."

"But . . ." one of the other zombies objected, which drew the king's angry attention.

"Does Ut-Ban have something to add?" Xa-Tul asked the complaining zombie.

Ut-Ban shook his green head.

"Perhaps Ut-Ban was promoted too soon," the king of the zombies said. "Now, Ut-Ban will be called Su-Ban until the zombie's actions match the title."

"Thank you . . . sire," the newly demoted Su-Ban said, bowing his head.

"The zombie army will come together and move against this village," the zombie king commanded.

"Xa-Tul, the village's defenses are formidable," Ur-Kil said. "The walls are tall and the archer towers many. Zombies may not be enough to breach the defenses."

Xa-Tul flashed a dangerous stare at the general.

"Perhaps the skeletons will help?" one of the other generals asked.

"The skeletons cower in their tunnels, afraid to be seen," Xa-Tul explained. "The defeat of the Maker has robbed the skeletons of the little courage they had before Herobrine crafted their new king, Reaper. The skeletons will not help the zombies, but perhaps the—"

Suddenly, a commotion drew the zombie king's attention. Turning, he strode toward the blocky steps that led up to a dark tunnel. As he ascended the steps, Xa-Tul paused beneath the sparkling green HP fountain. For just an instant, he let the delicious HP splash across his back, nourishing his body. Feeling stronger, the zombie king continued. When he reached the dark tunnel, he found a zombie barely alive being carried by two of the tunnel guards.

"What is this?" Xa-Tul demanded.

"This zombie said there is critical information that is fit only for the ears of the zombie king," one of the guards grumbled. "The zombie would not tell anyone else."

"Hmm," Xa-Tul mused.

Stepping forward, he motioned for the guards to raise the weak zombie up so he could inspect him. The creature looked like any other zombie, green from head to toe with rotting skin and a decaying smell that would scare away even the bravest of NPC warriors. Reaching out, Xa-Tul lifted the monster's chin so he could look directly in the creature's eyes.

"What is this information that is befitting the ears of your king?" Xa-Tul asked.

"HP . . . Please . . . HP," the creature moaned.

The king growled, but grabbed the zombie and carried him to the HP fountain. He let the smallest of splashes coat the creature, then pulled him away from the life-saving spring. Setting him down against the stone wall, Xa-Tul glared at the weak monster.

"What is the information? Xa-Tul demands that it is given."

The zombie tried to stand, but was still too weak. So instead, he sat there and gave his report.

"The User . . . back to . . . another . . ." The zombie was so weak that he could barely speak.

Xa-Tul growled, then picked up the creature and allowed him to bathe in the HP fountain for another second. Kneeling, Xa-Tul glared at the smaller zombie, his red eyes glowing with anger.

"What was that?" Xa-Tul asked.

"The User-that-is-not-a-user was seen," he said.

"WHAT?!"

The zombie nodded his decaying head.

"The User-that-is-not-a-user was spotted though he was in user form. This zombie saw him riding horses into the village with another user and an NPC. The zombies were just about to attack."

"Was the enemy of the zombies captured?" Xa-Tul asked.

The zombie shook his head.

"The User-that-is-not-a-user helped the NPCs defend the village," the weakened creature explained. "The attack was not successful ... No zombies survived. If I hadn't left early, I would have been killed and no one would know this information."

Xa-Tul nodded his head, lifted the zombie, and placed him in the sparkling green HP fountain. As the healing embers danced across the zombie's body, the king turned and faced his generals.

"This is the kind of zombie needed to ensure victory," Xa-Tul boomed. "What is this zombie's name?"

"Fo-Lin," the creature answered as he stood within the HP fountain.

"Fo-Lin has earned a promotion for his decisive thinking. From now on, this zombie will be called Ri-Lin," Xa-Tul said.

"Thank you, King," Ri-Lin said as he stepped out of the HP fountain. "What commands are there for Ri-Lin?"

"It is important that Xa-Tul knows what is happening at that village," the zombie king explained. "Ri-Lin will go watch the village and report if anything changes, especially with respect to the enemy, Gameknight999."

The other generals growled at the sound of his name.

"The zombies of the Overworld will take revenge on Gameknight999 and his friends ... but first, his location must be known. Go, Ri-Lin and report what happens."

"Yes, Xa-Tul," the zombie said.

Standing up straight, the newly promoted zombie bolted back into the dark tunnel that led out of zombie-town.

"Zombies, revenge is at hand," Xa-Tul bellowed, causing a chorus of excited moans from the generals. "Gather the troops. It is time for zombies to declare war with anyone who gives aid to the User-that-is-not-a-user, starting with that village."

The generals all turned and headed back into zombie-town to gather their troops. As the growls and moans drifted up from the collection of homes strewn across the chamber floor, Xa-Tul smiled. Soon, his enemy would be on his knees, begging for mercy that would never come.

"I'M COMING FOR YOU GAMEKNIGHT999!" he shouted loud enough to make the very walls of the cavern quake in fear.

CHAPTER 7

INTO MINECRAFT ...
AGAIN

Gameknight's senses were completely overwhelmed by the bright light encompassing him. He couldn't feel or hear or see anything other than the brilliant white glow of the Gateway of Light.

When the glare finally faded, Gameknight surveyed his surroundings. It was dark and difficult to see, but as his eyes adjusted, he could make out some details. A tall oak tree was just barely visible to his right. The blocky leaves moved gently in the warm breeze that flowed across the land. They swayed in a synchronized dance with the blades of grass that covered the ground. Normally, the block would have just appeared green with a texture that represented grass, but from within the game, he saw the fine detail and subtle beauty of the land.

Something moved next to the tree.

Gameknight reached instinctively for his sword, but found he had no weapon. Taking a step closer to the tree, he saw there was something tied to it. A pair of horses were leaning their long heads down to the ground, munching on the thick grass. Each was saddled and ready.

Probably a gift from Hunter, he thought.

Off to the left, Gameknight could hear the splashing of water. It sounded as though it was falling from a great height, then pouring into a pool somewhere in a deep underground cavern. He knew exactly where he was, for he'd materialized here twice before. This was near his original hidey-hole, from the first time he'd come into Minecraft. The waterfall to his left was where he'd defeated the spider on his first day. And somewhere behind him, there was a secret entrance to the cave he'd carved into the side of the mountain that loomed over him.

Just as he was about to turn and find the entrance to his hidden sanctuary, a blinding sphere of light formed in the air. The intense illumination drove back the shadows and allowed him to see his surroundings for just a moment. When the light faded, he found his father standing on a grassy block in his monkey-skin and Superman outfit, a look of surprise on his face.

"Dad, over here," Gameknight said, but his father didn't move.

Walking to his side, Gameknight grabbed

his hand and pulled him to the mountainside behind him.

"Stay here until I find the entrance," Gameknight said.

Monkeypants mumbled something, but it was completely incoherent; he was probably in shock.

Ignoring him for the moment, Gameknight hopped up the blocky mountainside, looking for the entrance he'd hidden so long ago. Moving his hands across the shadowy blocks, he finally felt what he was looking for— grass-covered blocks stacked one on top of the other. They wouldn't have spawned naturally like that. He clenched his hand into a fist and punched. In a minute, he was through the first block. Light from lava and torches streamed out of the hidden room, making it easier to see.

"Dad, come up here," Gameknight said as he started to work on the second block.

Once it was shattered, he moved down to his father's side.

"Monkeypants, we need to get inside. We have no weapons and no armor. We're sitting ducks for any monster who might happen to walk by."

His father said nothing. He just stared at the oak tree standing before him, then turned and looked down at the cubes of dirt covering the ground.

"Dad . . . are you OK?"

"It's incredible," he mumbled. "We're in the game, we're really in the game."

"Did you think I was making it up?" Gameknight asked. "Come on, we need to get inside before some zombies come by."

"Horses . . . look, there are some horses," Monkeypants said, wonder twinkling in his eyes. "They're all boxy and square, like in the game, but they look so much more *alive* now!"

"Yeah, yeah, I know," Gameknight answered, putting his hand on his father's shoulders and shaking him, hard. "You need to snap out of it, Dad. Can't you see it's dark out? Monsters will sense our presence here soon. We need to get up there, NOW!"

Monkeypants looked at his son, then glanced around at their surroundings and realized that they were indeed exposed out in the open.

"Come on, follow me," Gameknight said.

Turning, he led the way up the blocky slope to the torch-lit entrance, his father following close behind. Once they were inside, Gameknight placed a block of dirt in the doorway to keep out any stray monsters.

"Did you build this room when you first came into the game?" Monkeypants asked.

"Yep," Gameknight answered.

Monkeypants went further into the room, moving to the back so he could see the pool of lava that lit the rear of the cave.

"Don't get too close to the lava," Gameknight advised. "You can't swim in it, just so you know."

"That is sage advice, thank you," his father answered. "What do we do now? Wait until the sun comes up?"

"No, we can't wait. Every second counts. We must get to the village as quickly as we can."

He moved to the chest he'd placed there long ago and opened the wooden box. He peered inside and then smiled up at his dad as he pulled a long iron blade from the chest.

"I think Hunter was here," Gameknight said.

"Why do you think that?"

"Because I didn't stock this chest with iron tools, weapons, and armor," Gameknight explained. "I think she came here and filled it up for us."

Gameknight pulled out pieces of armor and tossed them to his father, then carefully laid a sword, bow, and arrows on the ground. He then pulled the same out of the chest for himself.

"Put those on, quick," Gameknight said. "We have to go."

They both donned their armor and put their weapons into their inventory. Reaching into the chest one last time, Gameknight pulled out two loaves of bread and tossed one to Monkeypants. His father deftly caught the loaf and held it before his eyes. Carefully, he stroked the rough surface with his blocky fingers, then brought it to his nose and inhaled. A smile grew on his face as he placed the bread into his inventory.

"I can smell the bread—for real," Monkeypants said.

"Of course you can," Gameknight said. "This is for real and don't you forget it. The monsters are real as well, and every one of them wants to destroy us for no reason other than they're monsters and we aren't."

"Understood."

"You ready?"

Monkeypants nodded his head.

"OK, here we go," Gameknight said as he pulled out a shovel and dug up the blocks of dirt.

Putting away the shovel, he drew his sword and carefully stepped out of the hidey-hole. His father did the same.

"Take the blocks of dirt and seal up the hidey-hole again," Gameknight said. "We might need it . . . You never know."

Monkeypants sealed the entrance and followed his son toward the horses tied up near the oak tree. As they neared the animals, a growling, moaning sound filled the air.

"Zombies," Gameknight whispered. "Quickly, get behind me."

His father ran behind his son and drew his own sword, watching his back. Suddenly, a pair of wretched green arms reached out at him, the fingers tipped with razor-sharp claws. Monkeypants screamed and swished his sword around in the air, not coming close to scoring hit. One of the zombies stepped forward and swung at Monkeypants, its nails carving four deep scratches in his chest plate.

"They're behind you!" Monkeypants screamed.

Gameknight turned and lunged toward the monster. Spinning to the side, he swung his iron blade at the monster's ribs, then blocked the claws from reaching his father again. Moving to the monster's side, Gameknight swung his sword, scoring a strong hit that made the creature flash red and scream out in pain. Two more creatures moaned from the darkness as they shuffled forward.

"Dad, just watch my back and tell me if any of the monsters are trying to get behind me," Gameknight instructed.

"Ahh ... I mean ..." Monkeypants stammered.

Gameknight could tell that is father was overcome with shock and fear. He remembered feeling the same way when that first spider had attacked him so long ago.

Focusing on the nearest zombie, Gameknight faked an attack with his sword, then drove a hard kick to the monster's stomach. When it doubled over, he attacked with his blade, consuming its HP in seconds. It disappeared with a *pop*, leaving behind three glowing balls of XP. Not waiting, he charged at the next zombie, slashing at it with all his strength. After scoring multiple hits, it too disappeared, leaving only one monster remaining. Sprinting to this lone creature, Gameknight attacked its head. But before his blade reached the zombie, he knelt down and spun with his leg extended, taking the creature's green, decaying legs out from under him. Falling hard on the ground, the zombie released a sorrowful moan and disappeared as Gameknight finished him off.

Gameknight found his father shaking, his face pale and covered with tiny cubes of sweat.

"Are you OK?" Gameknight asked.

"That was terrifying," Monkeypants answered, his voice shaking.

"Welcome to Minecraft. Fortunately, it was only three of them," Gameknight said. "It could have been a lot worse. Now come on, we'll be much safer when we're on horseback."

Putting away his sword, Gameknight climbed atop the chestnut brown horse, then gestured for his father to do the same. The pair rode away from their hidey-hole, galloping as fast as their steads would carry them, heading southwest toward the village, which Gameknight knew would be waiting for them. Neither saw the zombie hiding in the darkness, watching them ride away, the long scar across his face and eye obvious in the moonlight.

"Xa-Tul will be pleased with Ur-Kil," the zombie said to no one. "The User-that-is-not-a-user has returned, and Ur-Kil knows his destination."

The zombie released a maniacal, guttural laugh as he headed back to zombie-town and his king.

CHAPTER 8

WELCOMING

"**Y**ou're telling me that this Herobrine character made all the monsters attack the Source?" Monkeypants asked as he rode next to his son.

"Shhh, lower your voice," Gameknight said. "We don't want to attract any more attention then necessary. And yes, that was Herobrine's plan. He must have figured that he could escape the server if the Source was destroyed."

"And you stopped all those monsters?" his father asked.

"Well ... it wasn't just me. I did have an army of NPCs with me as well as an army of users. So I wouldn't say that *I* saved Minecraft. There were lots of other people there as well."

"It sounds like that was dangerous," Monkeypants said. "Maybe too dangerous."

"A lot of people were in danger, Dad. I was just doing what I could to help."

"But it sounds like you were at the front

of the battle lines instead of being somewhere safe," Monkeypants said. "Why couldn't you let others be on the front lines? Must it always be you?"

Gameknight sighed with frustration.

"Because I can't help if I'm hiding at the back of the army. Dad, this is what I do—I help these people when they don't know what to do. I would have thought you'd be proud of me."

"Ahhh—" Monkeypants started to say, but was interrupted by the sounds of an angry spider.

They looked for the clicking monster, but it had moved away to hide in the shadows again.

They rode in silence for a bit, both of them watching the square moon move across the sparkling starlit canopy of the night sky. The pale moonlight illuminated the ground just enough to allow them to avoid deep holes that would have likely injured or killed the horses.

"Watch out for that hole," Gameknight said as he veered to the right.

Glancing behind, he made sure that his father was paying attention. Monkeypants steered his horse around the deep opening, but as he skirted the deep hole, he looked down into its depths. Gameknight could see his father start to waver on the horse, possibly becoming dizzy.

"Dad, you OK?" Gameknight said as he moved his horse next to his father's. Reaching out, he grabbed Monkeypants's armor and held him steady.

"What's wrong?"

"You know . . . my fear of heights?" his father asked. "That hole was pretty deep."

"Yeah, it's probably part of a deep crevasse just under the surface," Gameknight explained. "That's why we need to be careful."

"Thanks for steadying me," Monkeypants replied. "I might have—"

Clicking sounds suddenly came from the top of a large spruce. Gameknight glanced up at the treetop and could see multiple red eyes glaring down at them. Veering away from the tree, they detoured far around it to avoid an unnecessary battle.

"And the spiders," Monkeypants continued, his voice just a whisper, "they had a queen?"

"Yes, her name was Shaikulud. She was one of Herobrine's creations, as was the enderman king and ghast king."

"Malacoda and Erebus, right?"

Gameknight smiled. "You're starting to get it straight . . . almost."

"So after the battle with the spiders, you escaped in boats to another land," Monkeypants said.

"That's right," Gameknight affirmed. "That was where the Last Battle for Minecraft was held."

"It seems that you had the *Last Battle* a couple times before as well," Monkeypants noticed. "They can't all be the Last Battle . . . Maybe you haven't had the *real* one yet."

"I hope that's not the case," his son replied.

"But you didn't really destroy Herobrine, you just captured him in a pig's body ... Is that right?"

Gameknight nodded his head as he scanned their surroundings for threats. Over the next hill, the sky was brightening, but it was too soon for dawn. They were getting closer to the village.

"And you think Herobrine's evil is leaking out of this pig and infecting Minecraft?" Monkeypants asked.

Gameknight nodded again.

"Why don't you just kill the pig and be done with it?"

"Do you remember seeing the glowing balls of XP that came from the zombies that attacked us when we came into Minecraft?" Gameknight asked.

"Sure."

They started to climb a gentle sloping hill, the ground covered with long blades of grass. Blue and red flowers dotted the hill here and there.

"That XP would be infected with Herobrine's virus," Gameknight said. "It will infect anyone that touches it, letting Herobrine take over that new body. This is the difficult thing. We can't kill him; we must instead put him someplace where he can't hurt Minecraft anymore."

"And where is that place?" his father asked.

"I don't know ... but Crafter does."

"So we just ask him and put the pig there ... Is that right?"

"Sort of," Gameknight said. "I'm not sure Crafter can tell us anything. He was so weak when we left the game before. I don't think he'll be able to tell us what we need to know."

"Then what are we going to do?" Monkeypants asked.

"I don't know, but we'll figure it out."

"I'm glad you are so confident," his father said.

"I have to be. These people are my friends and my responsibility, and Crafter is my best friend. I'm going to do everything I can to make sure he is safe. I have no choice. If he gets any sicker, he may die. I'd never be able to handle that kind of guilt."

Monkeypants was about to reply, but instead stayed silent and just nodded his head.

"Keep your eyes open, Dad. The village is just over this hill," Gameknight said.

The two riders crested the top of the hill and were greeted by the sight of an NPC village lit with torches. A tall cobblestone wall surrounded the community, defenders walking along the barricade, bows in their blocky hands. Gameknight could see that the villagers had deepened the moat that surrounded the wall, making entrance into the village possible across only a narrow bridge. Archer towers had spouted up next to the wooden crossing since the last time Gameknight had been there. Narrow bridges arched from the towers to the fortified walls, allowing warriors easy access to the towers without having to go outside their protective stone cocoon.

"Wow, did you show them how to build this?" Monkeypants asked.

"No," Gameknight answered. "It was really Shawny. He designed the defenses for the village."

Suddenly, the growling moans of a zombie horde drifted out of the dark forest surrounding the area.

"What's that?" his father asked.

"Zombies—lots of them," Gameknight answered. "Come on, the time for stealth is over. Now we need speed."

Digging their heels into the horses' sides, they sprinted toward the village gate. As they streaked down the hill, Gameknight could see archers running to the towers, their prickly shafts pointing out toward the dark trees. Warriors were mounting the walls, their shining metal armor reflecting the light of the moon, making each appear to glow as they readied for battle.

"Two riders coming in!" shouted the watcher from the tall cobblestone that stood at the center of the village.

Gameknight could see the iron doors on the other side of the wooden bridge slowly open. Hunter and Digger stepped out and waved, then waited for the pair's arrival.

Not slowing to say hello, Gameknight shot through the gates with his father right on his heels. Once they were inside, he leapt off the horse and motioned for his father to do the same. Turning to the iron doors, Gameknight took a step toward the entrance, but suddenly started to hear the murmurings of the villagers.

"The User-that-is-not-a-user has returned," someone said.

More villagers were coming out of their homes, weapons in their hands. They ran for their assigned places, each having a task to do for the defense of the village. But as they headed for their positions, they saw Gameknight999 and stopped, smiles showing on their blocky faces.

"He's back!"

"The User-that-is-not-a-user is here!"

The NPCs slowly approached him, some of them gently touching his arm or shoulder in greeting.

"It's Gameknight999!"

"He's here again!"

More villagers approached until Gameknight was completely surrounded. They crowded so close to him that he could barely see anything. A voice rang out from the village wall, a high pitched voice that he knew well.

It was Stitcher, and she was yelling at the top of her lungs.

"The User-that-is-not-a-user has returned!" she shouted, raising her enchanted bow high over her head.

The villagers cheered.

"FOR MINECRAFT!" Stitcher screamed.

"FOR MINECRAFT!" the NPCs echoed, and the village filled with shouts of courage and joy.

"Hey! The reunion is over!" Hunter yelled

from atop the fortified wall. "Get to your positions! A mob of zombies is attacking and they weren't invited to this party!"

The villagers shouted as they ran to their positions, ready to take up the defense of their home once again.

"So much for the celebration," Gameknight said as he drew his diamond sword, a look of determination on his square face.

CHAPTER 9

ZOMBIES!

A growling, moaning horde of zombies charged toward the village. The sound made little square goosebumps form along Gameknight's spine. He would have been happy to never hear that sound again. Glancing over his shoulder, Gameknight looked at his father.

"Come on, let's get to the top of the walls," Gameknight said.

Not waiting for a reply, he ran to the steps and climbed them until he was atop the fortified wall and standing next to Hunter. Her curly hair now looked as it was meant to appear—like coils of crimson springs glowing in the moonlight. She had her enchanted bow out and was firing arrows out into the open plain. The arrows instantly lit aflame as they left her magical bow, for she had the Flame enchantment on her weapon, as well as Infinite.

Suddenly, Monkeypants was at his side. His

monkey-face looked white when he looked over the edge of the tall fortified wall to the ground below. Gameknight could tell that his father's acrophobia made this difficult for him.

"You OK?" Gameknight asked.

What's wrong? Is Dad OK? Jenny asked through the chat.

Yeah, it's just his fear of heights, Gameknight thought, his words appearing on his sister's screen.

His father nodded and turned away from the precipice. Trying to ignore his fear, he faced the other NPCs.

"This must be the *real* Hunter," he said in a shaky voice. "Pleased to meet you."

"No time for pleasantries right now," she said. "We're kinda in the middle of a battle. If you want to make yourself useful, then grab some buckets of water and dump them against the walls where zombies are trying to climb."

"Water?"

"It will push them back down the wall," Gameknight explained.

"Ahh," Monkeypants said, nodding his head.

The zombies advanced across the open plain and were within range of the archers. Countless arrows flew through the air toward the creatures who were unfortunate enough to be part of the initial charge.

"I wish you'd left some blocks of TNT out there when you came in," Hunter said to Gameknight999.

"You didn't leave me any in my hidey-hole," he chided.

"Do I still have to do everything?" she replied, smiling.

A zombie splashed across the watery moat, drawing her attention. Hunter turned, aimed, then fired three arrows in quick succession, each of them hitting their target. The creature disappeared.

Suddenly, Gameknight felt someone tugging at his sleeve.

"Gameknight ... Gameknight ... GAMEKNIGHT999!"

"What?" he snapped as he turned.

In front of him was Herder, his long black hair dangling down to his shoulders, the sweat-soaked strands sticking to his forehead and neck. The lanky youth was out of breath.

"Slow down, Herder. What's wrong?"

"It's Crafter," the young NPC said. "I think he's getting worse."

"What do you mean?" Gameknight asked.

"The shadow of evil just attacked again and he's really weak," Herder explained. "We need to do something."

"Did you give him a potion of healing?" Stitcher asked as she approached. The young girl was half the size of the other warriors on the wall, but they all bowed to her as she walked by; her skill with the bow was legendary and she'd saved many lives with it on countless occasions. Everyone respected Hunter's younger sister.

"The healing potions aren't doing much good anymore," Herder said, a look of fear on his face. "I don't know what to do."

Digger now approached, having seen the discussion from below.

"We need to do something," the big NPC said. "Crafter was attacked so suddenly that he didn't have time to transfer his crafting power to me. If he dies, so does our village, and every villager will become Lost."

"What is Lost?" Monkeypants whispered to his son.

"If a village loses their crafter, then the NPCs are called Lost, and they must strike out across the land to find a new village. Few survive."

"Oh no," his father said.

Gameknight nodded his head solemnly.

"If I can interject," Monkeypants said. "I have some rules I've taught my son over the years."

"Daaaad," Gameknight whined, embarrassed.

LOL, Jenny typed.

Hunter looked at Monkeypants, then glanced above his head.

"That's right, *my dad* came with me into the game," Gameknight said. "He likes computer games, alright? He's been playing them since he was young and wanted to see what Minecraft was all about."

"Uh-huh," Hunter replied, not listening to her friend's explanation. She giggled then gave the User-that-is-not-a-user a mischievous smile. "Your family seems to enjoy coming in here with you. One would think they don't trust you very much."

"It's not like that," Gameknight complained. "He plays my favorite games sometimes and I play his."

"Like Wing Commander," Monkeypants blurted out with pride. "Only the greatest first-person space dogfight game ever when it came out in 1990."

Gameknight cringed with embarrassment as Hunter laughed.

"Hunter, don't goof around right now and be nice," Stitcher said.

"Please, Mr. Monkeypants, share with us your rule," Hunter said with a grin.

"Rule number two—If something isn't working, try something different," Monkeypants stated. "If the potions you are making aren't helping Crafter, then you need a different potion. Who makes them for you?"

A huge growling roar suddenly came from the tree line. Gameknight knew who made that sound. Glancing at the trees, his worst fears were confirmed: Xa-Tul stepped out of the shadows just as the sun's square face was rising from behind the eastern horizon. On his head, the monster wore a crown that looked as if it were made from golden claws. It sparkled in the morning sunlight.

"Great. Just what we need ... Him," Gameknight said.

"Brewer," Stitcher said.

"What?" Gameknight asked.

"Your dad," she looked above his father's head and read the name, "Monkeypants271 asked who makes the potions. Brewer has been doing it, but he's running out of Nether Wart and that's the main ingredient."

"It seems to me," Monkeypants said, "that you need some stronger medicine for Crafter. Where do you go to get stronger healing potions?"

"We'd have to go the Nether to get more Nether Wart," Stitcher said.

"No, that would give you the same thing you have now," Monkeypants said and pointed to Herder. "This fine young man here said that your healing potions were not strong enough. We need to take it up a level. Where can we get stronger healing potions?"

"We need potions of rejuvenation for Crafter," Herder said. "And I know only one source for those."

"Where?" Digger asked.

"A witch," the young NPC said, his voice edged with fear. "We need a witch."

"A witch?" Gameknight asked.

Witches were dangerous NPCs with ideas of their own. It was never clear whose side they were really on: the villagers or the monsters. They can't be trusted.

"I don't like it," Gameknight said.

Just then, Hunter notched an arrow and fired it at another group of zombies storming the village. Across the battlefield, Gameknight could see Xa-Tul sitting atop his zombie horse just out of bowshot, his golden sword pointing directly at him.

"I see you, Fool!" the zombie king bellowed. "Why don't you come out here and play?" Xa-Tul urged his mount forward a step, then glared up at his enemy. "Xa-Tul holds the User-that-is-not-a-user responsible for what happened to the Maker! GAMEKNIGHT999 WILL BE HELD ACCOUNTABLE!"

"Son, that large zombie seems to know you," Monkeypants said.

"We run into each other from time to time," Gameknight said.

Hunter laughed.

Looking across the grassy plain, the User-that-is-not-a-user could see that the archers were keeping the zombies at bay. None of them were able to cross the bridge with the hail of steel points raining down upon them. The village was safe … for now. Gameknight headed down the steps and to the ground and the others followed.

"I guess we have no choice," Gameknight said. "We need to get Crafter to the witch. Do you know where one is at?"

"There is an old witch in the southern swamp," Digger explained. "We'll go there."

"But how do we get past all those zombies?" Gameknight asked.

"Don't worry," Digger said, "I've already taken care of that."

Then Digger did something they didn't see very often: he smiled.

"Everyone collect what you need," the big NPC said. "I'll get Crafter."

His friends disappeared, leaving Gameknight and Monkeypants standing there, listening to the moaning zombies. When his friends returned, each had a horse in tow. Herder pulled two mules on leads, a chest strapped to their backs, as well as a mount for himself. The last to arrive was Digger. He came pulling two horses, a large gray for him and a white horse with Crafter lying across its back. Ropes had been wrapped around their friend, holding him firmly to the saddle.

Swinging up onto his mount, Digger tied the lead from Crafter's horse to his own saddle and faced the main gates.

"Come on!" he shouted to the party. "We get out this way. Smithy, you take command of the village and the battle."

"Just like the old days," the blacksmith said, his sword held high over his head. "Except I can only hold one sword."

"Like the old days," Digger agreed and headed to the rear of the village.

Gameknight and his father leapt up onto their horses. They followed Hunter and Stitcher, who were right behind Digger. Herder moved up next to Gameknight999.

"I wish it were happier circumstances bringing you back to us," Herder said.

"Yeah ... me, too," Gameknight answered.

He glanced at the pack mules, then back to Herder. "What do you have in those chests?"

"Well, potions for Crafter, as well as stuff that we might need," the young boy explained. "I'd been studying with Crafter before he became sick, and he taught me that there are always things you need when you leave the village."

"Like TNT?"

The lanky boy nodded.

"As well as buckets, rope, and some of his fireworks. Crafter taught me that you could never have enough of these."

Gameknight nodded and looked toward Digger at the front of the party. The NPC seemed to sink down, going lower and lower until both he and Crafter disappeared. Kicking his horse to trot faster, Gameknight moved up next to Hunter and then understood what happened: a massive set of steps had been carved into the ground wide enough and tall enough to allow a mounted rider to descend down into the shadowy depths. Pulling back on his mount, he let Hunter and Stitcher go down the steps, then waited for Monkeypants and Herder to follow. After the pack mules moved past, Gameknight brought up the rear.

As he descended, the dusty, damp smell of the tunnel filled his senses. It was much cooler in the passage, but that was to be expected. He did not expect the secret passage to seemingly stretch out forever. Gameknight could see torches glowing in the distance, the flickering flames casting a circle of light that lit only a portion of the tunnel. He watched his friends disappear into the darkness between the warm glow of the torches, only to reappear again a few moments later.

Where is Digger leading us? Gameknight thought.

He'd never seen this secret tunnel before, and he'd been in their village a hundred times. But then something that Xa-Tul said suddenly resonated within his mind:

Gameknight999 will be held accountable.

Once, just once, he'd like to come into Minecraft and not have an army of monsters chasing him all across the server. Sighing, he urged his horse forward into the darkness.

CHAPTER 10

THE KING'S DISAPPOINTMENT

Xa-Tul sat atop his zombie horse, watching the battle unfold. Before him stood the village of the User-that-is-not-a-user. A thick wall of cobblestone surrounded the wooden structures, denying the zombie-king the vengeance he rightfully deserved. Twin towers stood like giant sentinels on either side of the wooden causeway that spanned the watery moat, balls of XP and piles of zombie flesh littering one side. He had sent a company of zombies to take that bridge, but the last of them were now perishing at the foot of the crossing, none of them having even set foot on the wooden planks.

"General Ur-Kil, send a squad of zombies through the moat," he commanded. "Let's see if they can get close to the doors that way."

The zombie shuffled off to his warriors.

Xa-Tul watched the newly promoted commander and laughed when he reached his troops. He was a small monster, and his diminutive height compared to the other zombies looking comical. But this Ur-Kil had two things all the other monster lacked: courage and intelligence. The other zombies followed him willingly, his compassion winning over their hearts and loyalty.

Xa-Tul must watch this Ur-Kil; he could be a threat, the zombie king thought.

The zombies shuffled off to the edge of the battlefield, then moved toward the moat that encircled the NPC village.

"General Ta-Vin, send a battalion of zombies across that bridge," the zombie king ordered.

"But the zombies won't stand a chance against those new archer towers," the general replied.

Xa-Tul glared at the insubordinate fool, his eyes glowing a dangerous, bright red.

Ta-Vin quickly turned and gave the order.

"Ta-Vin will personally lead the charge," Xa-Tul said, his voice growling with anger.

"But . . ."

The zombie king slowly drew his huge golden sword, letting the sharp blade drag across the edge of the scabbard so that it made a scratchy scraping sound. He then leaned down from his green decaying zombie-horse, the sword extended toward the terrified general.

"If the order must be repeated, it will not end well for Ta-Vin," Xa-Tul said in a low, angry voice.

The general quickly drew his own golden sword. It looked childlike next to Xa-Tul's massive broadsword, but Ta-Vin held it high overhead as if it were Excalibur itself. Glancing toward his fellow generals, the doomed commander turned and ran off to join his warriors, his decaying face covered with sad acceptance of his fate.

"Where is Ur-Kil?!" bellowed the king.

"Here," came the response.

The small commander shuffled toward his king. He had been watching his warriors from the top of a small hill, but now quickly approached Xa-Tul.

"Here is a lesson for Ur-Kil," the king said. "The larger group of zombies approaches the bridge, drawing the attention of the NPCs. An attack of this size will draw the User-that-is-not-a-user to the ramparts, but the Fool will not see Ur-Kil's zombies swimming across the moat."

Ur-Kil nodded, understanding the deception and strategy.

Ta-Vin's zombies charged across the bridge, and as expected, were fired upon by the archers in the two new towers that stood on either side of the wooden crossing. NPCs from the wall also fired upon the battalion. But Xa-Tul did not see Gameknight999, nor the red-headed girl archer, step forward atop the fortified wall . . . Something was wrong.

While the defenders focused their attention on the assault from the bridge, Ur-Kil's zombies made it across the moat without a single shot fired in their direction. Pressing their backs against the rough cobblestone wall, the monsters moved along the barricade until they reached the iron doors. But just before their pointed claws reached the metallic gates, the doors suddenly burst open and a group of warriors, led by a blacksmith, charged out and quickly destroyed the small company. Moving back inside their village, the NPCs closed the doors again and continued their defense from the top of the battlements.

Something was definitely wrong.

"They have fled!" Xa-Tul bellowed, his voice echoing off the trees and making it sound as if it came from all directions.

"What do you mean, sire?" Ur-Kil asked.

"The User-that-is-not-a-user and his friends have fled the village!" Xa-Tul screamed. "They somehow escaped!"

He wanted to punch something, anything, but the other zombies had stepped back out of arm's reach. Putting his heels to the zombie-horse under him, he galloped across the battlefield to get a closer look at the NPCs atop the fortified wall. Some of the villagers tried to shoot their pitiful arrows at him, but the king had been careful enough to remain out of bow range. The pointed shafts stuck harmlessly into the ground five blocks in front of him.

Glaring at the defenders, Xa-Tul noticed that none of them had letters over their heads, nor did they display the confident, commanding presence that Gameknight999's friends always seemed to have.

My true enemies have definitely fled, he thought.

Pulling on the reigns, Xa-Tul spun his zombie mount around and brought it back near his generals.

"There is no point to this battle," the king grumbled. "We cannot breach these walls without creepers or skeletons or endermen."

"Should the attacking zombies be withdrawn?" one of his generals asked.

"No, let them fight," Xa-Tul explained. "The foolish villagers will think that they had been victorious and will become complacent in the defense of their walls. When the zombie army returns with ten times this number, the NPCs will not know what hit them.

"Come, let us return to zombie-town. Xa-Tul will gather all the zombie forces needed to erase this village from the surface of Minecraft," the king said.

Ur-Kil looked up at his leader and grinned a toothy smile, his dark eyes filled with hatred for the NPCs.

"But Ur-Kil will not return to zombie-town quite yet," the zombie king said. "In fact, none of my generals will return to zombie-town right now." He glared down upon his commanders. He could see that they all had fear in their eyes—all except Ur-Kil.

Ur-Kil is brave, and a brave zombie could be

dangerous to Xa-Tul's reign, the king thought. *This one must be watched closely.*

"Each zombie general will take a company of warriors and hunt for our true enemies, the ones who have fled," Xa-Tul continued. "When they are found, one warrior will be sent back to zombie-town to report their position, while the others will destroy the friends of the User-that-is-not-a-user. Xa-Tul wants Gameknight999 to witness the destruction of his friends, starting with the crafter. And when the User-that-is-not-a-user is overcome with grief, then Xa-Tul will strike and punish him for the destruction of the Maker." The king paused to lean down from his horse and glare at his commanders, his eyes glowing bright red. "Vengeance for the death of Herobrine will belong to the zombies of the Overworld!"

Xa-Tul let out a deep, maniacal laugh, and the hate-filled sound of it resonated across the landscape like evil thunder. Yanking on the reins, he spun his horse around and headed back to zombie-town alone, leaving the surviving zombies to follow their individual generals across the land in search of their prey.

CHAPTER 11

ESCAPING XA-TUL

Gameknight and his friends emerged from the secret tunnel far from the village and the prying eyes of Xa-Tul, spilling out onto a cold, snow-covered ice plain. The crisp air instantly bit into their cheeks as puffs of fogged breath billowed from horse and rider alike.

They rode in silence, listening to the distant sounds of battle, all of them hoping their friends and neighbors were safe. Thankfully the village eventually grew quiet, and no smoke billowed into the sky. That meant that the NPCs had won and the zombies must have been destroyed or retreated.

"Maybe Xa-Tul was killed?" Stitcher asked.

"Not likely," Gameknight replied. "I don't think we've seen the last of him."

They rode through the rest of the day in silence. Gameknight eyed the occasional tall spruce tree with suspicion, knowing that spiders liked to hide in their leafy foliage. He didn't like being out in the open like this, but at least, with the snow covering the ground, monsters would be easy to spot in the distance.

"By the way, Gameknight, I have something for you," Stitcher said.

She reached into her inventory and pulled out a diamond sword, purple waves of magical power running down its length.

"You dropped this when you took the Gateway of Light back to the physical world, after the Last Battle," she said.

Tell her I said hello, Jenny typed.

"Oh yeah, Monet113 says hello," Gameknight said to the young NPC.

Stitcher smiled, then looked up into the air and waved.

:D, Jenny replied.

Extending the blade, hilt first, she handed the weapon to Gameknight. He held it close to his face, inspecting every inch. Moving his hand down the flat side, he caressed it as if it were an old friend, its razor-sharp edge gleaming in the setting sun.

"Thank you, Stitcher," Gameknight said. "I really appreciate this."

She smiled, then moved out a bit and watched the sun off to the right slowly setting, the sky turning from a deep blue to a warm crimson that matched her own curly locks. The landscape was absolutely silent as the sky grew dark, the only sound being the crunch of the horses' hooves as they pierced the frozen layer of snow. When the light of the sun was fully extinguished and the heavens were painted with a million stars, a full moon began to peek its pale face above the eastern horizon, covering the landscape with an eerie, surreal glow.

Moving from the grassy plains, the party passed from the snow-covered grassland to cold taiga. Snow began to fall as they moved into the new biome. The shining flakes felt clean and pure, as if the bad things of Minecraft could not penetrate the purity of this landscape.

"Oh no," Hunter shrieked, "It's followed us!"

Gameknight looked in the direction she was pointing. In the distance, a blotchy dark stain moved erratically across the snow-covered ground, heading toward them.

"It found us," Gameknight said, his voice filled with fear. "Everyone, ride as fast as you can!"

Kicking his horse into a gallop, Gameknight moved up next to Crafter just as Digger's horse started to sprint forward. Drawing his sword, the User-that-is-not-a-user readied himself for battle—a battle against Minecraft itself.

The shadow of evil sensed its prey escaping and streaked across the ground. Moving like a jagged bolt of black lightning, the darkness skidded across the surface of the ground, heading straight for Crafter's horse, moving faster and faster. Gameknight could hear Hunter's bow make a *thrummm ... thrummm ... thrummm* sound as she fired arrows at the shadow, but they did nothing to slow it down.

When it found Crafter's mount, the horse flashed red as dark, jagged shapes shot up from the ground into the horse and rider. Crafter moaned in agony as the shadow of evil stabbed at him again and again with its blades of darkness. Herder threw potions of healing onto him, splashing the horse as well, but the shadow took a terrible toll on both.

"Gameknight," his father shouted, "you need move back and forth! You know, evade like in my the old computer game, Wing Commander."

"What?"

"Evasive action! As if it were homing in on Crafter," Monkeypants yelled.

And then Gameknight realized what his dad was talking about. Bolting forward, he grabbed the reins of Crafter's horse from Digger's hand, then shot off to the right. The shadow was slow to respond and fell behind. Just as it moved toward them, Gameknight turned to the left, then turned again. The shadow passed slightly under its target and was able to stab up at them, but it was a glancing blow and did little damage.

"Here it comes," Monkeypants said. "Break right!"

Gameknight turned to the right and sprinted forward.

"Here it comes again," his father reported. "Break left . . . now!"

He turned left, then drove his horse to sprint with every bit of speed the big animal could muster.

"It's starting to dissolve!" Stitcher said as she raced up to Gameknight.

Glancing over his shoulder, he could see the dark patch of evil was breaking apart and evaporating. It tried to make one more run at Crafter, but Gameknight dodged to the right as soon as it approached, causing it to miss its target.

And then the shadow of evil was gone.

Herder moved up next to one of the pack mules and pulled out another splash potion of healing and threw it on Crafter. The bottle shattered, throwing the reddish liquid across the horse and rider.

"That was good thinking, Monkeypants," Gameknight said.

"Well, the whole point of learning is to apply your knowledge and experience in new situations," his father said. "But I have to tell you, I never expected to apply my experience playing Wing Commander twenty years ago to evading a shadowy monster of evil while being trapped inside Minecraft."

They laughed, Hunter slapping Monkeypants on the back.

"I don't care where it comes from," she said, "as long as it helps. You're OK, Monkeypants271 ... though I wish we could do something about that name. It's kinda silly."

"Yeah . . . well . . ." Monkeypants said, a little embarrassed.

"You see? I told you," Gameknight said.

His father shrugged.

"That's enough, let's get out of here," Digger said. "Herobrine knows that Crafter is here; he'll be back as soon as he can."

"Why do you think it disappears like that and doesn't keep attacking?" Herder asked.

"Maybe Herobrine only has enough strength for these quick bursts," Gameknight suggested. "But they seem to be coming more frequently. Crafter told me that they were first attacking every other day, then every day, now multiple times a day."

"I think the shadow of evil is getting larger," Herder said.

"What do you mean?" Gameknight asked.

"I remember seeing it when it first attacked Crafter," Herder explained, "and it's bigger now. It's growing."

"Herobrine must be getting stronger," Gameknight added.

"That can't be good," Hunter added.

"It just means that we have to hurry," Digger said, a determined look on his square face. "Let's keep heading to the south."

Urging his horse forward, Gameknight followed Digger, the lead to Crafter's horse still in his hand. Looking about the landscape for threats, Gameknight noticed it had stopped snowing at some point during the attack, and everything was still. It was as though Minecraft itself was holding its breath as it watched the party pass through the frozen land.

Moving to take up flanking positions on either side of Crafter, Hunter and Stitcher positioned themselves to the right and left, their enchanted bows out and ready. The iridescent light from the magical weapons cast a strange purple illumination on the area, making it easier to see the snow-covered ground ahead.

Suddenly, a howling sound pierced through the silence, echoing throughout the forest. Turning to look at Herder, Gameknight found that the young boy was already gone, his horse streaking through the woods, a skeleton bone in his outstretched hand. Looking up into the sky, Gameknight noticed the square face of the moon climbing up from behind a group of trees, sparkling stars decorating the night sky. A faint halo of light surrounded the lunar face, caused by the wispy square clouds passing overhead.

"So what was the deal with that zombie king back there at the village?" Monkeypants271 asked.

"He is one of Herobrine's creations," Hunter explained. "His name is Xa-Tul, and he's just as evil as his Maker."

"What does he want?" Monkeypants said.

"To destroy everything," Digger said over his shoulder. "Herobrine created the monster kings and all they care about is destruction and attacking the Overworld again."

"What do you mean *again*?"

"There is very little written about that time in Minecraft, but the stories say that apparently a hundred years ago, all of the monsters of the Overworld could move about in the light of day without bursting into flames," Digger answered. "They lived on the surface with the NPCs, but something happened. They started attacking all the villages and destroying everything in sight. Nobody was really sure what started the Great Zombie Invasion, but they almost succeeded in obliterating everything. Then one NPC came forward and led the villagers to victory over the monsters."

"Smithy of the two swords," Gameknight said.

"Exactly," Digger replied. "Villagers all across Minecraft pause to remember him at the start of every new year."

"So the NPCs stopped the Invasion?" Monkeypants asked.

Digger nodded. "Yep, but then something happened to the monsters. The ghasts were banished with the zombie pigmen and blazes to the Nether. The skeletons and zombies were changed so that they would burst into flames under the light of the sun, forcing them underground. The endermen were banished to The End with their Ender Dragon. The Overworld was purged of the most violent of monsters, leaving only the spiders, creepers, and slimes to safely walk through the daylight. Somehow, though, the monsters have figured out how to come back into the Overworld. The zombies and skeletons still burn in the sunlight, but as you saw at the village, they've learned to wear hats to keep themselves from catching fire."

"What are the monster kings?" Monkeypants asked.

"Herobrine created monsters to lead his army," Gameknight answered. "He first made Erebus—the king of the endermen, Malacoda—the king of the ghasts, and Shaikulud—the spider queen."

"We managed to destroy those three," Hunter said as she scanned the snow-covered forest with her keen hunter's eyes.

Small white flakes of snow started to float down from the sky; it was snowing again. Gameknight marveled at the beauty of the scene. When just playing the game, the flakes of snow looked like regular star-like shapes. But here, inside the game, each snowflake was a unique pattern, one impossibly complex shape after another, gracefully floating through the air and settling on the ground.

In the distance, the sound of hooves galloping through snow drifted across the landscape. Gameknight thought he saw Herder returning alone, but as he neared, a dozen fluffy white wolves emerged through the falling soft white flakes. The furry animals blended in perfectly with the snow, making them nearly invisible. As he neared, the User-that-is-not-a-user saw that each wolf was now wearing a bright red collar; they were tamed and now were Herder's servants—no, his companions.

Gameknight smiled, but his smile evaporated when Crafter moaned behind him.

"It's OK, Crafter. We're getting you help," he said softly.

"Are there more kings?" Monkeypants asked.

"Yep," Hunter replied. "There's a whole new group of them, and they all want to play with us." She gave Monkeypants a sarcastic smile, then continued. "Xa-Tul, the zombie king that you saw back at the village, was one of his new leaders, but there's also Reaper—the king of the skeletons, and . . ."

"Charybdis, the king of the blazes," Stitcher added.

"And Feyd," Gameknight said, his voice filled with dread, "the king of the endermen."

"Yep, Herobrine's Four Horsemen, as he called them," Hunter said.

"The Four Horsemen of the Apocalypse," Monkeypants said in a low voice, his forehead creased with worry.

"But right now, it seems that we only have to worry about Xa-Tul," Stitcher said as she moved a little closer.

Ahead, they could see through the falling snow that they were reaching the edge of the cold taiga, and the next biome looked like sunflower plains. The yellow flowers were just becoming visible through the hazy snowstorm.

Suddenly, the wolves all started to growl, making everyone draw their weapons and scan the darkness for enemies.

Gameknight's skin felt prickly as tiny square goosebumps formed down his arms and neck. If the wolves were growling, it meant some kind of surprise was lying in wait for them up ahead ... and it probably wasn't a good one.

CHAPTER 12

ENDERMEN!

"**D**oes anyone see anything?" Gameknight asked.

Everyone shook their blocky heads as they continued to scan the forest.

"I can see something, but it doesn't make any sense," Monkeypants said.

"What do you see, Dad?"

"You know that game you play with the tall skinny monster?" Monkeypants explained. "It's called Slenderguy, or Slender . . . something."

"Slenderman?" Gameknight asked.

"Yeah, I thought I saw something like Slenderman, but all I could see was his shadow," Monkeypants said. "The shadow was completely black against the snow, making it easy to see in the moonlight."

The others looked at Gameknight, confused.

"What does that mean?" Digger asked.

"Endermen!" Gameknight hissed. "Come on, we need to move."

Gameknight kicked his horse into action, driving it as fast as he could. But suddenly a dark figure appeared before him. It was a tall nightmare of a creature with large white eyes and lavender pupils filled with hate. Its skin was as black as midnight, as black as the void.

"Everybody stay together and go around him!" Digger shouted. "There's only one of them."

As if on cue, a dozen more endermen materialized, each surrounded by a mist of purple particles. They stood in a ring around the party, making it impossible to escape.

"Everyone stop," Gameknight said. "They can't attack unless we provoke them."

They brought their horses to a halt and clustered together, Herder's wolves forming a circle around the NPCs, their angry red eyes and pointed bared teeth facing outward.

Suddenly a new enderman appeared outside the ring of monsters. This one was riding a tall dark horse, the animal's eyes filled with an evil purple light. The enderman rider glared at Gameknight999, the monster's eyes glowing bright red.

"I told you at the Last Battle that your time would come, User-that-is-not-a-user," the monster screeched. "That time is now. The Maker will be avenged."

"Feyd, you are nothing, just like your lame predecessor Erebus," Gameknight said, struggling to hold his voice steady, trying to mask his fear with artificial confidence.

He looked around at the endermen that surrounded them and felt himself start to shake. If these monsters attacked, they would prove impossible to defeat. Many of his friends would perish. Thankfully, they had not been provoked.

Slowly, he put away his sword and motioned to the others. They all returned their weapons to their inventories, with the exception of Monkeypants. He was looking toward one of the endermen, trembling. His father looked petrified with fear.

"The battle for Minecraft is not over, User-that-is-not-a-user," Feyd said, his screechy voice sounding like shards of glass scraping together. "The mobs will be united by the monster kings, and we will cleanse Minecraft of the infestation that is the NPCs and users."

"You sound tough, but I don't see any of your little monsters doing anything," Gameknight said, careful to keep his voice calm and not look directly at Feyd. "We know you can't attack unless you are provoked and we aren't going to do that, so why don't you just go away."

Suddenly, one of the endermen started to shake. Glancing at the creature, Gameknight realized that Monkeypants had been staring at the creature.

"Dad, NOOOO!"

The creature opened its mouth wide and let out a blood-curdling screech that was so loud Gameknight had to cover his ears. This made the other endermen screech in unison as their eyes all turned bright white; they were now enraged, which meant they could fight.

Gameknight and his friends were in trouble.

The first enderman teleported next to Monkeypants and reached out to punch him in the head, but just as it was about to make contact, a flaming arrow shot through the air. It struck the dark creature in the shoulder. The impact made the monster twist slightly, causing his attack to miss its target.

Feyd cackled evilly as the other endermen started to attack. Drawing his diamond sword, Gameknight moved forward to protect Crafter, but out of the corner of his eye, he saw the yellow sunflowers staring at him, the rain falling lightly on open plains.

And then he realized the answer.

"Rain!" he said aloud. "Everyone follow me! Ignore the endermen and RIDE!"

Reaching down, he slapped the back of Monkeypant's horse, making it bolt forward toward the flowery plain. With Crafter's lead firmly in his hand, he streaked out of the snowy forest. Behind him, Gameknight999 could hear the crunch of horses' hooves breaking through the snow. Behind him, he knew his friends were following, all of them riding hard. The twang of a bow sounded, followed by another, then a flurry of twangs filled the air. Gameknight knew that Hunter and Stitcher were firing on the pursuing monsters, keeping them back.

The endermen then teleported ahead of them, forming a wall of dark bodies, their fists clenched and ready.

"Hunter, Stitcher, fire ahead of us!" Gameknight shouted.

The sisters turned and fired their bows, aiming at the center enderman. The creature was forced to teleport away to avoid being hit. They then turned their fire on the next enderman and then next and next until they'd carved a hole in the monstrous barrier. Behind him, Gameknight could still hear Feyd cackling with evil glee.

"You cannot escape us, User-that-is-not-a-user," the king of the endermen said.

"Oh yeah?" Gameknight yelled back, laughing. "Let's see your pitiful endermen catch us."

Digging his heels into his mount, he shot forward, passing from the snowy forest and into the plain of bright yellow flowers. Instantly, he could feel the temperature change from a skin-tingling cold to something pleasant and warm. Rain fell on his face and arms, splashing little square droplets of water all over him.

The endermen, now furious at his taunting laugh, teleported to get to closer to their prey. They didn't pay attention to their surroundings. As the monsters materialized on the sunflower plain, they were instantly exposed to the rain. Where square drops of water touched them, their dark skin sizzled. The monsters cried out in pain as the water burned them more and more. The endermen had no choice but to teleport back to the snowy forest, their skin still sizzling, cries of pain coming from the enraged monsters.

"What's wrong Feyd?" Gameknight shouted. "You aren't gonna come out here and take your revenge?" He laughed at the dark monster again.

"Gameknight, you might want to take it easy on him," Stitcher said.

"Why?"

"Because there is no sense in getting him angrier," Stitcher explained. "This rain could stop at any moment. We need to keep going and put distance between us and those monsters."

"She's right," Monkeypants said. "Let's get out of here, quick."

"Fine," Gameknight said as he started to gallop southward. "Come on everyone, let's get to that swamp."

CHAPTER 13

TWO KINGS

The king of the endermen materialized in a tunnel lit with orange light. Lava flowing from a hole in the rough stone wall illuminated the cave with a warm glow, allowing Feyd to see the bats hiding in the corners, fluttering here and there. In the distance, creepers were moving about, hoping for some foolish user to stray to these depths where they could be ensnared in their explosive grasp. Spiders clicked in the shadows and the sounds of zombies echoed through the tunnel. Their sorrowful moans were filled with sadness for being exiled to these underground passages a century ago. Feyd knew that the green creatures longed to live under the sky again, but its burning rays kept the decaying monsters always in the shadows, a perpetual imprisonment likely never to end.

Just a few blocks away, a stream of cool, blue water fell from the ceiling, splashing the area—something that the enderman gave a wide berth. Where the water and lava met, the molten rock was transformed into obsidian by the cooling effects of the water. This formed a large field of the dark blocks, their purple flecks shining bright in the orange light.

This was the place, Feyd thought. *They always put their zombie-towns where the lava and water formed obsidian.*

Moving to the flat wall that stood on the other side of the obsidian plane, the king of the endermen approached a lone block of stone that protruded out from the flat surface. Pressing the block with his dark fist, Feyd felt it move slightly, causing a grinding sound to echo through the tunnel. He could hear stone sliding against stone as the wall slowly opened, revealing a long dark tunnel.

This is the place, my friends, Feyd thought to the other endermen.

Suddenly, he was enveloped in a cloud of purple teleportation particles as twenty endermen materialized around him.

Light from the nearby lava filled the passage with a warm orange glow, allowing Feyd to see the other end. Gathering his teleportation powers, he made the jump through the stone corridor and appeared at the edge of the zombie-town. The other monsters followed suit, all of them moving as one to the entrance of the giant cavern.

Before the endermen king stretched a massive cave at least a hundred blocks across and twenty blocks tall. All across the uneven floor of the chamber were boxy houses made of every material imaginable: zombie-town. The varied structures formed a patchwork of colors that spread across the cavern like a multihued blanket. Along the edges of the town, Feyd could see the green sparkling HP fountains. Within the shimmering flow stood many zombies, the decaying creatures bathing in the emerald sparks, looks of rapture on their hideous faces. At the center of the cavern, Feyd could see a clearing—a circle of stone free from any of the ramshackle structures. A platform of obsidian sat at the center of the assembly area, its dark blocks standing out in contrast to the gray stone on which it sat, sparkling green HP fountains surrounding the clearing.

"That must be where they have their gatherings," Feyd said to the other endermen, his long crooked finger pointing to the shadowy platform. "Come my brothers and sisters, but be on guard—these stupid zombies cannot be trusted."

He disappeared, then materialized on the dark stage, a mist of purple particles clouding his vision for just an instant. A moment later, the other endermen joined him. They turned and faced in all directions, a protective ring of dark fists surrounding their king.

"Be at ease, my friends," he said to his troops. "The time for battle may be near, but it is not now. Relax, and do not respond to anything the foolish zombies say or do unless I command it."

The endermen, unclenched their fists, but were still ready to move at lightning speed.

Just then, a booming voice echoed across the cavern.

"Who dares come into zombie-town without permission from Xa-Tul?"

A massive zombie mounted on a green decaying zombie-horse approached the platform. He was covered in iron chain mail, the links reflecting the green sparks from the HP fountains, making it look as if it were decorated with the tiniest of emeralds. Atop the monster's head sat a crown of gold that looked to be made from a ring of long deadly claws, each golden talon razor sharp. Feyd knew this zombie to be Xa-Tul, one of Herobrine's creations, and technically an ally, though zombies and endermen had never been friends.

"What are you doing here, endermen?" Xa-Tul demanded.

Zombies filed into the clearing. Some of them wore shining golden armor and carried gold swords, but they looked childlike compared to the massive broadsword that hung at the zombie king's hip. The zombies growled as they came forward, some of them moaning in anticipation of battle.

Drawing his sword, Xa-Tul leapt off his horse and approached the platform. At the sight of the gigantic weapon, the endermen surrounding Feyd gathered their teleportation powers, causing a mist of purple particles to form, wrapping around the shadowy creatures like a protective cocoon. Black fists clenched as they waited for the king of the zombies to approach.

"Everyone be at ease," Feyd said in a loud screechy voice that echoed off the stone walls. "We are here as friends, not enemies."

Xa-Tul looked at the endermen and growled.

"Endermen, relax—I order it," Feyd commanded.

The mist of purple particles faded away. Feeling the tension slowly ease, the dark monster turned and faced the zombie king.

"Why is the king of the endermen here in zombie-town?" Xa-Tul growled.

"We have a common enemy," he screeched. "The User-that-is-not-a-user is back."

"Xa-Tul knows this," the zombie king boomed. "These zombies have already attacked the village of his friends, but my incompetent generals were unable to capture him. The Fool and his friends escaped the village. They ran away at the height of the battle ... Cowards."

"I have seen him out in the wild," Feyd said.

This shocked the zombie king, making him take a step closer to the dark creatures. Some of the enderman around Feyd gathered their teleportation powers again, fists beginning to clench. Feyd looked at his troops, then back at the mighty golden broadsword that was still in the zombie king's hand.

"Perhaps you could put your little sword away while we talk?" Feyd said.

Xa-Tul looked down at the sword, then back up at the endermen king.

"Why should I?"

"The enemy of my enemy is my friend," Feyd said in a slow, deliberate voice. "We can pursue the User-that-is-not-a-user separately, and miss our chance to destroy him," Feyd said, his white eyes staring down into Xa-Tul's red ones. "Or we can work together and destroy Gameknight999 and all his friends. If we mix our endermen's teleportation powers with the zombies' ability to attack and fight, then we will become more powerful together than apart."

Xa-Tul considered these words. Sheathing his sword, the zombie king began pacing, his big hands linked behind his back, his armor clinking and jingling as he walked.

"Why should zombies do this thing?" Xa-Tul asked. "The zombie warriors can attack and destroy him without any help. What is being offered that the zombies do not already have?"

"I know where the User-that-is-not-a-user is going," the king of the endermen said. "We can lay a trap for Gameknight999 and his friends and destroy the ones responsible for the death of our Maker. Can the zombies do that?"

Reaching up to stroke his square chin with a clawed hand, Xa-Tul considered this information as he continued to pace. More of the zombies had come out into the open square, their growling moans getting louder and louder.

Xa-Tul stopped and faced the king of the endermen.

"The zombies will work with the endermen to destroy our common enemy," Xa-Tul said as he drew his sword and held it high over his head. He then turned and faced his own warriors. "Brothers ... sisters ... the endermen have agreed to aid us in our vengeance of the Maker. The User-that-is-not-a-user will soon be on his knees before Xa-Tul."

The zombies growled and moaned with excitement, their rotting fists held high up into the air. Xa-Tul looked about at his warriors and smiled a toothy grin, then turned back to the endermen.

"Say your plan, endermen king, and Xa-Tul will correct the errors and make it great," the big zombie said.

Feyd looked at the creature and shook his head.

Idiot ... but I must endure this zombie's ego only until I capture Gameknight999, Feyd thought.

"OK, here's my plan," Feyd said as Xa-Tul came closer, the zombie generals crowding the obsidian stand.

And as Feyd explained, the zombies growled louder and louder until the walls of the cave shook with fright.

CHAPTER 14

LAND OF DREAMS

Gameknight999 walked through a strange forest. Every tree was stripped of its leaves, the branches completely bare. It gave them a sickly look, as if some kind of terrible virus had infected them all, slowly squeezing the life from the trees and leaving just an empty husk.

This was not the forest the party had stopped in to rest. They had ridden all day through the sunflower biome, a constant drizzle of rain falling on their heads. None of them had been bothered, though, as it kept the endermen away, but after a hard ride through the wet weather, Gameknight and his companions had needed a rest. When they passed from the sunflower biome to the mega taiga biome, Gameknight found a depression in the forest floor where they could stop for the night without being seen.

Half the party fell asleep as soon as their

heads touched their pillows, Gameknight one of them. But as he looked around him, he could tell that these trees were not the super tall spruce trees that had surrounded him and his friends.

Something strange was going on.

Moving to one of the nearby oak trees, Gameknight ran his hand along the smooth branch. At his feet, piles of gray ash littered the ground, the remains of the deceased leaves. It was then that he noticed the silvery fog that circled about his ankles and knees.

He was in the Land of Dreams.

Instantly, his favorite bow materialized in his hand. It had Power V, Punch II, Infinity, and Flame enchantments. It had been the envy of every player in Minecraft, but back then, he'd used it to hurt others rather than help. He'd been the king of the griefers and had done terrible things with his bow, but Crafter and the NPCs of Minecraft had taught him about the value of friendship, ending his griefing days.

He smiled.

Suddenly, a sound came from behind. Spinning around quickly, he drew an arrow and notched it to the string. Drawing it back, Gameknight aimed at the sound. It was a crackling sound, like the sound of someone crumpling a piece of paper. Stepping forward slowly, the User-that-is-not-a-user moved from tree to tree through the silvery mist. The fog felt damp and cold against his square cheeks, chilling him to the bone. The crunching sound before him had his nerves on edge, and every one of his senses were focused to laser sharpness, directed toward the noise ahead.

Moving to a naked spruce, Gameknight peered around the smooth trunk. Before him, he saw what looked like an NPC wearing a dark smock, a black stripe down the center. The NPC's hair was as black as coal, the locks reaching almost to his shoulders. Reaching out, the NPC laid a hand on a tall oak, then stood motionless. His hand started to radiate a sickly yellow light that quickly spread, flowing over the branches until the tree was completely covered. The leaves then began to discolor, fading from their lush, healthy green to a darker shade that turned to an ashen gray. The leaves then crumbled and fell to the ground, leaving only piles of dust behind.

The NPC laughed, then turned and looked toward Gameknight999. His eyes were glowing bright white, just like . . .

Gameknight gasped.

"Ahh, my old friend has returned to visit me in my prison," the NPC said.

"Herobrine," Gameknight999 hissed as he stepped out from behind the tree, his arrow trained directly on the shadow-crafter's chest.

Kneeling, Herobrine blew a puff of air at the leafy remains. The dust billowed up into the air. He laughed.

"What are you doing here?" Gameknight asked.

"You thought you had me completely trapped

in that pig-body, didn't you," Herobrine said, then laughed again. "Xa-Tul named you correctly. You are truly the Fool."

He moved closer to Gameknight999, making the User-that-is-not-a-user take a step back.

"The prison you made for me is not strong enough to fully contain me," Herobrine said, his eyes glowing brighter. "I have found your little crafter friend and have been punishing him for knowing you."

"We're going to stop you," Gameknight said, trying to make his voice sound confident and strong.

Herobrine laughed.

"The Fool tries to sound like a man, but is still but a child," the shadow-crafter said with a sneer. "That pitiful pig-body cannot hold all of my powers."

"You mean hold in all of your evil," Gameknight added.

"Whatever," Herobrine continued. "My evil powers will continue to leak out into Minecraft until I've destroyed all the crafters ... everywhere. But the first one to be killed will be your friend as punishment. The villagers will come to understand my intent, for I will tell them in the Land of Dreams. They will try to stop me by attacking me in my prison, thinking that my death will save them. The fools will only be setting me free. When one of the villagers kills my pig-body, my XP will infect them and I will be free again. It is inevitable."

Herobrine took another step closer. Diamond

armor materialized on his body, the protective coating having some kind of enchantment on it, for Gameknight could see waves of sparkling black magic flowing across the chest plate and leggings. A diamond sword then materialized in the shadow-crafter's hand. He pointed it toward the User-that-is-not-a-user.

"The foolish NPCs cherish their crafters so much that they will unleash the instrument of their destruction just to save their leaders." He took another step closer.

Looking down at himself, Gameknight realized that he had no protection. Concentrating, he felt the cool presence of diamond armor materializing on his body. Dropping the bow, he imagined a diamond sword in each hand, each with Sharpness V and Knockback II.

Holding his swords out in front of him, he took a step toward Herobrine.

I refuse to be afraid of this monster, Gameknight thought to himself.

But he was afraid. He'd faced Herobrine multiple times in battle, but always had someone there to help him: Herder and his wolves; Shawny; his sister; then finally Herder and the pigs. But here, in the Land of Dreams, he was alone, truly alone. Gameknight knew that he could wake himself up, but he was tired of running from Herobrine and being afraid. It was time to stand up to this nightmare as he'd done with Erebus long ago.

"Let's see if you've gotten any better with your pathetic swords," Herobrine said. "I knew of another NPC who fought with two swords, you know."

"I don't care," Gameknight said as he moved closer.

"Smithy. He was a fool just like you, Fool," Herobrine said. "He tried to face me as you are doing, but do you know what happened? Not even your little Crafter knows. Smithy kept it secret."

"What?" Gameknight snapped. "What happened to Smithy?"

"He—ahhh, no, I don't think I'm going to tell you. I'll just show you."

Herobrine disappeared, then materialized right next to Gameknight999. Spinning, the User-that-is-not-a-user reached out with his sword as he moved away from the attack he knew was coming. Herobrine's sword streaked past Gameknight's shoulder and hit the ground, causing sparks to fly up into the air.

Not waiting for the Maker to recover, Gameknight rolled to his left, then slashed out at his armored legs. His diamond sword rang out when it smashed into the leggings, causing a chunk of diamond armor to fall off and clatter to the ground. But before Gameknight could swing his other sword at the exposed leg, the chunk of armor moved back to Herobrine and fused into the diamond coating, repairing itself.

"Ahh, another thing of which the great User-that-is-not-a-user is ignorant," Herobrine mocked.

Disappearing again, the shadow-crafter

appeared behind Gameknight999, slicing down with his own dark blade. The sword cracked Gameknight's chest plate in three places, causing pain to radiate throughout his body. He fell to one knee as he was overwhelmed with agony, but quickly rolled to the right just as Herobrine attacked again.

Standing, he faced his enemy, fear dominating his mind.

How can I defeat him? *Gameknight thought.* He's too strong and too fast.

Herobrine took a step closer, but suddenly stopped as his feet became tangled in the grass that covered the ground. The green blades of grass started to grow longer and longer as they entangled themselves around Herobrine's legs. Like tiny little emerald snakes, they slithered their way up his body until the long strands had wrapped around his arms as well, immobilizing his enemy.

Now's my chance, *Gameknight thought.*

But just as he started forward, a massive oak tree sprouted up out of the ground, followed by a pine right next to it and a spruce on the other side. Gameknight tried to move around the trees but more of the massive trunks appeared, trapping Herobrine in walls of wood on all sides.

Confused, Gameknight imagined a diamond axe. One instantly appeared in his hand, but before he could swing it at the pine, a rumbling splashing sound filled the Land of Dreams. Looking toward the sound, Gameknight could see a massive wave of water barreling down on them. It was a tidal wave at least twenty blocks high, and it tore through the Land of Dreams with the force of a giant's fist, tearing up trees and flattening mountains.

"Oh no," Gameknight said.

Herobrine laughed.

"Next time, you won't have any help," Herobrine said as the wave crashed down on them.

Gameknight tumbled around as the wave carried him away. Terrified, he did the only thing he could think of.

"WAKE UP ... WAKE UP ... WAKE UP ..."

Soaked and cold, Gameknight sat up on the bed and looked around. All of his friends were standing around him, looks of worry and concern on their square faces. Glancing up at the sky, Gameknight saw the twinkling stars peering down on him through the leafy canopy. It was still night.

"That's the second time I've done that to him," Hunter said proudly, giving him a huge smile, an empty bucket in her square hands.

"What is it ... what is it?" Gameknight asked. "What happened?"

"You were screaming," Digger answered, "Something about 'he's back' and that you were afraid."

"It was *him* ... in the Land of Dreams," Gameknight said as he wiped his face dry with his sleeve.

"I'm not surprised," Stitcher said. "That

pig-body can only hold his physical form, but it won't hold all of him."

"Wait a minute, why did you wake me?"

"You mean besides the fact that you were screaming?" Hunter asked.

"Because we have visitors," Digger said, his big pickaxe held in his hands, ready. "They say that they are friends of yours, and Hunter said that they were OK."

"Who are they?" Gameknight asked as he looked around. "Where are they?"

"By the horses," Digger answered.

Gameknight stood and shook his head, spraying Hunter with water. It was his turn to smile.

Putting on his iron armor, he drew his sword and moved off toward the picket line where the horses were tied. As he approached, he found that none of his friends were following. Glancing at them, he gave them a questioning look.

"They said they wanted to talk to you alone," Hunter said and then shrugged.

Gameknight gave her a nervous smile, then turned and continued. Gripping his sword tightly, he moved as quietly as possible, not wanting to give away his position until the last minute.

Ahead Gameknight could hear their horses. Their whinnying sounded strange, as if they were excited for some reason. He knew they were all tied to fence posts that Herder had placed into the ground and could not get away, but they didn't sound as if they were trying to escape. Rather, they sounded happy and contented. Sprinting from tree to tree, Gameknight moved closer. Ahead, there were shadows moving on the ground, the full moon overhead making them easy to see. There were two of them. Sheathing his sword, he drew his bow and notched an arrow.

I wish I had my enchanted bow right now, he thought.

Drawing the arrow back, he stepped out from behind the tree and faced two strange creatures.

"We finnnally founnnnd you," one of them said in a singsong voice Then both moved forward, straight toward Gameknight999.

CHAPTER 15

OLD FRIENDS

Gameknight smiled as the two strange-looking individuals approached, arms outstretched. Suddenly, Monkeypants was at his side, his iron sword held out in front of him.

"If you're here to hurt my son, you better think again," his father said, a scowl on his boxy face.

The two individuals stopped their approach and looked at Monkeypants, confused.

"Dad, it's alright, these are friends," Gameknight said as he laid a reassuring hand on his father's arm. "This is Grassbrin and Treebrin, two of the light-crafters that helped us defend the Source against Erebus and Malacoda."

"Light-crafters? I don't understand."

"Put away your sword and I'll explain," Gameknight said.

Monkeypants lowered his weapon, but his

son noticed that he kept it gripped firmly in his boxy hand.

He's learning to be cautious in Minecraft, Gameknight thought. *Good.*

"Dad, this one is Grassbrin," Gameknight said, pointing to the shorter of the two. "His job is to improve the grass and make it more realistic for the users."

Monkeypants nodded toward the light-crafter, but still stayed wary.

Grassbrin gave Monkeypants271 a deep bow, his long dark green hair drooping down over his face when he stood back up. Wiping the stringy locks from his face, he looked at Gameknight and his father with his bright emerald eyes. Gameknight could see the light-crafter still had a faint green tint to his skin. On any other NPC, it would have made them look ill, but on Grassbrin it made him look healthy, with the strong appearance of something alive and flourishing.

Grassbrin moved to the horses and plunged his hand into the soil. A glow enveloped his hands and wrists, the color matching the faint green hue to his skin and eyes. The iridescent glow spread to the neighboring blocks. As it flowed across the ground, long thick blades of grass sprouted up out of the ground beneath the horses. Bending down, the tall animals began to munch on the lush vegetation, feasting on the rich bounty growing around them.

Pulling his glowing hands out of the ground, Grassbrin stood and faced Gameknight999 and his father, then smiled as he brushed away dark green locks from his face again.

"It is a pleasurrrre to see you againnnn," he said, his melodic voice closer to music than speech.

Stepping forward, he wrapped his long arms around Gameknight999, hugging him tight. Then the light-crafter turned and faced Monkeypants.

"Grassbrin, this is my father, Monkeypants271," Gameknight said.

"Ahhh, the father of the User-that-is-not-a-user. It is a great honnnor to mmmeet you," Grassbrin said, the extended n's and m's making it sound as if he were humming while talking.

"Yeah, I guess I'm glad to meet you, too . . ." Monkeypants replied.

"The other is Treebrin," Gameknight explained. "His job is—"

"Let me guess," Monkeypants interrupted. "He's like the Lorax and he speaks for the trees?"

"He's not the Lorax," Gameknight grumbled, embarrassed, "but essentially you're right. He works on the trees."

Treebrin stepped forward. Towering over Gameknight and Monkeypants, the tall light-crafter bowed to the pair, then stood and gazed at the User-that-is-not-a-user. For the first time, Gameknight noticed that his skin had a mottled brown appearance that almost matched the pattern of the wood grain on the tall spruce next to him. He had spikey brown hair that stood straight up like tiny little branches, and his warm cream-colored eyes would almost pass for the color of the inside of a tree. Reaching up, he placed a knobby hand on the bark of the spruce and gently caressed it as if it were his own child. Gameknight could see muscles rippling beneath his strong arms and thick stout legs. Meeting Treebrin for the first time, the light-crafter's size and strength might be alarming, but the presence of the bright welcoming smile that was always plastered on his square face made the light-crafter appear peaceful and calm.

Looking down at Monkeypants, Treebrin said something, but Gameknight and his father could not understand any of it. The light-crafter's voice sounded like the rumbling of thunder, coupled with the cracking of bending strained branches. Nothing was intelligible.

"He said he's glad to meet the father of the User-that-is-not-a-user," a voice said from behind them.

Gameknight turned and found Herder peeking out from behind a bush.

"You can understand him?" Gameknight asked.

Herder nodded as one of his wolves stuck his white furry head out from behind the lanky boy's legs.

"Tell him that I'm glad they are—"

"He can understand you, Gameknight," Herder said, laughing.

"Ahh right, sorry." The User-that-is-not-a-user turned and faced the tall light-crafter. "I'm glad that you're here. We could use some help I think."

"Will you tell me what's going on?" Monkeypants asked, his voice sounding a little exasperated.

"Yeah, these two are light-crafters. They work on things for Minecraft, improving the code that runs certain parts of the game, as do all light-crafters," he explained. "The last part of their names, *brin*, means they are light-crafters. Their opposites, shadow-crafters, have a name that ends with *brine*. They improve the things of the dark: zombies, creepers, lava—creatures that typically live underground or in the shadows. It seems that these two are here to help us on our quest." Gameknight turned to face the two light-crafters. "What brought you to us?"

"The Oracle sent us to assist you," Grassbrin said.

Treebrin mumbled something and nodded his head.

"Yes, yes, I'll tell him," Grassbrin said to his friend. "There is an evil force attacking NPCs in a seemingly random fashion. The Oracle is trying to combat this force but she has so far been unsuccessful at stopping it or identifying the source."

"I know all about it," Gameknight said. "But I also know who's responsible: Herobrine is doing all this."

"Herobrine," Grassbrin hissed.

Treebrin trembled at the sound of his name, the warm smile changing instantly to an angry sneer.

"It was Herobrine that I was battling in the Land of Dreams," Gameknight explained.

"We know," Grassbrin said. "If you had killed him in the Land of Dreams, then you would have released his XP and infected Minecraft directly. We intervened to stop the battle. He was trying to goad you into destroying him."

"Ahh, the grass and trees," Gameknight said, everything suddenly making sense.

Treebrin nodded his head and grumbled something.

"He said that it was his idea to stop you in the Land of Dreams," Herder translated.

"Well, thank you," Gameknight replied, bowing to the tall light-crafter. "But back to the Oracle: She's still around?"

"Of course," Grassbrin replied. "All you have to do is close your eyes and listen."

Gameknight and his father closed their eyes and listened to their surroundings. He could hear the mooing of cattle in the distance, the occasional bleating of a sheep and the barking from Herder's wolves. Gradually, as if riding on a gentle ocean swell, harmonious tones filled his mind; gentle lyrical music that was calm and peaceful and beautiful. It gave him the impression of being wrapped in a warm blanket, safe from everything that was bad or hurtful.

"You hear it?" Grassbrin asked.

Gameknight nodded his blocky head as he opened his eyes.

"What was that?" Monkeypants asked, a smile on his face.

"That was the music of Minecraft," Gameknight explained. "Most users think that it's just a soundtrack to fill the silence, but it's actually the Oracle."

"What's an Oracle?" Monkeypants asked.

"It's an antivirus program that watches over Minecraft, keeping everyone and everything on the server safe," Gameknight said. "She helped us to battle Herobrine and capture him at the end of the Last Battle."

Monkeypants closed his eyes to listen again, but this time his smile faded to a worried frown.

"Something's wrong," his father said. "It sounds dissonant and scratchy now."

Gameknight instantly heard what Monkeypants meant—the music of Minecraft around them was under duress, and that could mean only one thing.

He's coming! Jenny typed. *The shadow of evil is coming!*

"Herobrine! He's coming!" Gameknight shouted.

Turning from the light-crafters, Gameknight ran to Crafter, but Digger was already there, lifting him off the cot on which he was resting and carrying him to the horses. With a length of rope, the big NPC tied this friend firmly to his horse as the others broke camp and ran to their own mounts.

As Gameknight climbed atop his horse, he looked down at the light-crafters.

"I'm sorry, we don't have horses for you, but—" he said.

"The pack mules," Herder interrupted. "Grassbrin and I will ride the pack mules. Treebrin, you can use my horse."

"Of course," the User-that-is-not-a-user replied as the light-crafters started moving toward their steads. Gameknight turned back to Herder. "Get some healing potions ready. I think Crafter is going to need them."

Herder nodded as he pulled a splash potion out of his inventory.

"Let's get out of here!" Gameknight shouted as he turned his horse to the south and kicked it into a gallop.

Moving up next to Digger, Gameknight reached out and took the lead to Crafter's horse, then sprinted through the forest. The others tried to keep up.

"Dad, get on my six," Gameknight shouted over his shoulder. "I need you to tell me which way to turn to avoid this thing."

"I'm already there," Monkeypants shouted. "Everyone yell when you see the shadow of evil."

The party sprinted to the south, driving their horses with as much speed as they could muster. They dodged around the towering spruces and blocks of mossy cobblestone as they shot through the mega taiga biome.

"I can't see the shadow of evil anywhere," Hunter yelled. "It's too dark to see it. The moon is down near the horizon and the tall trees are blocking its light."

"Great," Digger said. "We won't see it coming."

"How are we going to know when it gets here?" Stitcher asked. "I'm not sure Crafter can survive another attack."

"Scouts—we need scouts around us," Gameknight mumbled to himself.

"What?" Monkeypants asked.

"I said we need scouts around us, to warn us when the shadow of evil is close."

"Of course," Hunter said. "Everyone spread out, but stay close enough so that we can see each other. Herder, send your wolves out in a wide circle around us."

The skinny boy nodded, then wheeled his mule off to the right, a dozen wolves following close behind. Gameknight watched over his shoulder as Herder rode around their company, depositing a wolf at even intervals around their perimeter.

"Come on everyone, RIDE!" Gameknight yelled as he kicked his horse into a sprint.

Suddenly, a strange chill slithered down his spine, like tiny spiders with needles for legs crawling up and down his back. He knew Herobrine had arrived.

"He's here! Everyone look sharp!" Gameknight yelled.

Suddenly, a wolf yelped in pain.

"That's at our eight o'clock," Monkeypants said.

Gameknight turned to the right and rode hard.

Another wolf yelped, this time at his eleven o'clock.

Gameknight turned harder to the right and cut back along his own tracks. Just then, an explosion rocked the landscape. Someone had ignited some TNT.

"Maybe it will confuse it!" Stitcher shouted out from Gameknight's left.

The prickling along his skin seemed to dissipate for a moment, then returned.

"Worked for a moment," Gameknight shouted. "Give it some more!"

Zigzagging across the landscape, the User-that-is-not-a-user rode as hard as he could, pulling Crafter's horse with him as explosions rocked the landscape. More wolves yelped out in pain, but then Gameknight heard Stitcher cry out.

"It's on me!" she yelled.

Looking over his shoulder, Gameknight could see the shadow of evil stabbing up at the young girl with its dark shafts of hatred. Suddenly, Hunter came rushing to her sister. She smashed into Stitcher's horse with her own, snatched the girl from her saddle, and rode off, leaving the shadow behind. Stitcher's horse whinnied in pain as it was attacked, but soon quieted as the shadow of evil moved off in search of another target.

"This way—we'll be out of the forest!" Digger yelled, heading south.

Glancing to the east, Gameknight was glad to see the sun start to peek its square face above the distant horizon, changing the sky from a star-speckled black to a rosy pinkish-orange. Gameknight kicked his horse into a sprint and charged forward.

As the landscape grew bright, a swamp became visible in the distance, the shallow water sparkling in the morning sunlight. Large lily pads floated like tiny little green islands in the water, their wide surfaces quieting the gentle wind-driven waves. Swamp trees towered high in the air, their branches draped with long hanging vines that stretched all the way down to the water's surface.

Out there, somewhere, is the witch we need, Gameknight thought.

"Come on, everyone. Let's get to that swamp!" the User-that-is-not-a-user shouted.

Suddenly, a purple mist formed ahead of them, causing him to pull back on the reigns a little. Gameknight recognized it immediately. As the lavender cloud dissipated, fifty endermen materialized before him, each one with their arms wrapped around a zombie. At the center of the formation was Feyd, his long arms holding Xa-Tul.

It was a wall of monsters, with dark fists and razor-sharp claws all thirsting for Gameknight's flesh. As the endermen released their zombie cargo, the air filled with angry, hateful moans and vile, malicious chuckles. White endermen eyes blazed with fury in contrast to the dark lifeless eyes of the zombies. All of the creatures wanted to attack, but the only thing holding them back was their leader, Feyd. He stood out in front of the horde with Xa-Tul at his side. The two leaders glared at the User-that-is-not-a-user with venomous loathing that made Gameknight999 shudder.

Looking over his shoulder, Gameknight could see the shadow of evil had stopped and was hanging back, waiting. Likely Herobrine was reveling in the moment that was about to happen, the destruction of the User-that-is-not-a-user and his friends.

There's too many; we can't fight them all, Gameknight thought.

Some of the endermen grabbed their zombie friends and disappeared, only to reappear on their flanks, slowly boxing them in.

With the shadow of evil behind them, and a monster horde slowly circling them, they were trapped.

"Gameknight, what do we do?" Stitcher asked.

He said nothing, only stared at the two kings, his face pale with fear.

Suddenly, a cold wind blew across the landscape as a chilling snow began to fall.

"Great, just what we need—snow!" Gameknight said.

"Gameknight, how about one of your brilliant ideas?" Hunter asked. "I'd even settle for one of your foolish ones. Anything would do."

She looked at her friend, but Gameknight

could only return a blank stare. He had no idea what to do, and the thought of facing Feyd and Xa-Tul at the same time caused slivers of panic to stab at his soul.

They were trapped and the User-that-is-not-a-user had no idea how to escape. They were doomed.

CHAPTER 16

THE SOUTHERN SWAMP

"**G**ameknight, what do we do?" Stitcher asked, her voice cracking with panic. "We're surrounded."

"Maybe we could surrender and just explain that we're trying to help our friend get medicine from the witch," Monkeypants said. "There doesn't need to be violence here."

"Are you kidding?" Gameknight snapped. "Crafter is responsible for the defeat of Herobrine, as are everyone else in our party."

"But violence isn't always the answer," his father replied.

"It will have to be today," Hunter added as she notched an arrow to her bow. "Gameknight, what's your plan?"

Looking over his shoulder, Gameknight could see the shadow of evil waiting next to a tall spruce tree. The snow-covered ground made its terrible presence much easier to see against the fluffy white coating; the shadow looked like a malignant stain. Reaching out with an evil jagged shadow, Herobrine's evil presence touched the tree. Instantly, the leaves on the high branches started to shrivel and crumble. The lush green blocks of foliage turned ashen as they slowly died, their gray remains falling to the ground like a dark, sad rain.

Gameknight turned back toward the monsters. The zombies and endermen were spreading out, creating a wall to block any escape. Behind the monsters was the swamp that they so desperately needed, the witch that would save Crafter hidden somewhere out in the bogs. In the calm clear waters, the User-that-is-not-a-user could see the faintest of iridescent sparkles, as if some kind of strange magic was contained in those watery blocks.

"What do we do?" Stitcher asked again.

"I don't know . . . I don't know," the User-that-is-not-a-user whispered.

The falling snow had stilled the sounds of the forest, creating the crystalline silence that always made a gentle snowfall one of Gameknight's favorite things. But today, it just seemed to amplify the zombie growls and endermen chuckles.

"Snow . . ." Monkeypants said.

"What?" Digger asked.

"Snow . . . snowplow," Monkeypants said again. "I know what we'll do, but it's crazy and dangerous."

"I like it already," Hunter said with a smile.

"Form a wedge," Monkeypants said. "I'll be at the front and I'll—"

"No, you can't be at the front; you don't know how to fight endermen," Gameknight said. "I'll take the lead."

"But it will be dangerous," his father replied. "And when we—"

"Dad, I'm the User-that-is-not-a-user; this is what I do. I'm the best person to lead this charge, so that's what's gonna happen."

"But—"

"I know what I'm doing," Gameknight said. "You need to trust me."

"Fine," Monkeypants acquiesced. "Digger, you get behind him with Crafter. The others will be on the flanks. We're going to snowplow right through those monsters with the speed of the horses and swinging blades." He turned and looked at everyone in the party, waiting for objections. "Well?"

"I like this plan," Hunter said. "It has the crazy, what-were-you-thinking kind of feel to it—it's perfect." She turned and looked at Herder. "Send your wolves to the edges of the wedge, Herder, and bring up the rear."

"Nobody stops," Monkeypants said firmly. "Ready?"

"Waaaait," sang Grassbrin.

Gameknight turned to look at the light-crafter. The squat NPC had dismounted and plunged his hands deep into the snow-covered soil. As his arms began to glow a soft green, Gameknight could see the glow spread out between them and the monsters. Suddenly, a tangle of grass started to emerge through the fluffy snow right in front of the line of monsters. The leafy strands grew longer and longer until they were three blocks high. Driving his crafting power, Grassbrin made the fronds thicken and grow long until they formed a green leafy wall through which Gameknight could not see.

Smiling, the light-crafter withdrew his hand and jumped back onto his mount.

"Great, now we can't see the monsters," Hunter complained.

"And they can't see us," Gameknight said with a smile. "They won't know what's about to hit them." Turning in his saddle, he looked at his friends. "Are all of you ready?"

Everyone nodded and took up their positions.

"LET'S PLOW THE ROAD!" Monkeypants screamed. "Hunter, Stitcher, give them some presents to soften the wall."

"Oh yeah!" Hunter exclaimed.

Gameknight kicked his horse into a sprint and charged straight toward the green wall of grass, hopefully aiming for a section of the monster wall far from Xa-Tul; the last thing he needed right now was that massive broadsword. As he rode, flaming arrows streaked over his shoulder and disappeared through the curtain of grass. Angry growls and screeches came from the monsters as they closed on the grassy barrier. More arrows shot through the grass with more cries of pain coming from their adversaries.

And then suddenly, they punched through Grassbrin's obstacle.

Instantly, Gameknight could see zombies and endermen running around in a panic with magical flames licking their bodies. Some laid down in the snow to put out the flames, creating a small gap in the monstrous barrier. As more arrows flew past him, Gameknight gripped the reigns of the horse in his teeth, just like the Duke in that old movie, then drew both his swords.

Kicking his horse even harder, he picked up speed and headed for that tiny gap between zombie and enderman. As he rode, he found a battle cry starting to come out of his throat. It was not his normal battle cry, but it was appropriate for today.

"FOR CRAFTER!" he screamed as he smashed into the monsters.

Swinging both swords at the monsters on either side, Gameknight punched through the barrier of fists and claws, knocking down two of the creatures, their bodies flashing red with damage. Behind him, Digger and Crafter smashed through the dark barrier right behind him, Hunter and Stitcher on either side, their bows singing. Monkeypants, Herder, and the light-crafters brought up the rear with a circle of wolves surrounding the quartet. Not slowing a bit, they crashed into the monstrous barrier like a sledgehammer, knocking more of the creatures over as they sped by. In twenty strides, they were out of the mega taiga biome and wading through the still, shallow waters of the swamp, surprised looks on the monsters' faces.

Spinning their horses around, they all watched to see how the monsters would react. Gameknight could hear the creaking of drawn bows as Hunter, Stitcher, Digger, and Monkeypants all notched arrows to bowstrings and readied a pointed reply.

"The endermen won't follow," Gameknight said as he pointed down at the water. Around him, the swamp waters seemed to shimmer and sparkle, which seemed strange but was instantly forgotten when the sounds of zombie moans reached his ears. "But the zombies . . ."

As if on cue, a handful of zombies charged forward into the swamp. As soon as they waded into the water, blue iridescent bolts of lightning shot up out of the water, jabbing at the decaying creatures and making them flash red with damage.

"Go on, get them!" Xa-Tul bellowed.

The zombies, more afraid of their king than of Gameknight999, continued to move forward. Bolts of blue lightning continued to stab at them, smashing their HP with sheets of magical electricity. The zombies didn't last long. Their moans of pain and panic were drowned out by the thunderous blasts from the watery trap, but Gameknight could see their suffering and felt bad for the doomed creatures.

"I see that look in your eye," Hunter whispered into his ear. "Don't feel sorry for them; don't *ever* feel sorry for them. The first chance they get, they will destroy you and your father without a single hesitation."

"She's wrong, son. You should feel sorry for them," Monkeypants said. "War is terrible, and the warrior that forgets that lives are being lost on both sides, he becomes worse than the war itself. Fighting should be a last resort and always done with a heavy heart."

"He sounds like Crafter," Stitcher said.

Monkeypants looked at the younger sister and smiled. "Thank you, I think."

Glancing back at the zombies, Gameknight could see Xa-Tul scowling at him, a look of unbridled hatred in his red eyes.

"GET THEM!" the king of the zombies yelled.

None of the monsters moved.

"This is over for now," screeched Feyd. "There is some magic in the waters that stops your warriors from advancing. The water is deadly to my endermen and your zombies. We can go no further. We must retreat."

"NOOOOOO!" bellowed Xa-Tul.

Reaching out, Feyd grabbed the zombie king by the back of his chain mail. Stepping backward, he moved away from the deadly water, drawing Xa-Tul with him.

"This isn't over, User-that-is-not-a-user," Feyd screamed. "You will pay for the crime of destroying the Maker. Maybe not now, but soon. You can't stay in that swamp forever.

Eventually you will have to come out, and we will be waiting for you." Feyd laid a hand on the zombie king's shoulder. "It is time to go."

"No! I want to destroy Gameknight999!"

"Bye bye zombie king," Hunter mocked as she waved to him.

"Hunter, don't antagonize him," Stitcher said.

"Who cares?" the older sister replied. "He can't get us in here."

"Yes, but Feyd is right, we will have to leave eventually," Gameknight added.

"Whatever," Hunter added as she put her bow back into her inventory and pulled her horse around, facing into the swamp. "Let's start finding the . . . you know."

Her eyes darted to the monsters standing by the swamp's edge. Xa-Tul and Feyd both glared at Gameknight999 then disappeared in a cloud of teleportation particles. The surviving zombies each sought out an endermen and were also transported back to zombie-town, leaving only the shadow of evil behind.

The User-that-is-not-a-user looked at the dark stain. It moved closer to the edge of the swamp, but stopped.

"Maybe the magic of the swamp is keeping the shadow from attacking," Digger said.

"Or maybe it can't pass through water," Herder added.

"I don't know, and I don't care," Gameknight said. "As long as it isn't following us, I'm happy."

The shadow of evil shuddered for a moment, then disappeared, leaving the snow-covered ground unmarred and pristine. With its absence, Gameknight could feel the music of Minecraft relax, the harmonious tones sounding beautiful again.

"Come on, let's find that witch," the User-that-is-not-a-user said. "Crafter still needs our help, and I'm not going to stop until my friend is safe."

Monkeypants looked at his son and smiled, then urged his horse forward, following the rest of the party.

None of them noticed the dark creature hiding amidst the long, stringy vines hanging off the branches of a swamp tree a dozen blocks away. As the party cantered deeper into the swamp, the witch stepped out from behind the foliage and glared at the intruders. Her wart-covered bulbous nose wiggled back and forth with agitation as she glared at the trespassers, a hateful glare on her face.

"Enter the domain of Morgana at your own risk," she hissed, then moved stealthily from tree to tree, following the party through the shallow waters of the swamp.

CHAPTER 17

THE WITCH

They rode through the swamp in silence. The squishy soil under the thin layer of water was soft and spongy, the horses' feet sinking in a bit. Their hooves made a *squish-suck* sound, rather than the normal *clip-clop*, as they trudged through the mire. It reminded Gameknight of the noise his father's automated jelly dispenser had made on the day they had first tested the invention. The tiny pump had gotten stuck and shot globs of strawberry jam all over the kitchen walls.

Gameknight looked at his father and smiled. It was a good memory, even though the invention had failed. At least his dad had been home and they'd been inventing together that day.

Out near the edge of the swamp, they could hear the chuckling of endermen. The cackling sound brought an uneasy feeling to the group. Clearly Feyd had placed a ring of monsters around them, waiting for when they emerged from the watery domain. They all knew that they would have to deal with this threat eventually, and none of them looked forward to it; an endermen was a terrible foe to face in battle. With their teleportation abilities, it was like fighting Herobrine himself.

As they slogged through the swamp, Gameknight scanned the surroundings. They were heading toward a large copse of swamp trees, the drooping vines hanging off the branches making them seem sad and lonely. The ground under the trees was a mixture of brown dirt, pale sand, and large gray regions of clay, a single layer of water covering the colorful blocks. It was like a patchwork quilt up close, but in the distance, it all merged into a dull grayish-brown. Here and there, Gameknight could see sections of land standing defiantly above the still waters; lonely islands of dirt covered with life. Brown and red mushrooms poked their colorful faces through the tangle of tall grass as the occasional oak tree stood tall and majestic on the tiny isles. Every now and then, a chicken could be spotted walking on these isolated landmasses, their white feathery bodies standing out against the shining blue water.

Gameknight smiled as he tried to remember the famous YouTuber that used to call them spy-chickens ... Paul Somebody ... he couldn't quite recall.

"Son, I have to say, you took too much of a risk back there with the monsters," Monkeypants said.

"What do you mean?" his son answered.

"You always have to be at the front of the charge, the tip of the spear. It's dangerous, and you're just a—"

"A what? A kid?" Gameknight snapped.

"Well . . . yes," Monkeypants271 answered. "You're my kid and I have to keep you safe."

"How? By being away all the time?" Gameknight blurted out, then wished he hadn't.

He could tell that his comment had hurt his dad, but it was out there and he couldn't take it back.

Monkeypants looked down at the ground.

"I know you're young so you don't really understand, but—" Monkeypants tried to explain but was interrupted.

"I'm not that young. I'm almost an adult!" Gameknight snapped.

"You're twelve and still my child," Monkeypants replied. "And I have to do whatever is necessary to take care of you and your sister and mother. The way I can do that is by selling my inventions, you know that!"

"Yeah . . . I know."

"That's my job as a father," Monkeypants said. "And sometimes, that responsibility is difficult to bear, but I have no choice. I will never stop trying to take care of my kids and wife, for that's who I am."

Gameknight nodded his head. He'd heard this all before and knew the truth in his father's words, but still hated it when he was away from home.

"Responsibility is a heavy cloak that takes broad shoulders to support its weight," his dad said. "Some people take to it easily while others resist its challenges as they seek an easier path." His father moved his horse so that it was next to Gameknight's. Reaching out, he put a hand on his son's shoulder. "I'm able to take these trips to sell my inventions because I know that you are back home taking care of everything. Without you being there, I'd be stuck in a job I hate, being unhappy and dissatisfied with my life, and that would be bad for all of us. But because you are there, I'm able to do what I love and what I hope helps our family." He stopped his horse right near a large cluster of trees and stared straight at Gameknight. "Don't you see? Without you, I'd be a failure."

Gameknight999 looked up at his father.

"Sometimes we have to reach a little farther than we can, be a little stronger than we are, and do things that we normally wouldn't be able to, because we must, to take care of those we love," Monkeypants continued. "That's what I'm doing, and I need your help."

"I know but ..." Gameknight stopped and looked down at the ground.

"But what? Tell me."

"But sometimes I miss spending time with you. We used to spend hours together, working on your inventions in the basement. I'd take apart things that didn't work so you could use the components in something new. We'd build the contraptions together and see what would happen when we switched it on ... I loved those times together, but they don't happen anymore. You're always gone."

"I'm here now," Monkeypants said.

"You're here now because you feel guilty about being away," Gameknight replied. "I know—I heard you and Mom talking last night when you came home. You aren't really here."

"You feel that?" his father said as he reached out and patted his son on the shoulder. "That's me being here."

Gameknight glanced up at his father then looked away and sighed.

"It's not the same. I can hear it in your voice. You're always using your father voice in Minecraft, telling me what to do, lecturing me that I'm taking too many risks. You're doing the 'dad-thing' instead of just being you." Gameknight paused to look at him. "When we were inventing, your voice was filled with excitement. You talked to me not like a father to a son, but as an inventor to another inventor ... like I'm a regular person with smart ideas of my own.

"But instead of more great days in the basement, inventing, I've been down here, alone, playing Minecraft and taking care of everything at home. Now I invent things with redstone and command blocks instead of gears and springs with you. And because of the accident with the digitizer, I found these great people within the game. Meeting Crafter and Hunter and all these NPCs has made life bearable while you've been away. But you won't let me just be me here in Minecraft, the User-that-is-not-a-user. You don't trust me to handle this."

Monkeypants sighed. "Seeing you grow up is a difficult thing," he said. "One day, you were but a child playing at my feet, and now I see you as a grown, strong adolescent with his own ideas and own opinions. It's difficult for me. I hope you realize that."

His son nodded his blocky head.

"In life, we will always be forced to decide who we are, and what kind of person we want to be," his father said. "I chose to be the father who takes care of his wife and two children the best way he knows how: by selling inventions. I can't just stop being a dad and let you charge into danger every chance you get. I'm going to still worry about you, that's what I do. Who do you choose to be?"

Just as Gameknight was about to answer, Stitcher screamed.

"MONSTERS!"

Drawing his two swords in a smooth fluid motion, Gameknight turned and kicked his horse into motion. Ahead, a large group of green cubes bounced through the shallow waters—slimes. Each was a fluorescent green, with a transparent outer layer and a darker cube at their center, their faces buried inside. They bounced through the shallow waters of the swamp with surprising speed; this was their home and they had adapted to life in this biome. Many of the slimes were as tall as an NPC, but twice as wide, and there were some smaller ones as well. Their touch was like that of an iron sword, stealing HP in exchange for pain. They could be lethal.

Heading right into the group, Gameknight slashed at the smallest one. As his sword scored a hit, it flashed red, then divided into four smaller cubes.

"Go after the smallest ones first," Gameknight shouted.

Spinning his horse, he charged at one of the green cubes. It almost glowed in the bright sunlight, the translucent nature of the creature allowing him to see its internal structure. Swinging his swords with all his strength, he destroyed the small slime, then turned and pursued another.

Off to his left, the User-that-is-not-a-user saw his father attacking a large slime, but the monster scored a hit, denting his dad's iron armor. Monkeypants finally landed a blow, making it divide into smaller cubes, but he then turned and faced another large slime.

Kicking his horse to a sprint, he moved next to his father and guarded his side.

"Dad, go after the small ones first," Gameknight shouted.

"But the big ones are easier to hit," his father replied.

"Yes, but they divide into four. If you go after the big ones first, you'll quickly end up surrounded."

Reaching out with his sword, Gameknight blocked Monkeypants from hitting a large slime.

"The small ones, go after them!" the User-that-is-not-a-user shouted. "You know, like in your other favorite old game, *Asteroids*."

"Ahh . . ." his father said as realization came over him.

Monkeypants turned and attacked one of the smaller cubes. When he hit it, the gelatinous monster divided into four smaller cousins. He then attacked one of those and it divided again.

"The *smallest* ones," Gameknight reminded him.

Glancing at his son, Monkeypants271 nodded his boxy head, then charged at a tiny slime, slashing at it as he streaked by.

Across the swamp, the User-that-is-not-a-user could see his friends locked in battle, all except the light-crafters. They had moved their horses away from the battle and were dismounting.

Grassbrin plunged his hands into the soil and extended his crafting powers. Instantly, a tangle of grass grew out of the swamp, capturing one of the slimes and immobilizing it. From a distance, Stitcher was able to fire arrows at the captive monster, then shoot at the divided creatures still stuck in the long leafy blades.

At the same time, Treebrin was causing trees to sprout up out of the swamp water, the thick branches holding the slimes aloft so that Hunter could use her magic bow on the creatures.

Herder stood with his sword at his side, looking like some kind of magical wizard directing bolts of white lightning. Every time a slime approached, the lanky NPC gestured toward the green monster, and wolves shot out at the creature, destroying it with their sharp, pointed fangs. Pointing across the battlefield, Herder directed his furry white bolts of destruction into the monsters, always careful to attack the smallest or coming to the aid of an embattled friend. Without lifting his sword, Herder was responsible for destroying at least a third of the attackers.

Look how confident Herder has become, Gameknight thought.

He was so proud of the boy.

In minutes, the slimes were destroyed, leaving behind glowing balls of XP and green spheres of slime. Looking at the dropped items, Gameknight was always shocked: the curved spheres seemed out of place in the blocky world of Minecraft.

"Collect all the slimeballs, they could be useful," Gameknight said.

Herder and Stitcher ran across the battlefield, collecting the slimes and XP, the wolves howling with excitement as the chased after the lanky boy.

"They looked like jello," Monkeypants said to his son as the party continued on. "Those were goos, right?" his dad asked.

"No, that's a different game: World of Goo," Game- knight said as he rolled his eyes. "Those were slimes."

"They sort of reminded me of your mother's holiday jello," his father said.

"But without the marshmallows and pine-apple," Gameknight added with a chuckle.

Monkeypants giggled.

"What are you two laughing at?" Hunter asked, her enchanted bow lighting her face with a cerulean glow.

"Nothing," Gameknight answered, embarrassed.

"How about you quit goofing off and keep your eyes open," Hunter said with a scowl. "The witch could be anywhere and we need to be ready. If we stumble on her and get too close, she can throw splash potions on us and do real damage. We need to be ready."

"Sorry," Gameknight said, then chuckled again, drawing another scowl.

"There's the hut," Stitcher said in a low voice.

Gameknight looked in the direction she was pointing. In the distance, there was a wooden house built on top of four columns of wood; the witch's hut. A narrow porch marked the entrance to the hut, with a line of steps leading up from the waterline to the raised doorway. Extending over the porch was a flat roof. It stretched far over the edge of the dwelling, likely to help protect it from the rain, which was not uncommon in swamp biomes.

Through the windows on each side, Gameknight999 could see a warm glow of light coming from the interior, the illumination splashing outward and making the tree next to the hut appear to glow from within. Likely the witch had hung torches or a lit furnace to cook something. Whatever it was, the hut was clearly not abandoned; the witch would be inside or nearby.

Drawing his sword, Gameknight shifted his eyes to the left and right, looking for any sign of movement.

"Does anyone see anything?" Digger asked.

Everyone shook their heads.

Herder pulled out another flask of healing and threw it on Crafter. Gameknight could see that his friend was looking paler, his body slowly withering away.

We have to hurry.

"Let's see if she's inside the hut," Gameknight said as he kicked his horse into a gallop, charging forward.

When he reached the hut, he leapt off his horse and ran up the steps, both swords now in his hands. When he entered, his nose was instantly assaulted by strange aromas. Redstone dust, Nether Wart, sugar, melon, blaze powder, glowstone dust, fermented spider eye—all of these smells created a kaleidoscope of fragrances. Near the back of the hut, two brewing stations were running, the liquid in the bottles bubbling and changing color. Next to the brewing stations was a cauldron filled with water, some empty bottles lying nearby on the ground, as if suddenly dropped. The room was empty.

The stairs leading into the hut creaked and groaned under the weight of someone approaching.

Spinning, Gameknight readied himself for battle. If it was the witch, he'd have to strike quick and not let her throw her potions. Moving next to the door, he stood behind the brewing stand, hoping that the element of surprise would give him enough advantage to survive this encounter.

The stairs creaked again. Whoever or whatever it was, it was almost to the door.

Gripping his swords firmly, Gameknight could feel tiny cubes of sweat trickle down the back of his neck. Balancing his weight on the balls of his square feet, he got ready to spring out and attack.

He saw a foot step into the hut, colored red, and then blue pants, and in that last step Gameknight jumped forward. With his swords held high, he lunged forward, but was shocked to find the face of a monkey staring back at him.

"AHHH!" his father yelled.

He took a step back and almost fell down the stairs. If Digger hadn't been behind him, he'd likely have tumbled down the steps and into the swamp water.

"What are you doing?" Monkeypants said.

"Sorry, I thought you were the witch," Gameknight answered.

"Do I look like a witch?" his father asked.

"No, you look like a silly monkey in a Superman outfit," Gameknight replied.

"OK then—monkey, not witch, got it?" Monkeypants said, a wry smile on his face as he reached out and put a hand on his son's sword arm, causing Gameknight to lower his weapons.

"Sorry," he replied.

"What's going on in there? Let us all in," Hunter yelled from the foot of the stairs.

Monkeypants walked into the hut followed by Hunter and Digger, Crafter cradled in the big NPC's muscular arms. Stitcher and the light-crafters moved out away from the hut to watch for monsters. Herder and his wolves did the same.

Carefully, Digger laid Crafter on the bed that sat in the corner of the room. The young NPC groaned. Looking down onto his friend, Gameknight could see that he was looking even worse. Worried, he moved to the window. Gameknight could see Herder, standing out in the knee-high water, lean over and say something to the alpha-wolf, the leader of the pack. Instantly, the wolves started to spread out, forming a loose ring of fur and fangs around the hut. The boy then turned and came into the witch's domicile.

"She was here," Hunter said. "Look, there are potions still brewing and it looks like she's cooking some bread in the furnace."

"It's eerie," Monkeypants said.

Suddenly, the sound of splashing water came in through the window, as if something outside was moving through the swamp. Running to the door, Hunter shot out of the hut, then jumped into the adjacent tree. Climbing quickly to the top, she reached the leafy peak, then drew her bow and notched an arrow. Gameknight moved to the porch and looked up at her.

"You see anything?" he asked.

She said nothing, continuing to scan the surroundings.

Gameknight moved to the edge of the porch and looked about. Out in the swamp, the wolves out in the water bobbing up and down, their white fur making them look like tiny icebergs floating in the still sea. Out further, Stitcher and the light-crafters were spreading out, watching for threats.

"I think she's gone," Digger said. "We missed her."

"She's out there; I can feel it," Gameknight said.

"I think I saw something under one of the trees," Hunter said as she climbed back down from the tree.

"Where?" Gameknight said has he ran to the door.

"Don't look, she'll see you," Hunter explained. "Maybe ten blocks away—a large swamp tree with vines hanging down on one side. I saw something hiding within those vines when I was on top of this tree; it might have been her." She paused and turned to Gameknight999. "We need to let this witch think that she's hunting us when actually we're the ones doing the hunting."

Gameknight was confused and it showed on his face. Hunter gave an exasperated sigh.

"Digger, you have any armor stands with you?" Hunter asked.

"Sure, I have three," he replied.

"Good, here's what we're going to do ..." Hunter said and then explained her plan.

Gameknight smiled. It was a good plan, not as crazy and wildly dangerous as his own plans in the past, but it would do.

Once they were prepared, the party mounted their horses, Digger tied Crafter to his horse again, and they rode away from the witch's hut. They moved in a tight cluster, the horses bumping into each other as they trudged through the mucky swamp.

Headed away from the hut, none of the riders turned back to see the witch sprinting from tree to tree, following the intruders. Moving so as to draw the witch away from her hut, the party ambled toward a dry block of land. The riders stopped for a moment as one of the horses munched a bit of grass that was growing on a lone block of dirt protruding up from the still waters. Not more than a dozen blocks from the hut, Gameknight cantered toward Digger and spoke in a loud voice.

"Here's what I think we should do with the witch when we catch her," Gameknight said, then lowered his voice and mumbled something unintelligible.

Digger nodded.

"But first, we have to hide the potions that we found in that temple," Digger lied. "If she were to get these potions, it would give her more power than any other witch."

"That one potion . . ." Gameknight said, then lowered his voice again so that it would not carry across the swamp.

He heard a splashing sound behind him, but did not turn to look. They wanted to draw her in.

"But Digger, if she ever found these potions, she'd rule Minecraft. We have to . . ." He lowered his voice again, drawing the curious witch even closer.

Suddenly, a yell sounded as Hunter leapt out of the witch's hut with Herder at her side. A dozen wolves flowed out of the wooden structure like a furry white wave. They splashed down right behind the witch, the wolves quickly surrounding her. Hunter stepped back out of range of her throwing arm and drew back an arrow. The witch reached into her inventory and pulled out a dark green splash potion, getting ready to lob it at her attackers.

"Don't!" Hunter yelled.

"Wolves, ready!" Herder screamed.

The ring of animals snarled and growled as the witch raised her arm. They took a step closer, their red eyes all focused on her with laser accuracy. She might be able to throw one potion, but wouldn't get the opportunity to throw another.

Hesitating, she glanced down at the wolves, then slowly lowered her arm. Suddenly, a rope flew through the air and wrapped around her body, pinning her arms to her sides, the splash potion falling harmlessly into the water. Pulling the rope tight, Digger splashed through the water and wrapped another length around her arms, then tied it off behind her back.

"Into the hut, witch," Gameknight yelled as he led the horses with fully adorned armor stands tied to the saddles back toward the witch's home.

After tying the horses to the tree, Gameknight and Monkeypants carefully lifted Crafter from his horse and carried him inside. Herder, Stitcher, and the light-crafters stayed behind, guarding their perimeter.

Gameknight and Monkeypants carefully laid Crafter back down on the bed as Hunter pushed the witch into the corner. The young NPC's skin was ghostly white, almost transparent. His breathing was faint and irregular, as if he were fighting for his own life . . . and losing.

Gameknight reached down and brushed away a strand of sandy blond hair from his friend's face, then turned and faced their captive. Drawing his enchanted diamond sword, the User-that-is-not-a-user took a step toward the witch, his blade pointed at her.

"You are going to help us with our friend," Gameknight said.

The witch harrumphed and turned away, her pyramid-like hat sitting tilted on her square head.

Stepping closer, Gameknight drew his diamond sword and held it before him and then drew the iron blade with his other hand. The witch saw the two swords and a look of surprise came over her face. She glanced nervously at the intruders, then brought her gaze back to Gameknight.

"Let me ask nicer," Gameknight999 said, an angry scowl on his blocky face. "I am the User-that-is-not-a-user. Are you going to help us with our friend, or will this be the last day of your life?"

CHAPTER 18

MORGANA

The witch looked down at Crafter, then back up at Gameknight999.

"Why should I help you? The NPCs drove me from my village and made me live out here all alone," the witch said.

Monkeypants stepped forward and put a hand on Gameknight's blades. Carefully, he moved the weapons down and stepped forward. Moving back, Gameknight looked at the witch carefully. She wore a purple smock that covered her from neck to knees, a wide green striping running down the middle. Brown pants extended out from beneath the smock, covering her legs, with square gray shoes on her feet. Atop her head sat the stereotypical witch's hat; a pyramid-shaped thing that narrowed to a blocky point, with a gray band encircling it in the middle. What looked like an emerald sat in the middle of the gray band, adorning the black hat with a splash of bright color.

Gameknight looked at the NPC. She was old, with a wrinkled face and skin that sagged as if it were a little too big for her frame. Tiny blotches marked her skin here and there, likely scars from past adventures of burns from potion brewing gone awry. Her bulbous nose seemed massive on her face, a tiny wart on the side wiggling ever so slightly. She was easily the oldest NPC Gameknight had ever seen.

Looking away from the wart, Gameknight glared straight into her brown eyes. Just as he was about to speak, Monkeypants raised his hand to silence him.

"My impatient son is extremely concerned for our friend here," Monkeypants said, pointing down at Crafter. "We have need of your services, for as you can see, he is quite ill."

The witch looked down at Crafter, then moved a bit closer and sniffed, taking in his scent. Nodding her head, she turned and faced Monkeypants.

"He has the taint of evil on him," she said. "It is devouring his HP slowly. Your feeble healing potions will soon be ineffective."

"That is why we're here," Monkeypants said.

"Just make her give us what we need!" Hunter snapped, her bow creaking as she drew back an arrow.

Monkeypants moved in front of Hunter, putting his own body between her arrow and the witch.

"We cannot *make* her do anything, but we

can negotiate a solution here," Monkeypants said.

He turned back to the witch.

"A shadow of evil is pursuing us and attacking our friend," Monkeypants explained. "It is growing stronger while we grow weaker."

"Soon, this shadow will get big enough to take over everything," Gameknight added as he sheathed his swords. He leaned forward and spoke in a low voice. "It's Herobrine's shadow attacking us. If we cannot stop him, then all of us will die, you included."

The witch smiled as she returned Gameknight's gaze.

"Herobrine's shadow cannot enter my domain. My potions kept him out just as it kept out the zombies that were chasing you. Morgana is safe here."

"That's your name, Morgana?" Monkeypants asked.

The witch nodded, her tall hat bobbing up and down.

"We have seen the shadow getting bigger and stronger," Digger added, his booming voice filling the hut with thunder. "Soon, your potions will not be sufficient to hold it out of your swamp. You're in this with us whether you like it or not."

Morgana looked at the big NPC, then back to Crafter. Reaching up, she straightened her hat and took a step toward the bed. Instantly, Gameknight drew his sword and Hunter pulled back an arrow, ready to fire.

"Put your weapons away," Monkeypants said. "Morgana is on our side."

"Witches are not on anybody's side," Hunter said. "They are like the Lost; they're alone and cannot be trusted."

"That's because you NPCs chase us out of the village when we get transformed," Morgana snapped as she glared at Hunter. "It's not our fault that we get hit by lightning."

"What is she talking about?" Monkeypants asked.

"When NPCs get hit by lightning, sometimes they get transformed into witches," Digger explained. "It's true that it's not their fault; it just is what it is."

"That's why they can't be trusted," Hunter said. "So they get chased out of the village and into the wild. They become Lost—a villager without a village."

"That's terrible," Monkeypants said. "You should embrace them instead of excommunicating them . . . help them learn how to adjust to their new role as the village witch."

"That's not the way," Hunter said.

"Well, it should be," Monkeypants replied. "You see, when people who are different come into your life, you have to—"

"Silence!" Morgana snapped as she knelt down next to Crafter.

Reaching into her purple smock, she withdrew a bottle with some kind of sparkling purple powder. Pulling out a small amount, she sprinkled it across Crafter's forehead. When the glittering dust settled onto his pale skin, it glowed bright for just an instant, then disappeared, leaving behind a soft amber glow that slowly faded away. Putting the bottle back into her smock, she stood and turned to face the User-that-is-not-a-user.

"The evil still resides within this NPC," Morgana said. "Herobrine's left a sliver of his shadow within your crafter and it is attacking him from within. Soon, your pathetic healing potions will offer little relief to the internal war that is waging here."

"That is why we have come to you," Gameknight said as he put away his sword and stepped closer to the witch. He looked straight into her brown eyes and pleaded. "Please, you have to help my friend. He knows what we must do to stop this shadow of evil once and for all. Without his help, I fear that all of Minecraft is doomed."

The witch considered his words, then turned and looked at Hunter. Morgana glanced at the bow Hunter still held in her blocky hands, then raised her eyebrow. Sighing, Hunter put away the bow.

"I can help you. I have potions that will keep the shadow at bay within your crafter," she said. "This potion will not stop the internal battle, it will only delay it for a while. The only way to truly save your friend is to destroy the source of the evil. But for now, my potion will help. But it will not be given for free; I will ask something of you in return."

"What is it you want, witch?" Hunter growled.

Gameknight could tell that his friend did not trust her.

"I will not say now," Morgana said, "but you must agree to what I will ask or I will not help."

Hunter pulled out her bow again and drew back an arrow.

"Killing me will not give you what you need," Morgana said. "It will only guarantee the outcome you seek to avoid. If you want this crafter to live, then you must agree to whatever I require—now."

Gameknight looked at Hunter and motioned her to lower her bow, then he glanced down at Crafter. He was looking worse, his skin almost bone white. Glancing back at Hunter and Digger, the User-that-is-not-a-user could feel a square tear start to tumble down his cheek. As he started to speak, Hunter stepped forward.

"We agree, witch," Hunter said, an angry scowl focused toward her adversary. "But if you hesitate to keep your end of the bargain and help us, I will end your miserable life without a second thought . . . do you understand that?"

Morgana nodded, then moved to the brewing station. Removing one of the bubbling orange potions, she poured a small amount into an empty bottle. Pulling a blue potion from her smock, she added a small amount to the orange, then set it on the brewing station. Withdrawing a bright red potion, she poured a sizable amount into the mixture, then waited for it to begin bubbling. As it boiled, she pulled out the bottle of purple powder. Holding it up to see how much remained, she sighed as she poured the last of the powder into the mixture. As soon as the purple dust touched the liquid, it instantly turned a dark purple, almost black.

Gameknight looked at the potion as the bubbles slowly faded, leaving a calm surface. It looked like the color of an obsidian block but darker; it was just barely a shade brighter than an enderman. Tiny purple particles danced about on the surface of the liquid, and he knew this was something magical beyond all of their skill.

Morgana put a cork in the top of the bottle and shook it up. Moving to Crafter's side, she removed the cork and poured just the smallest amount into their friend's mouth. It glowed the softest blue as it flowed past his lips and into his mouth. After corking the bottle, the witch put the potion inside one of the hidden pockets of her smock. Gameknight could see that there were likely three more gulps left.

"Well?" Hunter asked as she looked worriedly down upon her friend.

"Have patience," Morgana replied.

"She doesn't have a lot of that," Gameknight said.

Hunter was about to reply, but stopped just as Crafter moaned and rolled onto his side.

"Crafter, are you alright?" Gameknight asked.

"What?" he said confused. "Where am I?"

"Just relax, Crafter," Digger said. "We're at the old witch's hut in the southern swamp."

"Old?" complained Morgana. "Who you callin' old?"

"I'm sure he was referring to your hut and not you," Monkeypants added.

"Hmm," the witch grunted.

"Crafter, can you hear me?" Gameknight asked as he knelt at his friend's side.

"Of course I can hear you; I'm not deaf."

Gameknight laughed.

"We were afraid you were going to die," Gameknight explained. "Herobrine's shadow of evil has been attacking you over and over."

"That's funny, I don't remember any of that."

"You've been a bit out of it," Hunter said.

"Morgana gave you something to make you feel better," Digger explained. "But we need to eliminate this shadow of evil before it claims more victims and destroys Minecraft."

"Hmmm," Crafter said, processing the information.

Feeling better, the young NPC sat up, then turned and put his feet on the ground, sitting on the edge of the bed.

"Crafter, you were going to tell me how we destroy this thing back in the crafting chamber," Gameknight said. "You said Herobrine had to be put somewhere so that he couldn't hurt Minecraft anymore. Please tell us—what do we do?"

"We have to put Herobrine where he can no longer touch anything in Minecraft," Crafter explained.

Gameknight looked at his friend, confused, then glanced at Digger and Hunter. They, too, had confused looks on their faces.

"It's not that hard," Crafter said as color slowly came back to his face. "Where can something be put and have it be gone from Minecraft . . . forever?"

"The void," Digger whispered.

Crafter nodded.

Hunter and Gameknight gasped at the same time.

"What's the big deal about the void?" Monkeypants asked.

"You can get to the void in only two ways," Gameknight explained. "You can dig down to the bottom limit of Minecraft, which is about 130 blocks deep. At that level is a layer of bedrock. Beneath the bedrock is the void."

"OK, so let's dig down and go through the bedrock to get to the void," Monkeypants suggested.

Hunter laughed.

"What?" Monkeypants asked.

"You can't dig through bedrock; it's impossible," Gameknight said. "Minecraft won't allow it unless you're in creative mode, which isn't possible on these servers."

"OK, so where else can you get to the void?" Monkeypants asked.

"The End," Digger whispered. "It's the most

dangerous place in Minecraft, and that's where we need to take Herobrine—to The End."

Gameknight shuddered. The Dragon—the thought of battling the Ender Dragon again made him shake. The last time, they had an entire army, but now there was only this small collection of friends to face off against that terrible beast. It would be impossible.

Gameknight sighed, fear and uncertainty rippling through his soul. But as he looked at Crafter, who was struggling to stand, he knew that he would do anything to help his friend.

"We're taking Herobrine to The End and getting rid of him once and for all," Gameknight said.

"You kidding?" Hunter laughed, but could see the look of deadly seriousness on Gameknight's face. "It isn't going to be easy for any of us, but I love this plan: a small group of NPCs and a pair of Users-that-are-not-users against the Ender Dragon. This is perfect!"

"Dragon?" Monkeypants271 exclaimed. "Who said anything about a dragon?"

Hunter and Digger laughed, but Gameknight remained silent, a cold, serious look on his face.

"Another great plan, Gameknight999," Hunter mocked. "But how are we going to get past those endermen? I don't look forward to facing an army of endermen and zombies as soon as we set foot out of this swamp."

"Leave that to me," Morgana said from the doorway. "I can get all of you past that rabble without a problem. Besides, I'll be glad to be rid of all of you and back to my own life."

"I don't think so," Monkeypants said. "You agreed to help us, well, get to The Ending."

"It's The End, Dad," Gameknight said, rolling his eyes.

"Whatever. Getting us to The End is part of your bargain," Monkeypants continued. "I saw how you looked at Crafter when he woke up. You and I both know that he is not fully healed, right?"

Morgana looked at the ground and nodded.

"He will need more healing before he goes to The End," Monkeypants continued, "and you'll have to be there to administer the correct potions. If you want your payment, then you must help us get to The End."

She sighed, then reluctantly nodded her blocky head.

Turning to his son, Monkeypants smiled a satisfied grin, making the User-that-is-not-a-user roll his eyes again.

Nine of us against an army of endermen and the Dragon, Gameknight thought. *Well, if that's what I have to do to protect my friends and save Minecraft, then bring it on.*

CHAPTER 19

SPIES

Feyd, the king of the endermen, surveyed his domain: The End. He ruled this land of pale yellow End Stone and tall obsidian pillars, glittering ender crystals floating atop each of the dark spires. Teleporting to the far side of the giant floating island, he smiled as he felt his HP increase. Moving carefully to the edge of the island, the enderman peered into the darkness. The void that surrounded his island seemed to go on forever, the shadowy expanse stretching out into infinity and then a bit farther.

This was their home, but also their prison. It was their punishment for helping the monsters of the Overworld after the Awakening: banishment to The End. If an enderman stayed away for too long from The End, their HP would decrease quickly. The only way they could rejuvenate their heath was to teleport across the landscape of The End. The teleportation particles that always surrounded the dark creatures would feed their health and restore their HP, but it only worked here, on this isolated island. As a result, it was their domain—their home—but it was also a cold, heartless prison.

Feyd wanted more. The evil, spite, anger, and greed that Herobrine had fused into him during his making had made Feyd greedy, always wanting more, but there was no more to be had—this was it. This fact filled Feyd with an overwhelming rage that he focused on the User-that-is-not-a-user. He knew this wasn't Gameknight's fault, but he didn't care. Herobrine had also built into him a strong hatred for his enemy, and any chance to exact revenge for the Maker's destruction was a welcome distraction.

Suddenly, an enderman appeared right next to him, the mist of teleportation particles nourishing the newcomer.

"The enemy and his companions have escaped the swamp," the enderman reported.

"WHAT?!" Feyd screeched. "How is this possible?"

"We don't know," the enderman replied, taking a step away from his king to position himself out of arm's reach. "One minute they were all there on horseback, riding through the swamp, and then they disappeared."

"Tell me everything!"

"Well, they headed straight for the witch's hut when they went into the swamp. Quickly, they captured the old witch that lived there."

"Why would they want to take a witch prisoner?" Feyd asked.

"I don't know; maybe they wanted to torture her for some reason?"

"Don't be ridiculous," Feyd said. "NPCs don't know how to torture other creatures. Now users, they know how to use mindless violence for no reason at all. That is a possibility, but why?"

Feyd moved away from the edge of The End and walked toward one of the tall obsidian pillars that dotted the landscape. This one was lower than most, and he could easily see the ender crystal on the top, the intricate cube bobbing in a bath of flame.

"Continue," the king commanded. "Tell me the rest."

"After the NPCs captured the witch, they left the hut and moved across the swamp. But the strange thing was, the witch was riding on the back of one of the horses, right behind the little red-headed NPC. She could have jumped off at any time, but she didn't."

"That sounds more like a willing accomplice than a prisoner," Feyd noted. "Continue!"

"They moved across the swamp to a place near a small island. One of them got off their horse—the big NPC—and it looked like he was digging something up. He dug for a long time with the others just standing there watching. And when we came back, they—"

"What do you mean *when you came back*?" Feyd asked.

"It wasn't very exciting just watching the big one dig, so some of us went out looking for them across the dry land," the enderman explained. Feyd could hear the idiot's voice crack with fear. "When we came back, they were gone. All we could see were their horses, they were just standing there eating grass and wandering about."

"So all of you just left your post to wander around for a while, and then just came back?" Feyd screeched. "I told you to stay there and watch them, not go off on a nature walk."

With lightning speed, Feyd punched the foolish enderman in the chest and then moved to his left side and attacked. He then teleported to his right, pummeling the idiot with a flurry of punches that quickly ate away at his HP. To escape the attacks, the enderman backed up one step at a time, Feyd driving him backward with his fists. Not watching where he was going, the doomed enderman was shoved off the island and fell into the void.

Feyd smiled as he watched the creature plummet into the darkness, too terrified to simply teleport back onto the floating island.

"The fool, he let them get away!" the king of the endermen screeched.

Gathering his teleportation powers, he zipped to the center of the island at the speed of thought, materializing right next to a large group of creatures.

"Listen to me, all of you," Feyd screeched, his voice echoing across the landscape. In an instant, all the endermen teleported nearby and moved close enough to hear. "The User-that-is-not-a-user has escaped the swamp and is somewhere in Minecraft. I am ordering all of you to go out and find him, then return here and report his location. Now GO!"

In an instant, the dark creatures disappeared in a massive cloud of purple particles, leaving Feyd alone in The End.

"You won't stay hidden for long, Gameknight999," Feyd screeched, his voice drifting out into the impenetrable void. "When I find you, I will make you suffer!"

And then he cackled an evil enderman laugh that made even the dragon flying high overhead cringe with fear.

CHAPTER 20

THE OCEAN VILLAGE

ameknight laughed again when he thought about how the endermen must be reacting. One minute, they were there in the swamp, and the next minute they were gone, leaving only their horses behind.

Morgana knew every inch of her swamp, including where an abandoned mineshaft was buried. Digger dug a set of steps downward until he intersected the wood-lined passages of the mine, then let the water fall down into the mineshaft so that the others could easily follow. Gameknight's father had been confused about the whole operation.

"What good does an abandoned mineshaft do us?" Monkeypants had asked.

"Abandoned mines are places where the minecart network of the NPCs had become visible to the users," Gameknight had explained. "Wherever there is an abandoned mineshaft, there is also a minecart network nearby."

And sure enough, he'd been right. Once they reached the abandoned mineshaft, Digger had been able to quickly find the minecart rails. Why Crafter had a dozen minecarts in his inventory was still a mystery; he always seemed to have what was needed. Each piled into a cart and sped down the tracks to the next village. Once they found their bearings, Crafter was able to point them to the correct minecart track that would lead them back to the ocean village and location of the Last Battle.

As he sped down the minecart track, Gameknight thought about that last confrontation with Herobrine. The battle had been close, and he thought for sure that he was going to die, but his friend Shawny and his sister, Monet, had saved him at the last minute and allowed Herder to capture the monster. Their salvation had been found in the lowliest of creatures: a pig. They'd managed to trap Herobrine within a pig-body, and there he sat, imprisoned in the small pink form. But still his evil nature was leaking into the fabric of Minecraft, allowing the shadow of evil to roam about the server.

Chills ran down Gameknight's spine as he thought about facing that pig again. It likely had those terrible glowing eyes of Herobrine's and an evil look on its normally cute face. He cringed but refused to give in to that monster's reign of fear.

Behind him, Crafter was sitting in his own minecart, the young NPC slumped over, still weak from Herobrine's attacks. Morgana's potions had helped, but his friend still remained fatigued.

Ahead of Gameknight was the bulky form of Digger squeezed into a minecart, his mighty pick held in his hands, ready. In the distance, the end of the tunnel brightened; they were finally reaching the next village, the ocean village. Tiny square goosebumps formed on his arms as he watched Digger's cart shoot into the crafting chamber. And then in an instant, he was there.

Leaping out of his minecart, Gameknight drew his sword and surveyed the surroundings. The crafting chamber was large, as most were, maybe fifty blocks across and easily as high. The walls were rough hewn, hand-carved ages ago by an army of diggers. They'd left torches high up on the walls when the original construction had been done, then dug down to the floor below. The light from high above splashed on the stone, casting a warm yellow glow throughout the huge cavern. Across the floor was a maze of minecart tracks. Each started near a cluster of crafting tables, then shot off into the many tunnels that pierced the rock walls. On one side of the room, Gameknight could see the steps that led up out of the chamber to a set of iron doors and tunnels beyond, which extended up to the surface. This was one of the great secrets in Minecraft that users did not know existed.

Scanning the chamber, Gameknight looked

for monsters, his memories of the Last Battle having put his nerves on edge.

"What are you doing?" Digger asked. "There are no monsters here."

Glancing around, Gameknight could see all the NPCs looking at him with curious stares.

"Ahh, sorry, I guess I'm a little nervous, being back here again," Gameknight said.

A clattering sound caused him to turn around just as Crafter's minecart shot out of the darkness. Running to the cart, he helped his friend out.

"I can do it myself," Crafter complained, but then stumbled as he walked away from the tracks.

"Yeah, not so much," Gameknight replied. "Come on, let me help."

Extending an arm to his friend, Gameknight helped Crafter walk to the side of the crafting chamber, then supported him as the weak NPC sat down on a block of stone and leaned against the cool rocky wall. Monkeypants rolled out of the tunnel followed by Stitcher and the light-crafters. The young NPC instantly ran from her cart and shot up the stairs. She, too, was nervous about being back here and went up to the watchtower to make sure all was safe, Grassbrin and Treebrin close on her heels. When Morgana's cart came through the entrance, suspicious glances from the other NPCs shot her way. Glaring back at them, she reached into her smock with a blocky hand, ready to draw out a splash potion if attacked.

"Be at ease, Morgana," Digger said. "As long as you are helping us, you are under my protection."

The big NPC had said it loud enough for everyone in the chamber to hear. Glancing around the cavern with his pickaxe in his hands, he glared at the villagers, forcing them to look away. Morgana eased her hand out of her smock and relaxed.

"So this was where you had that big skirmish," Monkeypants said as he moved next to his son.

"It wasn't a skirmish, Dad, it was a war," Gameknight said. "There were hundreds and hundreds of people there; monsters, NPCs, and users."

He shook almost imperceptibly at the memory of all those NPCs who lost their lives in the Last Battle. A tiny square tear leaked out of his eye and tumbled down his cheek.

"Yes, of course," his father replied. "I hope you were sensible and stayed in the back where it was safe."

"Your son saved a lot of lives that day," Crafter said. "You should be proud."

"Oh, um, yeah ... of course I'm proud," Monkeypants said as he looked about the crafting chamber.

Gameknight sighed.

He doesn't really mean that, Gameknight thought. *If I were an inventor, he'd be proud, but he still doesn't understand Minecraft. He thinks this is just some little game, and the way he treats me, he still thinks I'm still a little kid that needs protecting. When is he going to see the real me, here in Minecraft?*

Before Gamekniight could reply, his father walked off to watch one of the workers at a crafting bench.

Gameknight sighed and looked at the ground, his shoulders slumped down in defeat.

A soft hand settled itself on his shoulder. Slowly turning his head, he found Crafter looking up at him, a look of concern in his bright blue eyes.

"He still doesn't understand what's going on with Minecraft . . . with me," Gameknight said.

"Your father cares about you very much," Crafter said. "If he didn't, would he have come into Minecraft with you?"

"I know," Gameknight replied. "But when is he going see me as I really am? The User-that-is-not-a-user; the person who takes care of his friends, no matter how hard it will be?"

"Sometimes we see things through a certain perspective, Gameknight999," Crafter said. "When I see Monkeypants271 looking at you, he's using a father's glasses. He sees his young son who he raised from a baby, and you will always be his baby whether you like it or not. That's how parents are. He thinks about how he can protect you and take care of you in Minecraft, while at the same time he's trying to understand this new environment. It's his job in the physical world to make sure that you are cared for, fed, clothed . . . protected from anything that can hurt you. And from what I heard you say, he uses his inventions to do this. I can imagine that this is hard for him, because the only way he can protect you is to be away, selling his inventions. That sounds difficult.

"You, on the other hand, see your dad as someone whose respect you crave, but you want an adult's respect, not a child's. You want to be seen as someone who can be trusted, someone who can do hard things—even scary things. In short, you want to be grown up. I've seen this many times with kids in our village, like Fisher. He wanted to be treated like an adult, and he felt like an adult inside, but it takes a while for others to get used to him being an adult. That's what adolescence is, the transition from childhood to adulthood, where the child and the parents both start to recognize the new adult who is slowly emerging from the child's body."

Crafter paused as he stood up slowly. Gameknight reached out to help him, but the young NPC waved off his assistance; he wanted to do it on his own. Once he was up, Crafter turned and face his friend.

The sound of tools banging on crafting benches and anvils echoed through the rocky underground chamber. It was a sound that Gameknight had come to love; it was the peaceful noise of a village doing what it was supposed to do: make things for Minecraft. It reminded him of home. He glanced around the room, then brought his gaze back to Crafter. A faint smile grew on the young NPC's face, then his friend brought those blue eyes to his.

"You and your father are converging on the same vision of your relationship," Crafter continued, "but it takes time to reach the same destination, for parents have a hard time giving up images of their babies and seeing the adults who stand before them." Crafter put a hand on Gameknight's shoulder. "Give him time, and soon you'll find that you're both at the same place."

Gameknight nodded his head as he considered his friend's words.

"What are you two doing, dancing?" said a voice from behind.

Spinning around, Gameknight found Hunter staring at them, her deep brown eyes showing a twinkle of mischief.

"You'd think we have enough to do right now," she added, "but if you want to spend some time dancing, that's OK with me."

She laughed as Herder giggled at her side.

Crafter dropped his arm as he smiled at the NPCs. Gameknight gave her a scowl as he moved toward his father.

"Come on, all of you," Crafter said. "We have a pig we need to collect."

CHAPTER 21

HEROBRINE'S PRISON

Gameknight followed Crafter up through the tunnels and to the surface. Behind him walked the others, their footsteps echoing down the long stone passages. When they reached the village, a bright morning sun greeted them. The blue sea in the distance reflected the light and sparkled as though the rippling surface were covered with brilliant gems. On the other side of the village, a dense forest of birch trees loomed tall and proud, their white bark standing out against the morning shadows cast by the thick, leafy canopy.

Between the village and the forest, Gameknight could see a tall hill made from just about every block imaginable. Stone, cobblestone, sand, mycelium, wool, granite, podzol, wood, iron—every kind of block found in Minecraft was placed on this mound. It looked like some kind of gigantic patchwork quilt had been laid down, marking the spot where Herobrine had been captured.

On four corners of the hill, tall towers had been erected out of birch wood and stone. Atop each stood a collection of archers and watchers, their keen eyes never leaving the pile of cubes that sat at their feet, ensuring their prisoner's permanent residence would not be disturbed.

As they approached the hill, Gameknight could see the village crafter approaching. Instantly, Crafter moved away from the group to talk to the elder, explaining what it was they were here to do.

"So this is the place where the Maker was captured," a scratchy voice said from behind.

Looking to his side, he found Morgana walking next to him.

"Yep," Gameknight answered. "There were hundreds and hundreds of monsters lined up over there," he pointed to the edge of the birch forest, "an army of users positioned off to the left, over there, and the villagers behind fortifications right where we are standing. The painted zombies and iron golems came out of the forest from the right."

"I'm surprised anyone survived," she croaked. "Usually, when a lot of people come together with weapons in their hands, the only outcome is mutual destruction. What stopped the carnage?"

"I battled Herobrine, and with my friends' help, we trapped him in the pig-body," Gameknight explained as they walked toward the massive mound. "Once the monsters saw their Maker captured, they realized that nothing good was going to come from continuing the fight. They just left."

"And now they think you've killed their Maker and want revenge?" Morgana asked.

"Something like that," the User-that-is-not-a-user replied.

"You users and NPCs seem to always be battling something in Minecraft. I don't understand why you can't just live in peace like the witches," Morgana said.

"But you live alone, isolated from everyone else," Gameknight said. "You are at peace because there is no one else around."

"I did not choose to be alone," she snapped. "The villagers chased me away; they don't trust me."

"Maybe because you throw poison at them."

"They started it first!"

"Hmmm, it doesn't seem as though your life is as peaceful as you suggest," Monkeypants added from behind.

Morgana turned and glared at him, Herder at the monkey's side.

"Sometimes misunderstanding grows and festers when not dealt with and becomes a bigger problem," Monkeypants said. "Maybe a peaceful dialogue would help."

"Witches cannot talk with villagers," Morgana growled. "Just like the User-that-is-not-a-user cannot talk to the monsters—there is no common ground."

"Hmmm," Gameknight said, considering her word. "But when—"

Suddenly, a howling sound came from the woods—wolves. Herder looked at Gameknight, a skeleton bone in his hand. The lanky boy had to leave his wolves back in the swamp since they could not ride in the minecarts.

"You know we'll need to take the minecarts again," Gameknight said.

Herder nodded.

"This village needs a pack of wolves to help protect it," the NPC said.

"OK, but be quick," Gameknight said. "We need to get out of here as quickly as possible. I don't know how long the potion is going to last for Crafter."

Herder nodded again, this time his long black hair flinging over his face. Pulling the locks from his eyes, he bolted off into the forest, a skeleton bone held in each hand.

"That boy loves his wolves," Hunter said next to him.

Gameknight nodded.

Off to the right, corrals and animal pens held the village's livestock: cows, chickens, and sheep. With a grin on his face, Grassbrin approached the pens and gently petted one of the cows. He then knelt and stuck his glowing hands into the ground. Instantly, grass sprouted out of the ground beneath the animals. Eagerly, they munched on the thick blades as Grassbrin smiled. Looking back at Gameknight, the light-crafter gave him a nod, then caused the grass to grow even longer. Near the edge of the forest, Treebrin did the same, causing trees to sprout up out of the ground, replenishing the woodland for the village. The two crafters looked to be in joyful bliss when they cared for the grass and trees of Minecraft; it was their task and sole reason for their existence. They had no responsibilities other than creating life.

Gameknight envied them.

He wished he had such clarity of purpose, for he was conflicted. He wanted his dad home and with him, but he really didn't want him in Minecraft; they were two opposing sides of the same coin. He wanted to be treated with more respect, like a big kid, but he also hated all the responsibility that was heaped upon him as the User-that-is-not-a-user. There had been a time when he had no responsibilities; he could just be himself and play, but that had been his child-self. Now, he wanted to be more, but missed the child he used to be. All of these aspects battled with each other like a philosophical tug-of-war continually happening in his mind.

Suddenly, Crafter was at his side. He looked terrible. Gameknight could see that his skin was starting to lose some of its color, the rosy red cheeks fading to a pale, almost ashen look. Stitcher appeared out of nowhere and put an arm through Crafter's, offering a little support; he did not object.

"OK, I explained to the village's crafter what

we are doing," Crafter explained. He paused to take a breath, then continued. "He's notified the archers to hold their fire so that we can get in there and retrieve Herobrine." He looked around at their companions, then back at Gameknight999. "Where's Herder?"

"He went into the woods to get some wolves for the village," the User-that-is-not-a-user explained.

"We need him to get the pig out of that mountain," Crafter explained. He paused again for a breath. "He's the best person to take charge of the animal."

Gameknight nodded.

"I'll go get him," Hunter said as she ran off into the birch forest.

"It's not a good idea for her to go out there on her own," Stitcher said. "Monkeypants, come help with Crafter."

Gameknight's father moved to Crafter's side, helping support the young NPC, allowing Stitcher to run off and help her sister. As she streaked away, Digger moved toward the large pile of blocks, his big pickaxe in his hands. Swinging it with all his might, he started to tunnel his way to the center of the pile. A couple of villagers moved in to help. They weren't really sure where Herobrine's prison was under all those blocks, so the three of them dug parallel tunnels a few blocks apart, hoping one of them would find the cobblestone chamber that lay buried under the monument.

While they dug, Gameknight could see

Hunter and Stitcher emerging from the forest with Herder between them. A line of eight wolves followed the trio, each of them with a red collar around their necks. This signified that they'd been tamed and were now friendly. As they approached, Herder leaned down to the largest of the wolves and spoke a single word.

"Protect."

Instantly, the wolves ran off, placing themselves around the village, their tiny eyes scanning the terrain for monsters.

Suddenly, one of the villagers emerged from the narrow tunnel, his eyes bright with excitement.

"We found it!" he exclaimed. "Does someone have a rope?"

"Herder, go bring him out," Gameknight said.

The boy looked up at the User-that-is-not-a-user with fear in his eyes.

"You're the best with animals; you have to do this," Gameknight said. "I know you're afraid but I have faith in you."

This brought the faintest of smiles to Herder's face, but he was still afraid.

"Come on, I'll go with you," Gameknight999 added. "We can do this together, I know we can. Are you ready?"

Herder looked nervously at Crafter and Monkeypants, then back to Gameknight999 and nodded his head.

"Let do this," Herder said, standing a little

taller as he pulled out a rope and headed for the pile of blocks.

Gameknight ran right next to him, then followed him into the tunnel. It was a narrow passage, only one block wide and two blocks high. Torches had been placed on the walls, offering a small amount of light. This lit the multicolored corridor with a golden hue that allowed Gameknight to see all the different blocks that made up the monument to the Last Battle. NPCs from all over Minecraft must have come to place these blocks. The walls of the passage were like the inside of a kaleidescope, with netherrack, End Stone, stained clay, red sand— every possible block from every possible biome making up these prison walls. It was amazing.

At the end of the tunnel, Gameknight could see shapes moving in the dim light. Reaching for his sword, he was ready to draw it, though he knew it would be useless against the Herobrine-pig. If anyone had to kill the pig, then they'd likely be infected by his evil XP, and they would turn *into* Herobrine. So hurting the pig at all was out of the question. They had to protect the pig until they could get it to The End.

"Herder, Gameknight, here!" Digger's voice boomed through the tunnel.

As they neared, Gameknight could see that they'd cleared out a large chamber around a small cobblestone structure. It was the prison that Digger had built just after they'd captured Herobrine with the pig.

"Herder, you ready?" Gameknight asked.

The lanky boy nodded his head, the rope held out in front of him.

"OK," Gameknight said, "let's open it up. Be careful not to hit the pig. He'll likely try to get himself killed if possible."

"Understood," Digger said, then turned and faced the other villager. "Use a wooden shovel on that end of the enclosure. He'll think we're digging through there and move to that end."

The villager nodded and pulled out the tool. He started digging into the cobblestone with the shovel. Of course it was doing almost nothing. After a few hits, Digger moved to the opposite end and quickly smashed through the blocks with his iron pickaxe. As the wall crumbled away, Herder leapt forward and threw the line around the pig's neck before it knew what was happening.

As Herder pulled the pig out of its cobblestone prison, Gameknight was shocked at what he saw. The tiny little pig had piercing bright glowing eyes that lit the chamber like it was noon on a cloudless day. The pig looked up at Gameknight999, then made some angry pig noises and charged, its blunt grass-eating teeth snapping together as if it wanted to kill the User-that-is-not-a-user right at that moment.

Herder pulled back on the line, keeping the little pink animal away from Gameknight, pulling it back to his side.

"It's OK, little fella," Herder said as he reached down to pet him on the head.

With lightning speed, the pig turned its

head and snapped at Herder's hand, clamping down on a square finger. Herder yelled out in pain, but did not let go of the rope. Reaching into his inventory, Herder pulled out another rope and attached it to Herobrine's neck, then tossed the free end to Digger. Slowly, they led the pig out through the tunnels, with Herder pulling the creature forward and Digger keeping tension at the back so that Herobrine could not get to either of them.

As they emerged from the tunnels, Gameknight was surprised to find the entire village standing around the edge of the monument. They all gasped when they saw the glowing eyes of the pig. Many villagers reached for their weapons, but the village's crafter kept the NPCs calm.

Moving Herobrine carefully through the streets, they headed for the secret tunnel that led to the crafting chamber. As they walked, a strange cold feeling moved through the village. It felt to Gameknight like a chilling breeze, as if tiny shards of ice were poking at him, but the sensation was not on his skin—it was coming from within.

The shadow, Gameknight thought.

"Crafter, quickly, get on a stack of blocks!" Gameknight shouted.

"Just do it!"

Confused, Crafter leapt up into the air and placed a block of dirt under him.

"Higher, go higher—as high as you can," Gameknight exclaimed.

"What are you doing?" Hunter asked.

"The shadow of evil is coming," Gameknight said, his voice filled with fear. "Crafter, go higher!"

Crafter went up another four blocks, then stopped. He was eight blocks up in the air.

I hope this works.

He knew in his weakened condition, Crafter might not survive another attack and Herobrine certainly knew where they were.

Just then, a shadow moved at the edges of his vision. It was twice the size as it had been on the edge of the swamp. Moving along a jagged path, it stabbed up at as many villagers as it could while it closed on their position.

Pulling out his shovel, Gameknight broke the blocks out from under Crafter, while the ground on which Crafter stood stayed in place. The block of dirt hovered there, floating on air with Crafter safely held aloft. Working with a fury, Gameknight dug out the dirt beneath his friend, quickly moving him even farther up and away from the surface of Minecraft.

And then suddenly Gameknight's nerves were aflame with pain as the shadow of evil enveloped the ground beneath him. Waves of agony flowed through him, causing his legs to fail. He started to crumble to the ground, but someone reached out and caught him as he fell, lifting him high in the air as they ran for safety. Looking down, Gameknight realized it was his dad who was holding him high over his head. The shadow of evil was stabbing up at Monkeypants with its dark jagged shadows as he ran, trying to reach Gameknight999. His monkey face flashed red as Herobrine tore into his HP, his teeth gritting with pain, but his father did not stop. He ran to the left, then right, then left again as he evaded the specter. Losing interest in Monkeypants and his son, the shadow moved back to its intended target, Crafter, but he was too high up in the air.

The shadow shot erratically to a nearby house and moved up the wooden wall. It reached out for Crafter from the side of the house, its jagged shards of evil extending like a nest of writhing sinister snakes, but again the NPC was out of reach. Moving off, it sought other victims.

Gameknight looked down at Herobrine-pig and could see the animal smile cruelly as it watched the shadow move from companion to companion, stabbing at them with his hatred. The pig's eyes glowed bright with evil glee as he heard the screams of NPCs echo across the landscape.

And then suddenly, the shadow evaporated into nothing—it was over.

Gameknight glanced at the pig and could see that Herobrine was tired; he'd exhausted all of his evil powers—good.

"Quickly, Dad, put me down," Gameknight said.

His father slowly lowered him to the ground.

"Are you OK?" Gameknight asked.

Monkeypants wiped his sweat-covered brow and nodded.

"Yeah," his father replied. "No big deal."

"It *is* a big deal. I've had that thing attack me and I know how much it hurts, so thanks. Now you need to eat something so your HP will get replenished—here."

Gameknight offered him an apple and the monkey happily accepted. His father ate it in a few quick bites and color and health returned to his face.

Sprinting to Crafter, Gameknight built a set of steps out of dirt, allowing his friend to climb down from his perch. When he reached the ground, Morgana moved to his side. Placing a hand on his square forehead, she felt his temperature then pulled out a flask of blue liquid and held it to his lips. Crafter drank slowly at first, but quickly gulped down the potion. Color blossomed in his cheeks again, but just faintly.

Morgana looked at Gameknight, and he could tell that she was worried.

"What is it?" he asked.

"The shadow grows stronger, we must hurry," she said and headed for the cobblestone watchtower.

"Come on, everyone, to the crafting chamber."

Gameknight reached down, scooped up Crafter, and carried him as he ran.

"I don't need to be carried. I'm older than you are. This is ridiculous."

"Be quiet and let your friends help you," Gameknight snapped.

Crafter stopped his complaining, but a scowl remained on his brow.

They moved quickly to the watchtower, then through the tunnels to the crafting chamber. When they reached the minecart tracks, each of the companions grabbed a minecart. Gameknight watched as Herder took out another length of rope and wrapped it around the pig's nose and mouth, making it impossible for the animal to bite anyone. He then picked up the animal as it squirmed in his arms.

"You won't get away from me, Mr. Pig," Herder said. "I've held onto many an animal in my days and you are nothing compared to an injured wolf with a fever, so just stop your wiggling and do as you're told."

He flicked one of the pig's soft, velvety ears. It winced but stopped its struggles.

Carefully, Gameknight put Crafter on the ground.

"OK, where do we need to go to get to The End?" Gameknight asked his friend.

"We need to get to the stronghold in the ice—ice spikes—biome . . ."

"Crafter, are you all right?" Stitcher asked. "You look pale."

Gameknight looked down at his friend and could see that most of the color had already drained from his face and a ghost-like hue covered his skin.

"We just . . . just have to pick the . . . pick the right track to . . . to get to that . . ."

And then Crafter collapsed, unconscious.

"CRAFTER!" Gameknight screamed as he reached out and caught him just before he hit the ground. "Morgana, please, help me."

The witch came to Gameknight's side and looked into Crafter's face. She pulled the bottle of sparkling black liquid from her smock and uncorked it. Pouring half the remaining liquid into Crafter's mouth, she put the bottle away and placed a wrinkled hand on his pale brow. Slowly, color flowed back to his cheeks and face, then his eyes fluttered open. Gameknight looked down on his friend and smiled and then glanced at Morgana.

"Thank you, Morgana. You saved him," he said.

"I saved him for now," the old witch said. "There is enough for one more treatment, then he will have to face the shadow of evil on his own."

"Can't you make more?" Hunter asked.

"I used up the most critical ingredient, essence of endermen," Morgana explained. "It took me years to acquire what I had. I cannot make more elixir. We must be quick. There are still a few tricks I have that may be of use, but you must remember our bargain if you want me to continue with this journey."

"Yes, I remember it, witch," Hunter snapped. "You're going to ask for payment later. I get it. Let's just get this done. If we can get rid of Herobrine, then it will be worth any price."

Carefully lifting Crafter to his feet, Gameknight put an arm around his friend and moved him toward the minecart tracks.

"Crafter, which one do we take?" Gameknight asked. "Which one leads to the stronghold?"

He pointed to a tunnel far to the left. Moving to that track, Gameknight stepped up to the rails. Monkeypants placed a minecart on the track, then another one directly behind it. Reaching out, he helped his son place Crafter in the first minecart, then Gameknight climbed in behind him. Digger ran ahead of them and placed a cart for himself and shot down into the dark tunnel, his big pickaxe across his lap.

Gameknight pushed off, shoving his and Crafter's carts forward. When they hit the powered section of track, they rocketed into the darkness. As they moved through the tunnel, he could hear Crafter moaning. Suddenly, a bottle of purple liquid shot through the darkness from behind and splashed on Gameknight and Crafter. It was a potion of healing, likely from Morgana. Instantly, his friend's moaning stopped as the rejuvenating liquid went to work restoring his HP. Slowly, as his strength returned, Crafter sat up in the cart.

"Crafter, you have to hang in there," Gameknight said. "We'll get to the next village, then use some horses to get to the stronghold. You'll be in The End in no time."

"I never thought I'd ever say it," Crafter said

in a weak voice as he looked over his shoulder at his friend, "but I'm looking forward to getting to that land of endermen and dragons." He smiled, then curled up and fell into a peaceful sleep.

"Don't worry, Crafter," Gameknight said in a low voice. "Nothing will stop me from getting rid of Herobrine and saving you."

But as they shot through the dark tunnel, he thought about all the endermen who would be waiting for them with Feyd, the king of the endermen, right there at the front. And then there was the Ender Dragon, as well.

How are we going to do this with just a handful of NPCs? he thought.

But as Gameknight999 looked at Crafter, he knew that there was nothing in this universe that would stop the User-that-is-not-a-user from trying to save his friend.

CHAPTER 22

THE HOUNDS FIND THE FOX

Feyd moved through The End, sometimes walking, sometimes teleporting to his destination. He didn't really have anyplace to go, but he was too anxious to just stand still.

The User-that-is-not-a-user had disappeared from the face of the Overworld and most of his endermen were now back from their search; none of them found any trace of his enemy.

"He has to be out there somewhere," the king of the endermen screeched.

Overhead, he could hear the flapping of heavy leathery wings; the Ender Dragon could sense his agitation. Its purple eyes shown like two bright beacons in the darkness of The End. They were always searching the land for intruders—two lavender searchlights forever scanning the pale landscape from above.

As the dragon curved gracefully through the sky, a small endermen suddenly materialized right in front of Feyd, nearly smashing into his king.

"What are you doing, you idiot?" Feyd said, pushing the young enderman back a few blocks.

"I'm ... I'm sorry, sire," the youth stammered.

"What are you doing here?" Feyd demanded. "Why did you nearly collide with me?"

"I saw them ... I saw them," the young enderman exclaimed.

"What are you talking about?"

"The User-that-is-not-a-user ... I saw them," he repeated.

"What? Where?"

"Riding toward the ice spikes biome," the enderman reported.

"Hmm," Feyd said as he paced back and forth in front of his subordinate. "There is no village in that biome, nothing of interest unless they know about the—ENDERMEN, COME TO ME NOW!"

In an instant, all the endermen in The End disappeared and materialized before their king. As the mist of teleportation particles slowly evaporated, Feyd looked out upon the sea of dark monsters. There were probably a hundred of them on the floating island, all of them focusing their rectangular eyes on him.

"Gameknight999 and his cowardly friends have been found," Feyd said.

The endermen chuckled with excitement.

"They have been seen in the ice spikes biome, and that can mean only one thing." Feyd paused while he let his subjects process this information. "They must be going to the stronghold hidden in that land."

"Do we stop them from getting there?" one of the endermen asked.

"No, we let them enter," Feyd explained. "Once they have gone inside, we will send in an army of zombies to chase them through the labyrinth of passages. We will seal off the exit while they are running from the zombie horde—they will have no place to hide. Any who survive the zombies will find us waiting for them."

Feyd's laugh—maniacal and screechy—brought fear to all of his subjects.

"How many of us will you use to guard the entrance of the stronghold?" another asked.

"All of us will go," Feyd replied. "The Maker underestimated the User-that-is-not-a-user and was destroyed. We will not make the same mistake. All endermen will be there to see our triumph, with the Ender Dragon guarding our domain."

Feyd looked upward and could just barely make out the flying monster high overhead. He knew that Gameknight999 would not be foolish enough to come to The End with only a handful of NPCs; that would be suicide.

"This will be the greatest moment in endermen history!" Feyd shouted in a loud piercing voice. "We will see the end of the User-that-is-not-a-user, and the death of the Maker will be avenged."

The other endermen started to shake with excitement, many of them opening their wide, toothy mouths as they grew enraged.

"Come, brothers! We go to zombie-town to collect our zombie cousins, then we will wait for our prey near the stronghold."

Feyd held his long arms high into the sky, gesturing for his army to go. Sporadically, his endermen disappeared in tiny little puffs of purple mist as they teleported to zombie-town. When the last of them had gone, he summoned his ender-horse and mounted the beast. Looking high up at the dragon, Feyd smiled.

"Don't worry, Ender Dragon," Feyd shouted. "We will not be gone long."

And then Feyd, king of the endermen, disappeared, chuckling with glee at the thought of finally destroying Gameknight999.

CHAPTER 23

THE STRONGHOLD

They rode their horses carefully across the frozen landscape, their hooves crunching the ice that covered every part of the land. Gameknight exhaled, creating a white, billowing cloud before his face. Puffing his breath, he tried to make smoke rings out of the fog, but was not successful. Rubbing his slightly numb checks, he urged his horse to increase speed. A chilling wind blew up from the east, carrying with it tiny little shards of ice and snow. The breeze froze his cheeks and the tip of his nose, as well.

He looked at Monkeypants. Gameknight could still see shock in his father's eyes as he looked at their surroundings. They had crossed into the ice spikes biome about an hour ago, and Monkeypants was amazed at the beautiful ice sculptures that Minecraft had created.

"You see, Dad, not everything in Minecraft is about monsters and fighting," Gameknight said.

Monkeypants remained silent, his mouth held agape as he gazed at the frozen wonders standing majestically around him. Columns of ice decorated every inch of the landscape, some short and squat while others were tall and narrow. Each was different in their shape and size and height. Some of the spikes had arms sticking out from the side, allowing secondary spikes to shoot up into the air, while others abruptly stopped just a few blocks above the ground. The diversity of ice sculptures stretched out as far as the eye could see, each slightly different.

The one thing in common was the color. Everything had a glacial blue hue, giving the landscape a diamond-like appearance. The sparkling ice facets reflected the light from the soon-to-be setting sun and made the terrain glitter as though covered with the rarest gems.

When they reached the gigantic two spires named The Twins, Monkeypants wanted to stay and just stare up at the mighty shafts of ice, but Gameknight drove them onward. Morgana's potion was still working, but they could all see that Crafter was getting weaker. If they didn't hurry and get to The End, he'd likely not survive.

"Come on, I can see The Father up ahead," Gameknight said, pointing off into the distance.

Monkeypants turned and looked in that direction and gasped. Ahead of them was the tallest of the ice spikes: The Father, as it was named, stretching high up into the sky. Driving their horses to a gallop, they crossed the icy landscape quickly, approaching The Father along the same path they'd used the last time Gameknight had been here.

The User-that-is-not-a-user had led an army of NPCs to this stronghold the last time he'd been stuck in Minecraft. They had needed to find the Oracle and had found the location of the ancient mystic in the stronghold's library, but at the cost of some NPCs' lives. Now he was back, but not for books. Within this stronghold lay a portal that would take them to The End—and the void. That was their destination and the only thing that would save his friend.

Looking up at The Father looming overhead, Gameknight knew the entrance was near. Moving cautiously forward toward the massive ice spike, he turned in his saddle and surveyed the landscape.

It was quiet—too quiet.

"I don't like this," Gameknight said in a low voice. "Feyd would have sent some of his endermen at us by now, but where are they?"

"There is no pleasing you is there, User-that-is-not-a-user," Hunter said with a smile. "First, there are too many monsters, and now there's not enough."

Gameknight scowled at her as he approached the entrance to the stronghold. Dismounting, he moved close to the spiral staircase Digger had cut into the soil. It seemed an eternity ago when they'd been here last. Much had happened since then. Looking down into the stairway, Gameknight expected it to be dark, but the torches that had been placed there by Digger so long ago were still burning bright.

Funny how torches never seem to go out in Minecraft, Gameknight thought.

"Maybe they're still back at the swamp looking for us," Digger suggested.

"No . . . it just doesn't feel right," Gameknight replied.

Suddenly, an eerie swooshing sound rode in on the cool breeze, followed by another, and another.

"Endermen!" Stitcher shouted, "And zombies!"

Suddenly, a hundred endermen materialized around the party, each holding a zombie within their dark skinny arms. In a huge cloud of purple mist, Feyd materialized on his ender-horse, Xa-Tul at his side on his own vile zombie-horse.

"Everyone, off your horses and into the stronghold!" Gameknight shouted.

But before they could move, the zombies moved closer, forming a solid ring of claws and flesh around them and the stronghold entrance. Closing the circle, the rotting creatures moved close enough so that their decaying stench made the NPCs choke with disgust. Behind the zombies, a ring of dark endermen closed in, forming a dark, impenetrable wall of black fists.

They were trapped.

"So we meet again, Fool," Xa-Tul bellowed as he drew his massive golden sword. Urging his decaying horse forward a step, he pushed through the circle of monsters. "Don't worry, Xa-Tul hasn't forgotten the pathetic friends of the Loser-that-is-still-a-loser. These zombies will take care of them while Xa-Tul is finally ridding Minecraft of Gameknight999."

"Now you listen here," Monkeypants said as he stepped forward in front of his son. "You aren't going to do anything to my son, not without going through me first."

He reached into his inventory and nervously pulled out his sword, but he pulled out the wrong one. Instead of drawing his iron sword, he accidently pulled out an old chipped and cracked wooden sword in his hand. With his hand shaking nervously, he dropped the sword on the frozen ground, then stooped over and picked it up quickly.

Xa-Tul and Feyd started laughing, almost falling off their horses. This made the zombies and endermen laugh, some of them dropping their golden swords.

"Dad—" Gameknight said, embarrassed.

"Now! Down the stairs," Monkeypants shouted.

They shot down the steps with Gameknight taking the rear. As his friends disappeared down the steps, Gameknight looked up out of the steps and stared at the zombie-king.

"There is nowhere to go down there," Xa-Tul shouted. "Keep running, but it will only delay the inevitable; Xa-Tul *will* catch the Fool—soon."

"We'll see, zombie," Gameknight replied.

Reaching into his inventory, he placed a block of TNT next to the entrance, then lit the striped block with flint and steel. As the explosive cube started to blink, he bolted down the steps and into the stronghold.

CHAPTER 24

TRAPPED!

The musty smell of the ancient stronghold instantly assailed his nose. The aromas made Gameknight sense the timeless nature of this structure; it was older than anything he'd ever seen. Likely it was from the very first version of Minecraft, pre-alpha or earlier.

Breathing in again, the dusty smell made his nose tingle and itch. It brought the memories from the last time they'd been here instantly to the forefront of Gameknight's mind. He could almost hear the breaking of the blocks that held the spiny little monsters—silverfish. They had chased them from the library and out of the stronghold the last time they'd dared invade these solemn halls; but not everyone had made it out alive.

And now they were back.

Looking at his friends, Gameknight wondered if they would suffer the same fate.

Would some of them never see daylight again? Gameknight thought.

A thunderous explosion from above rocked the stronghold, dust and dirt falling from the walls and ceiling, choking the corridor; Gameknight's TNT had sealed the entrance behind them.

"That should slow them down a bit," the User-that-is-not-a-user said as the cloud of dust cleared. He turned to his father. "Dad, you embarrassed me back there, pulling out your wooden sword and then dropping it."

"No, I distracted the monsters *on purpose* so that we could get inside," Monkeypants said. "There's a saying: 'all warfare is based on deception.' That's what I just taught all those zombies."

I bet now you wish I'd come along instead of him, Jenny typed in the chat.

:-) Gameknight sent back. *I'm not sure which of you would be more annoying, LOL.*

When the air had cleared, he found Hunter smiling at him, her enchanted bow held in her hand. It cast an iridescent glow on the corridor, painting the walls with shimmering sapphire light and creating eerie, flickering shadows.

"Before we continue," Stitcher said, her voice piercing the silence in the dimly-lit passage, "I have something for you, Gameknight."

The User-that-is-not-a-user turned and faced his friend.

"I retrieved something else you left back at

the ocean village after the Last Battle." She reached into her inventory and pulled out a set of armor, magical enchantments making them shimmer and pulse with life. "Here is your old diamond armor, all repaired and given a few enchantments. The NPCs back at the village repaired it with diamonds they mined. I forgot to give it to you earlier because of the shadow of evil."

Gameknight reached down and picked up the iridescent chest plate, then quickly put on the armor. Instantly, he felt somehow stronger and more confident.

"Thank you," Gameknight said to his friend. "There's nothing like diamond armor."

He smiled, then turned and looked down the passage. Torches lit the passage, casting a warm yellow light on the walls and floor. Around the entrance, Gameknight could see brown speckled blocks of soul sand; they were the cubes Crafter had placed to keep the silverfish from making it out of the stronghold.

THE SWARM!

"Everyone be careful around the blocks," Gameknight said. "Some of them contain silverfish and there are hundreds of them down here if not thousands."

"Hmm," grunted Digger. "That's right. If you see a creeper, it must be destroyed before it can explode. I don't look forward to facing the Swarm again. Last time we barely made it out alive."

"What?!" Monkeypants asked. "Barely made

it out alive? Is there something I should know, son?"

His father walked toward his son, stepping on the brown speckled blocks in front of him. Instantly, the soul sand slowed his progress to a crawl.

"What's going on? What's this stuff?" his dad asked.

"Yeah, there is something you should know—don't walk on soul sand," Hunter said with a smile. "It slows you down A LOT!"

She laughed, then turned and headed off down the corridor.

"I'm gonna scout ahead!" she yelled as she ran off, Stitcher following close behind.

"OK, here's the plan," Gameknight explained as Monkeypants struggled to get out of the soul sand. "The fountain room is off to the right, the way Hunter went. If we keep the torches on our right, we'll eventually get there. Somewhere near the fountain will be the portal room, but we must be cautious: there will be monsters all throughout this place, and they mean business."

"Monsters? Down here in these dark, shadowy hallways? How do you see them?" Monkeypants asked.

"You find them when they attack you," Digger said.

The pig in Herder's arms made a muffled squeal, the rope around its snout holding its mouth closed. Carefully, the lanky boy put the animal on the ground, holding the rope tied to its neck firmly in his hand. The pink animal instantly tried to flee, running the opposite direction as Hunter and Stitcher. Pulling on the leash, Herder brought the animal back to his side and took in the slack on the rope. Herobrine turned and tried to bite the young boy on the leg, but the pig's mouth could not open.

Gameknight smiled. Kneeling, he stared into the Herobrine's glowing eyes.

"Looks like you aren't so powerful anymore, are you?" the User-that-is-not-a-user said, a mocking smile on his face.

A growl sounded from overhead—zombies.

"We need to get going," Digger said, hefting his big pickaxe onto his shoulder.

"Right. Dad, you stay close to me. Those zombies up above are going to be hot on our trail. Let's go."

Before he could take a step, Grassbrin ran in the opposite direction and placed some blocks of dirt on the ground just at the edge of the flickering torchlight. Plunging his hands into the brown cubes, he brought some grass to life—the long green strands growing thick and healthy as they blocked off the passage. Satisfied with the growth, he pulled his hands out and returned.

"Theyyyy will think weeee went that wayyy," Grassbrin said in his lyrical sing-song voice.

"Perfect!" Gameknight exclaimed.

"Are you coming or are you planning on having a little vacation here?" Hunter's sarcastic voice said from the darkness.

"We're coming!" Gameknight shouted, then drew his two swords.

They plunged into the shadowy passages of the stronghold, running from torch to torch, always keeping the light on their right. Gameknight could hear Hunter far ahead of them, the sound of her armored boots echoing off the cold stone walls. Occasionally, he'd hear her stop, then the twang of her bowstring would resonate through the stronghold. Stitcher's bow often added to the chorus.

Suddenly, a creeper shot out of a side passage and moved straight for Herder and Herobrine. The young boy screamed as the mottled green monster started to hiss. Before it had a chance to detonate, Gameknight was there with his two swords. Slashing at the monster, he made the creeper stop its ignition process as it stepped back from the flurry of blows. Moving forward, it tried to ignite again, but Gameknight struck at it over and over. With a *pop*, it disappeared, leaving behind a small pile of gunpowder.

"You OK?" Gameknight asked Herder.

He nodded.

"Remember, we can't let the creepers explode or they will release the silverfish," Gameknight explained. "You have to hit them hard and fast."

"I got it," Herder answered. "I was just a little . . . surprised."

"It's OK to be afraid," Gameknight said, "but

you can't let your fear control you. Acknowledge your fear, then work around it."

He reached out and tussled the boy's long dark hair, then gave him a reassuring smile.

"Thanks," Herder said.

"Are you idiots coming?" Hunter yelled from the edge of a flicking circle of torchlight.

Gameknight turned and ran, Herder fast on his heels.

As they sprinted through the passages, a bellowing, angry growl suddenly shook the ancient structure.

Grassbrin smiled.

"I think they founnnd the falssse trail," the light-crafter said.

Treebrin patted him on the shoulder and gave his friend smile, grumbling something that none of them could understand. Grassbrin smiled and nodded at his fellow light-crafter.

"We have to hurry," Crafter said in a weak voice. "They know where we are now."

"Come on," Digger added. "We all need to run."

Reaching for Crafter, Digger scooped up his young friend and started running, the rest of them following close behind. They passed dark shadowy doorways that led off into the confusing depths of the stronghold. Some of these doorways held the occasional spider or zombie, but Gameknight and Hunter took care of these quickly.

The growls grew louder as the pursuing horde closed in.

"Faster!" Gameknight exclaimed.

They shifted from running to sprinting as they followed the glowing torches to the fountain room, but many of them quickly grew tired.

"We have to stop and rest for a moment," Monkeypants said.

"I agree," Digger replied.

"Fine, but just for a minute," Gameknight said.

"I'm going to see what's ahead," Stitcher said as she disappeared into the shadows.

"Going alone isn't a good idea," Monkeypants said.

Standing, the monkey dressed in the Superman outfit drew his iron sword and followed the young NPC around the corner. They were gone for no longer than a minute when Stitcher's voice suddenly could be heard echoing through the hall.

"Oh, no, we're trapped."

"What?" Gameknight asked.

Drawing his diamond sword, Gameknight followed them around the corner, the rest of the party on his heels. As he rounded the curving passage, he stopped in his tracks next to his father and Stitcher, shocked at what he saw.

Ahead of him the passage was ... missing.

It was as if some kind of giant had just scooped up this section of the stronghold and left behind a deep hole. It was maybe twenty blocks deep, the walls on their side steep and sheer. On the far side of the hole, Gameknight could see the edge sloping upward; it was climbable. But this side of the hole was nearly vertical. If anyone jumped, they were dead.

All around, Gameknight could see small piles of gunpowder. Likely this was the result of a lot of creepers exploding sometime in the last few days. Moving to the edge of the hole, Gameknight peered down at the bottom. He could see small spiny things scurrying about, their segmented tails dragging across the ground: silverfish, hundreds of them.

Stepping away from the hole, the User-that-is-not-a-user turned and faced his friends. He knew his face gave away his fear and uncertainty.

"Can we climb down?" Digger asked.

Gameknight shook his head.

"The bottom is covered with silverfish. We wouldn't stand a chance," he replied.

"What are silverfish?" Monkeypants asked.

"They're tiny little monsters that swarm over anyone idiotic enough to get close to them," Hunter said. "Fighting them is impossible, especially with as many as I hear down there."

She sighed.

"We're trapped," Hunter said, dejected.

Moving to a wall, Hunter placed a block on the ground, then pulled out arrows and placed them on the ground so that she could get to them easily.

"What are you doing?" Monkeypants asked.

"Preparing," Hunter replied. "I think we'll be playing out something Gameknight once explained to me a long time ago."

"What was that?" Monkeypants asked.

"I think he called it Custer's Last Stand," she said.

Stitcher moved next to her sister and placed a block of dirt on the ground from which she would shoot. Digger put Crafter down, then moved out into the passage and started digging deep holes that would slow the zombies in their attack.

"You all act like this is over, and it's not!" Monkeypants exclaimed.

They ignored him.

Monkeypants looked toward his son. Gameknight stared back at his father, a look of sadness and defeat on his face.

"Dad, we have to get ready to fight," Gameknight said.

"You two should go back to the physical world," Crafter said in a weak voice. "No sense in you dying here if you don't have to."

"NO!" Gameknight snapped. "I won't leave you."

"You have no choice," his friend said. "You can always just bounce back into Minecraft when this is all over and help the villagers after Herobrine has escaped."

"Blue paint," Monkeypants said as he peered into the chasm.

"What?" Gameknight asked.

"What we really need is some blue paint

from that other game you play—Portal 2. Yeah, that's it," Monkeypants said.

"What did you say?" Gameknight asked, his voice filled with excitement.

"I said Portal 2," his father answered. "You know, that game with the portal guns and Glados and—"

"Blue paint! Of course! You're a genius!" Gameknight exclaimed as he put away his swords.

The moans and growls of the approaching zombie horde grew louder, their sorrowful wails echoing off the walls.

"Ha ha," Gameknight laughed as he pulled out a crafting table and placed it on the ground. Instantly, his hands were a blur as he crafted something green.

"What are you doing?" Hunter asked.

"Making blue paint, of course," Gameknight replied with a knowing smile.

"What?" Hunter replied, an angry scowl on her square face. "Are you going insane?"

"Son, what are you doing?" Monkeypants asked. "You can't use something from another game in Minecraft, right?"

His father looked confused as he glanced from his son to the other NPCs.

Gameknight ignored them and crafted as fast as his stubby square fingers would allow. When he was done, he looked at his friends triumphantly. Moving to the edge of the sheer cliff, he peered down in to the hole.

Walking back to the crafting bench,

Gameknight took about eight steps from the sheer edge and then turned and faced the cliff. Bending his knees, he got ready to sprint.

"Gameknight, what are you going to do?" Hunter asked.

"Something incredibly dangerous and stupid," he replied with a smile.

"I LIKE IT!" she shouted with a smile.

"I don't. What's going on?" Monkeypants asked, his monkeyface looking scared.

Gameknight looked at his father and gave him a wink, then sprinted toward the cliff and jumped out into the open air, the squeaks and squeals of the approaching silverfish filling his ears.

CHAPTER 25

CLAWS WITHIN REACH

Xa-Tul rounded the corner and peered from the darkness at his prey. Stepping back, he whispered to his generals.

"The NPCs are trapped," Xa-Tul grumbled in a low voice. "There is a deep hole behind them and they cannot escape."

The zombies growled in excitement.

"Generals, bring your warriors forward," the zombie-king commanded. "Get ready to attack."

The zombies shuffled forward, their claws shining in the torchlight.

Xa-Tul looked again at the NPCs, but was shocked when he saw Gameknight999 run toward the edge of the chasm. After his enemy jumped into the air, the zombie-king saw the User-that-is-not-a-user pull out a green slime block, then disappear over the edge. Seconds later, Gameknight bounced high up into the air, his hands empty. When he reached his apex, the User-that-is-not-a-user pulled out another slime block, then disappeared again into the massive hole.

"What's he doing?" Xa-Tul grumbled as Gameknight bounced up again and again, slowly traversing across the silverfish-filled hole.

Finally, the User-that-is-not-a-user landed on the far side of the obstacle. Climbing up the jagged hill, he stood on the opposite side, then waved to the other NPCs.

"They're escaping!" Xa-Tul bellowed. "Get them before they're gone. CHARGE!"

Drawing his massive golden broadsword, the zombie-king charged forward, a growling wave of angry zombies on his heels.

CHAPTER 26

FOLLOW THE LEADER

Gameknight looked toward his friends and waved them forward.

"Come on! The zombies are coming," he yelled.

Digger looked over his shoulder, then scooped up Crafter in his thick arms and ran for the edge of the cliff. Leaping with all his strength, he soared out into the open air and plunged toward the chasm floor.

The User-that-is-not-a-user watched, holding his breath, as his friends plummeted toward the awaiting swarm of silverfish. As they fell, Gameknight could see Digger correct his fall so that he landed square on the slime block. Bouncing high up into the air, Digger flew to the next block that Gameknight999 had placed. He sprang high up into the air as if propelled by a trampoline, bounding across from slime block to slime block until he landed on the far wall.

Reaching down, Gameknight held out a

hand for Crafter, helping the still weak NPC to safety. Digger followed right behind. When the big NPC stood next to Gameknight, he drew his bow and started firing at the approaching zombie horde. The User-that-is-not-a-user did the same.

"Come on, everyone!" Digger yelled.

Stitcher streaked toward the cliff and flew through the air, repeating Digger's path. When she landed on the far side, she added to the flurry of arrows arching high overhead.

The witch turned and threw a couple of splash potions at the approaching monsters, then ran for the cliff and slime blocks. The potions flew through the long tunnel and smashed against the lead zombies, causing them to slow down instantly. Those behind smashed into them, making some of them fall to the ground, creating a green decaying zombie pile-up.

"Just step over them," Xa-Tul bellowed. "GET THEM!"

"Everyone, hurry!" Gameknight yelled, but he could tell that there wasn't enough time for all of them to cross.

The witch landed safely on their side of the chasm and moved to the side to give others more room.

"HURRY!" Digger yelled.

Grassbrin turned and looked at Gameknight999. He gave him a quick smile, then ran straight for the zombies, placing blocks of dirt as he ran.

"What's he doing?" Crafter asked in a weak voice.

"I don't know," Gameknight answered truthfully.

The light-crafter placed a few more blocks, then knelt and placed his hands in the dirt. As his hands began to glow a deep forest green, blades of thick grass slithered out of the blocks. Growing longer and longer, the grass began to look like thin, flat snakes as they spread across the stone passageway. But as the grass grew, the blocks of dirt behind Grassbrin blossomed with thick blades, as well. In seconds, a tangled green barrier spread across the tunnel, completely obscuring the zombies as well as Grassbrin.

"Where did he go?" Gameknight asked. "I have to go back and help him."

Putting away his bow, Gameknight ran toward the cliff, but Digger grabbed him by the arm and held him tight.

"Your place is here, Gameknight999," Digger said as he pulled him back.

Gameknight sighed as he stood back from the chasm and pulled out his bow again. They couldn't shoot at the zombies and risk hitting Grassbrin, so they waited.

Treebrin, seeing the opportunity, grabbed Herder, who was now holding the pig in both arms, and ran toward the cliff. They soared through the air and bounced across the deadly hole, the squeaking of the excited silverfish filling the air.

When they landed, Gameknight reached

down and grabbed Herder by the collar, helping the youth up the rough wall as the pig struggled to get free. Looking up at his idol, Herder gave Gameknight999 a huge smile as he finally stepped onto the ground.

Looking back at the writhing overgrowth of thick grass, Gameknight could see sickly green arms trying to push through the plants. Dark claws sparkled in the torchlight as their growls filled the air.

They must have gotten Grassbrin, Gameknight thought.

Just as he was about to raise his hand and give the salute for the dead, Grassbrin burst out of the thick growth, a huge smile on his face. Not waiting to be told, he shot straight for the cliff and soared through the air, bouncing across the lethal ravine.

This left Hunter and Monkeypants.

"Dad, come on!" Gameknight screamed.

Monkeypants looked at his son, then glanced over the edge of the sheer cliff below him. Looking back up, Gameknight could see his face was white with fear.

"Oh no, my dad is afraid of heights," Gameknight said softly. "He can't do it."

"You better get moving, or I'm leaving you here," Hunter said as she drew an arrow and fired it at a pair of arms struggling to get through the tangled strands of grass.

"I can't. You don't understand," Monkeypants mumbled. "I have a fear of . . . I mean this is too high . . . umm . . ."

"I've heard enough," Hunter said.

She put away her bow and turned to face Gameknight's father. Reaching out with one arm, she started to push him toward the edge.

"What are you doing?" the User-that-is-not-a-user shouted, but she ignored him and focused on Monkeypants.

"What's wrong? You afraid of heights?" she asked.

Monkeypants didn't answer; he just stared at the nearby cliff.

"Well, I'm going to help you find the courage you need," Hunter said. "You see, we don't give into our fears in Minecraft. We stare them straight in the eye and say, '*I refuse to be afraid!*'"

She gave him another push.

"You either run and jump, or you fall and get attacked by all those silverfish," Hunter stated. "Decide, fast! I'm sure the spiny silverfish love the taste of monkey."

Monkeypants looked down into the deep chasm, then glance at his son. Gritting his teeth, he sprinted for the edge. As he fell through the air, he yelled a string of words that Gameknight999 could not understand. Landing on the first slime block, he shot up into the air, then landed on the next and the next until he crashed to the ground safely on the other side.

Suddenly, the zombies were through the barrier of grass and charged straight at Hunter. She streaked for the edge of the cliff. Gameknight watched her soar gracefully through the air and land on the first slime block, but when she bounced up, she left behind a striped block on top of the gelatinous green one. Soaring high into the air, she gracefully landed on the next, leaving another striped block behind. Continuing on, she landed on each slime block, depositing a present on each until she made it to the far side of the chasm.

Looking down at the slime blocks, Gameknight could see that she'd placed blocks of TNT on top of them. Before he could ask, she fired her enchanted bow at the red and white cubes. They exploded in a shower of stone and dirt, destroying the bouncy path and stopping the zombies from following.

A choking cloud of smoke and dust filled the tunnels as the explosion echoed through the stronghold. When the air cleared, Hunter stepped to Gameknight's side and looked across the ravine. They could see Xa-Tul standing at the cliff's edge, growling in frustration.

"You aren't safe yet, Fool," Xa-Tul bellowed.

In frustration, he turned and shoved his way through the zombie horde that was right behind him.

"Zombies, follow me," the zombie-king screamed. "We'll use the rear entrance to the fountain room and catch the NPCs. There is no place for them to run now."

"Bye bye," Hunter mocked. "It was nice seeing you again."

"Hunter, don't antagonize them," Stitcher chided.

"Whatever," the older sister replied. "Let's get going."

She moved down the tunnel, following the string of torches still on the right side of the passage. Her sister followed close behind.

"Grassbrin, that was very dangerous, what you did back there," Gameknight said.

The light-crafter shrugged his shoulders.

"I just imaginnnned what the Userrrr-that-is-not-a-userrrr would do," he said with a smile, then turned and followed the sisters down the tunnel.

Digger bent and helped Crafter up, then continued down the tunnel, the witch and Treebrin following close behind.

"Dad?" Gameknight asked.

"Yes, son?"

"What was it you were saying while you were flying through the air?"

"I was trying to explain to Hunter about my fear," Monkeypants explained. "It's not that I'm afraid of heights; I'm just afraid of hitting the ground."

His father laughed, completely unashamed, unconcerned if anyone saw him. It was the first time that Gameknight had ever seen him like that. Usually he was always careful and calculating. Letting out a fat, loud belly laugh like that was something he never did. But after he'd made it across that silverfish-filled chasm, his dad seemed a little different. It was as if he were a little taller, somehow.

Reaching out, he patted his dad on the

back, then took off running, following the others. But Gameknight could not be as joyous as his father, for he knew where they were heading. A terrible beast waited for them with razor-sharp claws and frightening purple eyes.

CHAPTER 27

THE FOUNTAIN ROOM

They raced through the cold passages of the stronghold. Ahead, Gameknight could hear Hunter's bow singing out as she fired enchanted arrows at some hidden foe.

"Take that!" she screamed as she fired again and again.

"Everyone keep on coming," Stitcher yelled. "It was just some spiders. They're gone now."

Her voice echoed through the passages, making it unclear if it was coming from ahead or behind, but Gameknight knew where they were. Continuing through the maze of corridors, he kept going, keeping the torches on his right. Pausing for a moment, Gameknight glanced over his shoulder, looking for Xa-Tul and his army of crazed monsters. He hoped they'd lost them and they were gone, but he knew better than to count them out.

Sprinting ahead, he tried to keep up with his father. As they streaked through the corridor, a zombie jumped out of a dark passage. Its sharp claws slashed into Monkeypant's armor, leaving a set of deep scratches. As his father stopped and drew his sword, Gameknight slammed into the monster, knocking it to the ground. The decaying monster struggled to stand, but Gameknight gave it no quarter. He fell on it with both swords, making the creature flash red over and over again. Stepping to his side, Monkeypants added his sword to his son's, depleting the monster's HP in seconds. It disappeared with a *pop*, leaving behind three glowing balls of XP.

"Come on, we need to keep going," Gameknight said.

Monkeypants nodded and continued down the passage. Following his father, the User-that-is-not-a-user turned at the next corner and found his companions stopped next to an ornate chest, slabs of cobblestone placed around the dusty old chest. A torch on the wall cast a golden circle of illumination around the ancient wooden box.

"What are we waiting for?" Gameknight asked.

"We need a break," Digger said. "We'll rest for a few minutes, then we'll—"

"No," Gameknight snapped. "This is a race and only the winner survives. If Xa-Tul gets to the portal room before us, then Crafter is doomed. We must get to The End so that we can destroy Herobrine and save our friend."

"But—" Digger said

"There is no 'but,'" Gameknight interrupted. "We have to go—now!"

His weary companions stood and followed him as he raced down the dusty tunnel. Following the passage, the User-that-is-not-a-user could hear the sound of water splashing. They were close. Speeding up, he turned and glanced over his shoulder. Digger was carrying Crafter in his burly arms, his young friend's skin getting whiter and whiter.

We have to hurry!

Running with all his might, he shot down the corridor and bolted into the fountain room. Stopping before the flowing spring, Gameknight scanned the chamber, looking for threats. It was empty. Behind him, he could hear Digger enter the room, his heavy footsteps sounding like thunder as they echoed off the cold stone walls.

The big NPC carefully placed Crafter next to the fountain, sitting on a block near the watery flow. Morgana quickly knelt next to the infirmed NPC and felt his forehead. Looking to Gameknight, she shook her head.

"He does not have long," she said with a scratchy voice. "He'll need the last of the potion soon."

"I'll be OK," Crafter said, his voice barely loud enough to be heard over the trickling fountain. "Don't worry about me."

Gameknight gave him a smile, then cast a worried look toward the witch.

"Can you do anything for him?" he asked.

"I could give him the last of the potion I made in my hut," she explained. "But if it wears off before you destroy Herobrine, then the evil that resides within your friend will win."

"What do you mean *it* will *win*?" Stitcher asked as she moved to the other side of Crafter.

"I mean it will devour that last of his HP," Morgana explained. "He will die."

The young girl looked toward Gameknight and gazed at him with worried eyes. Glancing about the room, he noticed the same expression on all of their faces; they expected the great User-that-is-not-a-user to do something clever and save the day.

But what can I do other than get to The End? he thought.

The last time they'd been in The End, an army of NPCs had been with him. There had been hundreds of endermen there, all of them thirsting for violence. The thought of facing off against Feyd made Gameknight's blood run cold.

Moving to Crafter's side, the User-that-is-not-a-user placed a hand on his friend's arm and gave him a smile. The young NPC was about to say something when a ghost-like appearance came across his face, his skin now bone white. Slowly, he slumped to the ground as his strength evaporated.

Gameknight dashed to his side and caught his friend. Cradling his friend in his arms, Gameknight looked up at the witch, tears falling from his square cheeks and landing on Crafter's dented armor.

"Morgana, HELP!" he cried.

The witch pulled out the last of the sparkling black potion. Carefully she poured it into Crafter's mouth, then closed his lips until all the liquid ran down his throat. Instantly, color came back to his skin, drawing him back to the world of the living.

Slowly, Crafter opened his eyes.

"Ahh ... what was I saying," Crafter said, his voice just a whisper. "Sorry, I guess I dozed off."

"Ha," Hunter laughed, startling everyone in the room. "You didn't doze off, you passed out. The witch here gave you the last of her potion."

She turned and faced Gameknight999.

"We need to do something, quick," Hunter said, worry filling her dark brown eyes.

"Don't worry, I'll think of something," he said.

Just then, the music of Minecraft swelled, filling him with a calm peace. At the same time, the smallest cube of water splashed out of the fountain and landed on his cheek. Looking at the fountain, the User-that-is-not-a-user realized that this was part of the solution for surviving the impending battle in The End.

"Water—we need water," Gameknight said.

"What are you talking about?" Hunter asked.

Turning, the User-that-is-not-a-user faced Herder.

"You said you brought buckets?" Gameknight asked.

"Of course," Herder replied. "Crafter taught me you should always have a good supply of buckets with you."

"And splash bottles," Gameknight added. "We'll need something to use against all the endermen that will be waiting for us."

"I have splash bottles with me," Morgana said.

She pulled them out of her smock and filled them at the fountain. Herder did the same with his buckets.

As the other NPCs took bottles and buckets and began filling them, a plan started to come together. The puzzle pieces tumbled around in his head, then slowly fell into place and showed him what he had to do. It was dangerous, but everything hinged on getting past the endermen so they could get to the edge of The End.

"From what I understand, the water is for the endermen, right?" Monkeypants asked. "But isn't there a dragon there, as well?"

"Don't worry, Dad," Gameknight said. "With all those endermen there, the Ender Dragon will be flying high overhead. It won't be able to pick us out amongst all the endermen. I'm sure it won't bother us until after we've gotten rid of Herobrine."

"But what if you're wrong?" his father asked.

"You taught me not to worry about the *what if's*," the User-that-is-not-a-user answered. "I'm only focused on *the now*."

But he was lying. When he thought about the dragon, Gameknight was terrified. But he couldn't show it. Right now, everyone needed confidence and courage—even though he had neither.

CHAPTER 28

THE PORTAL ROOM

Hunter and Stitcher led the way out of the fountain room as Digger and Morgana helped Crafter shuffle through the corridors. Herder followed close behind with Herobrine straining on his leash, trying to run in the opposite direction.

"Is there anything you can think of to get the pig to be more cooperative?" Gameknight asked Treebrin.

The tall light-crafter looked down on him. His spiky dark hair looked like a bramble of twigs as he moved through the circles of torchlight, his dark brown skin allowing him to blend into the shadows and almost disappear. He mumbled something that sounded like words coupled with the cracking of branches; it was completely unrecognizable to Gameknight.

"What?" the User-that-is-not-a-user asked.

"Heee said that heee has sommme ideas," Grassbrin said, a devious smile on his face.

Holding out his dark hands, Treebrin held a cube of dirt between his thick, knobby fingers. He then started to hum. It was a strange, mysterious tune that echoed off the stone walls, then reflected back to harmonize with the tall light-crafter. As he sang, the cube of dirt seemed to radiate with a curious golden glow.

And then a branch started to grow from the dirt. It emerged, not as the smallest sapling, but as a fully formed branch, the bark of the tree limb covering the sharp thorny spines.

As Treebrin sang louder, the branch grew thicker and longer, the glow from the cube of dirt lighting the shadowy passage. Gameknight watched with amazement as the long barbed tree branch grew from the cube, and then suddenly, it was done. The golden light from the dirt extinguished, leaving the companions in the dim light from the torches.

Grasping the thorny branch from the smooth end, Treebrin pulled it from the cube of dirt and gently tapped Herobrine from behind. The pig squealed and jumped forward, the sharp spines poking into the pig's skin, but not doing enough damage to make it flash or lose HP.

"This is perfect," Gameknight said. "We can goad it forward without doing damage to its HP."

Herobrine made a loud angry oink as it glared at Treebrin. The light-crafter gave the pig a mischievous grin, then tapped the little animal again, making it squeak even louder.

Scurrying faster, the little animal moved out of reach from the pointed tree limb and up closer to Herder.

Gameknight looked up at Treebrin and smiled. The light-crafter glanced down with his warm cream-colored eyes and gave him a big toothy smile that warmed his heart.

"We're there!" a shout came from ahead.

Looking forward, Gameknight could see the orange glow of lava within the portal room spilling out into the dark passage. A crunching sound echoed through the tunnel, then the breaking of something metal. He knew that Hunter and Stitcher had just destroyed the silverfish spawner that sat on the steps up to the portal. Squeaking cries of pain sounded through the passage as Gameknight entered the room. Hunter and Stitcher were chasing the few silverfish that patrolled the room. Working together, they'd corner the creatures, then hit them quickly, taking their HP before they could call out to more of their kind.

Looking around, Gameknight surveyed the room. Two small pools of lava that sat in cobblestone-trimmed basins on either side of the doorway, a large wooden chest nearby. The light from these two pools lit the dark hallway, creating an island of illumination in the shadowy passage, marking the entrance to the infamous portal room. On either wall, there were windows carved into the cobblestone with iron bars filling their interior; Gameknight always found these curious. There was nothing to see out of the windows—they were underground.

At the center of the room was a large pool of lava that cast an even brighter glow on the ancient cobblestone ceiling and walls. Sparks leapt up as ash floated into the air. The heat from the pool was intense; a stark contrast from the cold and clammy stone passages through which they'd been traveling.

Floating above the pool were twelve end portal blocks, each with sides colored a pale yellow, their tops rimmed with deep green. At the center of each block was a dark, ominous hole. As he climbed the steps to look down, Gameknight shuddered. The portal blocks looked like sightless eyes, all staring up at him.

"What do they do?" Monkeypants asked from his son's side.

"These blocks form the portal that will take us to The End," he replied. Turning, he looked down at the chest that sat against one wall. "Stitcher, bring the Eyes."

"The what?" Monkeypants asked.

Gameknight ignored the question. He knew they were about to go past the point of no return, and every one of his uncertainties and fears concerning their plan ... Herobrine, Crafter ... everything was magnified.

Stitcher opened the chest that sat next to one of the lava basins and took something from its dusty interior, then climbed the steps and moved out onto the end portal blocks. Carefully, she placed the green spheres in each block. Instantly they transformed into something that looked like a strange alien eye. Gameknight could feel them staring at him, daring him to venture into their domain—The End.

When she finished placing the last Eye of Ender, the portal sprang to life. A dark, endless space filled the portal, with bright stars twinkling in its depths. Monkeypants gasped as he looked into the infinite chasm that stretched out before him.

"Is that . . . The End?" his father asked.

"No, it's just the portal that leads to it," Gameknight explained.

Looking down, he faced away from the portal and to his friends.

"Here's the plan," he explained. "Typically, you spawn near the edge of The End. As soon as we spawn, we'll drop Herobrine over the edge and—"

The pig squealed and pulled against his leash. Reaching down, Herder picked up the animal and wrapped his long arms around the beast, squeezing him tight. Herobrine tried again to bite the lanky boy, but the rope around the creature's nose and mouth was still holding, though Gameknight noticed it was starting to look a bit frayed.

"As I was saying, we'll drop Herobrine over the edge and be done with him. Crafter will then be safe. Any questions?"

"Is there anything I should know about The End?" Monkeypants.

Gameknight shook his head.

"There is one thing," Hunter added.

"What's that?" Monkeypants asked.

"Don't get killed," she said with a smile.

Stitcher punched her sister in the arm.

"Be nice," Stitcher chided.

Hunter smiled and was about to respond when the sound of a hundred growling and moaning zombies suddenly filled the air.

"They found us!" Digger exclaimed as he pulled out a block of obsidian and tried to place it on the ground.

But before he could, Morgana stepped out into the hallway. Pulling bottles of splash potion out of her smock, she threw them into the hallway, causing a brown, stinking cloud of gas to form. Stepping back into the portal room, she smiled.

"That should slow them a bit," the witch said with a mischievous smile.

"I'm starting to like her," Hunter said under her breath.

Digger looked at Morgana suspiciously, then placed a block of obsidian in the doorway and stacked another on top, sealing up the entrance to the portal chamber.

"What good is that going to do?" Monkeypants asked the stocky NPC. "If they can't get through the doorway, they'll just break through these stone walls."

Digger smiled as he patted the stone blocks that lined the doorway.

"I don't think so," the big NPC said, a

mischievous grin on his boxy face. "I think a little surprise is in store for the zombies within these blocks."

Gameknight looked at the big NPC, confused, but didn't have time to worry about it.

"Time to go," Gameknight said. "Remember, as soon as we're in, throw Herobrine over the edge."

He turned and faced the witch.

"Morgana, are you coming with us?" the User-that-is-not-a-user asked. "You aren't an NPC or user. The zombies might let you leave unharmed."

"No, I think I'm in this with you," she replied in a scratchy, aged voice. "Besides, there is still repayment to discuss after this mission is successful." She turned and faced Crafter. "I'm not letting you NPCs off the hook. You owe me a lot and I mean to collect."

"OK, let's do this thing," Gameknight said as he turned and faced the portal.

Grabbing his father's hand, he looked into his monkey-face.

"You ready?" he asked.

Monkeypants looked down into the endless expanse of space that filled the portal. Gameknight could tell that his fear of heights was overwhelming his mind.

"It's not real; it's just an illusion," Gameknight said.

"Tell that to my brain, which is terrified," his father answered.

"I know an easy way past this fear," Hunter

said as she approached, one hand outstretched in front of her.

"No, not that again," Monkeypants said and leapt into the portal.

Gameknight smiled, then stepped into the portal, his two swords in his hands, ready for battle.

CHAPTER 29

THE END

They materialized on a flat piece of obsidian, completely surrounded by End Stone and buried underground. The pale yellow stone hugged close to their dark platform, a roof pressing down on them just three blocks high.

Without waiting to be told, Digger pulled out his big pickaxe and started digging a set of steps to the surface. Herder and Stitcher did the same.

"Remember, the edge of the floating island is likely near these walls," Gameknight said. "So everyone must be careful."

Hunter pulled out her own pickaxe and began digging. Moving to her side, Gameknight helped her carve into the soft walls, shattering through the End Stone as if it were glass.

"Collect as many of these blocks as possible," Gameknight shouted over the sounds of iron shattering blocks. "As soon as we're to the surface, Herder, take the pig to the edge and throw him over. Remember, don't bump into any of the endermen. We want to keep them out of this fight as long as possible." He turned and faced Herder. "For now, tie the pig to a post so you can help with the digging."

Herder pulled out a fence post from his inventory and placed it in the ground. The pig's leash was tied firmly to it, though Herobrine was testing the strength of the rope, pulling against the knots with all his little piggy strength. Treebrin moved next to the pig and tapped it with his thorny branch. Grumbling something to the small pink animal, he wagged a gnarled finger at Herobrine, then swatted him again with his barbed stick. Oinking in pain, the little pink monster moved away from the light-crafter and stood near the fence post, his eyes glowing bright white with hatred.

"I'm through," Digger said.

"What do you see?" Gameknight asked. "Which way is the edge? How many endermen are nearby?"

Instead of answering, Digger came down the steps, a look of confusion and fear on his square face.

"What is it?" the User-that-is-not-a-user asked.

Digger said nothing, just stared back at Gameknight999. Shoving past his friend, Gameknight put away his pick and drew his diamond sword.

"Come on, everyone," Gameknight said as

he bolted up the makeshift stairs. "Let's get this done!"

When he emerged from their hole, he was shocked at what he saw. The landscape was completely empty—no endermen were visible anywhere.

Great, the dragon will pick us out almost instantly, Gameknight thought.

He scanned for the edge of the island and couldn't find it. The pale yellow stone stretched out into the distance. They had spawned in the largest End landscape he'd ever seen, and worse yet, they were in the middle.

"We'll have to make a run for the edge," Gameknight said as he scanned the sky for what he knew was up there. "Herder, get up here with the pig. We have to—"

GROAR!

A growling roar pierced through the silence of The End, shattering any remote thoughts that they might be alone in this land. Overhead, Gameknight could see two bright purple spots of light floating on unseen currents of air. Turning in a graceful arc, the purple eyes turned and headed down to the ground. As they neared, the body around the glowing orbs emerged through the darkness. Gameknight could see the dragon's massive head as it approached, its sharp, white teeth somehow glowing bright in the pale light of The End. Gray thorny horns protruded from the creature's head, matching the spiky ridges that ran down the monster's neck and back.

Spreading its wide leathery wings, the Ender Dragon banked slightly as it lined up to attack the new intruders. Gameknight shuddered as it extended its clawed paws, the razor-sharp talons gleaming with deadly intent. Locking its purple eyes on the User-that-is-not-a-user, the monster tucked in its wings and accelerated toward its target, another mighty roar coming from its throat.

"DRAGON!" Gameknight yelled.

Sprinting away from the hole, he dove to the ground just as the dark claws swiped at the air just above him. The dragon beat its heavy wings and climbed back into the sky, but he wasn't fast enough. Hunter emerged from the hole with an arrow already drawn. The flaming projectile leapt from her bow, curved through the air and hit the creature on the back, making it flash red. The flying demon yelled out in pain.

"Did you get him?" Monkeypants asked as he emerged from the hole.

"I hit him alright," Hunter said with a smile.

They watched as the dragon flew to one of the many tall obsidian towers that dotted the landscape. Atop the nearest, a pink crystal floated in a bath of fire, bobbing up and down as if it did not need to follow the commands of gravity. As the dragon flew near, a purple shaft of light shot out of the crystal and hit the flying giant.

"What's that?" Monkeypants asked.

"On top of each obsidian pillar is an ender

crystal," Stitcher explained as she moved next to her sister. "They heal the Ender Dragon. We have to destroy all those crystals before we can take on that dragon."

"But we don't have to fight the dragon," Monkeypants said. "We just throw Herobrine over the edge and we're done, right?"

Stitcher tried to give Monkeypants a reassuring smile, but did a poor job.

"What?" Monkeypants asked.

"We have to destroy the dragon so that a new portal will appear that will take us out of here," Hunter explained. "No dead dragon, no portal. Got it?"

"Here he comes again!" Digger yelled.

Spinning around, Gameknight could see the monster coming straight at them. But before he could move, Treebrin stepped in front and placed a block of dirt on the pale ground. Plunging his hands into the cube, he made a tall oak tree suddenly burst into life. The leafy giant shocked the dragon, making it climb upward and out of reach. Hunter and Stitcher fired their enchanted arrows at the beast, but it climbed too fast and was quickly out of range.

"Nobody told me about fighting a dragon," Monkeypants complained.

"Well, we don't have a choice," Crafter said in a still weak voice. "We can't make a run for it; the dragon will pick us all off. It's time to fight."

Crafter reached into his inventory for his sword, but just as he did, a shadow of evil materialized under him. Dark jagged shapes jutted up from the ground and hit the young NPC over and over, making him cry out in pain.

Moving without thinking, Gameknight streaked to his friend side and lifted him up off the ground. Holding him as high as he could, the User-that-is-not-a-user let Herobrine's evil shade jab at him with its evil, serrated shadows. Hunter moved next to his friend and placed a block of end stone on the ground, then placed two more next to it, then a stack of three, building a set of stairs. Gameknight quickly climbed the steps, getting as far from the shadow as he could.

But as quickly as the shadow appeared, it disappeared, evaporating into a dark mist. Gameknight came down from the steps and carefully placed Crafter on the ground.

"I don't think it will be back for a while," Digger said. "Herobrine seems to only have strength for so many attacks before he needs to rest."

Gameknight turned and looked at the pig Herder was dragging out of the buried end stone chamber. The pig looked exhausted, as if it had used all its strength to sustain this attack.

Pulling out a piece of bread, Gameknight ate it quickly, hoping it would help rejuvenate his HP.

"Herder, place a fence post here, next to the tree," Gameknight said as he chewed. "Crafter and Morgana are going to stay here and guard the pig. The rest of us are going after the Ender Dragon."

"But it's so huge," Monkeypants objected. "How are we going to do this?" His father turned and faced Gameknight. "No, this is just too dangerous. I forbid this."

"But dad, we have to—for Crafter, for my friends, for everyone."

"It's too dangerous," Monkeypants repeated. "I could lose you, my boy, my little Tommy. How could I live with that?"

"You told me I needed to decide who I am and what kind of person I want to be. Well, I want to be a person who is there for his friends and family. I'm a big boy, and I think I can shoulder the responsibility heaped on me, with the help of my friends, that is."

Hunter moved next to Gameknight's side and put a hand on his shoulder. Herder and Stitcher then moved to his side. They all looked at Gameknight999 and gave him a smile, then turned and looked at Monkeypants271.

"You don't get it," his father said. "If you were to die, then—"

"No, *you* don't get it," Gameknight snapped. "If I run away from my friends and just let them perish here in The End, then what kind of person am I?" He took a step closer to his father and lowered his voice. "Is that the kind of child you raised? One who would just run away when things got hard? One who would abandon his friends when they needed help?" He paused as Monkeypants considered his words, then continued. "These are the people I care about. If I abandon them, then I will regret it for the rest of my life. Is that what you want for me?"

Gameknight sighed. He felt trapped. The idea of battling an Ender Dragon again scared him all the way down to his toes, but he had no choice; he had to stay and help his friends. And then the realization hit him—this was probably how Monkeypants felt. His dad didn't want to travel, but he had to take care of his family and was willing to do anything he needed to do to make sure that they were safe, and fed, and had a roof over their heads. Even if it meant traveling all over the country to sell his inventions, his dad was willing to do it. Gameknight now understood that his dad had no choice; he had to be away from home to do what he needed to do, to sell his inventions.

A new appreciation for his father filled Gameknight. He was proud of him and was about to say something when the dragon roared in the distance. Turning to the sound, he could just barely make out the mighty beast in the darkness as it carved a graceful arc in the sky.

Monkeypants looked up at the dragon in the distance, then back to his son, worry and uncertainty still showing in his monkey-eyes.

"I knew all along that I'd need to stand up to the Ender Dragon to save Crafter, even though that monster terrifies me, but I don't care. All that matters is that I need to help my friends."

He moved next to his father and placed a hand on his shoulder. "Will you stand with me?"

Monkeypants smiled and a look of pride came across his square face.

"Let's do this," his father said. "How do you say it? GO, MINECRAFT!"

"No, it's *for* Minecraft," Gameknight corrected, rolling his eyes.

Hunter laughed.

"Oh, sorry," Monkeypants said, then drew his sword. "FOR MINECRAFT!"

"FOR MINECRAFT!" the others yelled as they ran toward the first obsidian pillar, the Ender Dragon's terrible roar echoing overhead.

CHAPTER 30

THE FIRST ENDER CRYSTAL

They sprinted toward the nearest obsidian pillar. Because the pillars of dark stone are randomly generated, one never knew how tall or how many of them there would be in The End. Smiling, Gameknight could see that the nearest was a small one, only four blocks across and short—good. They could get this one with arrows.

As they ran, Gameknight scanned the sky for purple eyes. He knew the dragon was watching them, planning when to strike, and he had to be ready. Then he saw them, the two blazing orbs of purple hatred. The dragon was coming in low, close to the ground, hoping to avoid detection.

"Digger, to the left," Gameknight said as he pulled out his bow. Digger did the same. "Hunter, Stitcher, focus on the ender crystal. Digger and I will keep the dragon busy."

Peeling off from the rest of the party, Gameknight999 and Digger ran straight for the dragon, arrows notched. As it neared, its terribly sharp white teeth could be seen against its black skin. It snarled, then beat its huge leathery wings, making the gray spikes that ran down its back curve like some kind of armored snake. The dragon sped up, beating its wings even harder while it gnashed its frightening teeth together.

"Ready?" Gameknight said.

Digger just grunted as he loosed his arrow, Gameknight's following close behind.

Not waiting to see if they hit, the pair continued to fire, their pointed shafts arcing through the air in a graceful curve. The first few landed short, but as they closed the distance, their projectiles began hitting their target. Gameknight's third arrow pierced a wing while Digger's fourth found a shoulder. The dragon roared in pain and dove at them, seeking revenge.

As Digger kept firing, Gameknight put away his bow and drew his two swords. Charging straight at the monster, he yelled at the top of his lungs.

"FOR CRAFTER!"

His ferocious charge, coupled with the damage the dragon was taking from Digger's arrows, made the monster break away and seek out the closest ender crystal. It approached the nearest pillar. Instantly, a purple beam of light shot out from the dancing crystal, but as the dragon neared, the crystal exploded.

"Take that!" Hunter shouted as her arrow found its target.

The dragon flashed red as the exploding crystal sent blast damage up the purple shaft of light, injuring the dragon even more. The monster roared in anger and pain, then curved and sought out another crystal.

"Hurry, it will be back soon," Gameknight said. "Let's get to the next one."

Gameknight followed the dragon to the next pillar. It was a tall one, maybe thirty blocks high. As they neared the next pillar, healing beams of light shot out to the dragon from the neighboring crystals, rejuvenating the beast until its HP was back to full. When it was healed, it turned and dived toward the intruders.

"Get ready to scatter," the User-that-is-not-a-user shouted. "He's coming in fast!"

Gameknight could hear the twang of Hunter's bow, Stitcher's adding to the melody, but the dragon was flying too fast and their shots were all missing.

The dragon was now like a winged missile, streaking straight at him, but Gameknight knew that the monster had traded agility for speed. It was going so fast that it wouldn't be able to turn quickly.

"Swords out!" Gameknight yelled.

The monster was getting closer. He could now see the dark pupils within the blazing lavender eyes.

"SCATTER!" he shouted.

Everyone shot out in a different directions and dove to the ground, except for Gameknight999, who stood his ground. With his two swords extended, he ran toward his attacker, yelling at the top of his lungs.

The dragon smiled and beat his wings even harder. The User-that-is-not-a-user saw the monster reach out with its pointed talons, ready to tear into his prey. But at the last instant, Gameknight laid on the ground and extended his two swords straight upwards. His pointed swords dragged across the dragon's stomach as it flew over his body, its dark claws lightly scratching across his chest plate. As it zipped over his head, Gameknight999 saw it flash red, his weapons tearing its long dark body.

The monster roared in frustration as it climbed into the air.

Smiling, Gameknight stood and continued to run toward the pillar.

"Look out!" Monkeypants yelled.

Looking over his shoulder, Gameknight found the dragon almost upon him. It hadn't flown off to get healed. Instead, it turned and attacked.

Rolling to the side, Gameknight avoided its sharp claws, but as the dragon passed, the monster whipped its long, pointed tail. It smashed into Gameknight's chest, knocking him to the ground and filling him with pain. Struggling for air, the User-that-is-not-a-user tried to get up, but found he was too stunned to stand.

The dragon roared.

It was coming closer. Gameknight could hear its panting breath getting near. Then a *twang* sounded, followed by another and another. The dragon roared as arrows struck his body, making him flash red. Leaping into the air, it flew off toward its ender crystals and their healing rays. But as it soared upward, the creature glared hatefully down at Gameknight999, its eyes burning with purple fire.

Finally able to stand, Gameknight turned and faced his friends. He rubbed the diamond chest plate and knew the armored coating had probably just saved his life.

"We have to hurry," he said.

"Are you OK?" his father asked. "It looked like the dragon hit you."

"Yeah, I'm OK. Let's get these crystals."

They ran to the nearest pillar and stood at its base. It seemed impossibly tall. Gameknight knew he had to go up there and destroy the crystal; their bows would not reach. Pulling out a stack of End Stone, he jumped up into the air and placed a block under his feet, then paused for a moment. He looked at his friends.

"Digger, I'll come down either on this side or the opposite side, be ready," Gameknight said.

Digger nodded, then grabbed Herder's arm and whispered into his ear.

"What's happening?" Monkeypants asked. "Is this dangerous?"

"Of course not," Hunter added. "Gameknight does this all the time."

"Yep," his son replied with a smile.

"Come on, Monkeypants, you're with us," Hunter said. "Our job is to encourage the dragon to go away."

"Treebrin, Grassbrin," Gameknight shouted. "Go out and plant grass and trees all across the land. It will confuse the dragon about where we are."

"It willll be donnne," Grassbrin said.

Treebrin grumbled something unintelligible, then the two light-crafters ran off. Pausing for just an instant, they placed blocks of dirt on the ground, then brought forth lush plants that grew long and tall on the barren landscape.

GROAR!

The dragon bellowed as it approached.

Not waiting to see where it was at, Gameknight continued jumping and placing blocks, slowly scaling the tall obsidian tower. The *twang* of bowstrings let Gameknight know that the monster was close, and fear nibbled on his nerves as he imagined those terrible purple eyes swooping down on him—maybe from behind, maybe from his left side, or maybe his right. He could feel the creature out there, stalking him, waiting for an opportunity to strike. It made the User-that-is-not-a-user want to stop and go back to the ground, but he knew he couldn't—Crafter was depending on him, and they had to destroy the dragon before they could get rid of Herobrine.

He was almost there.

The top of the pillar was now visible. He

was going to make it without getting attacked by the dragon.

Suddenly, the sound of huge leathery wings sounded off to his left. Currents of air buffeted him as the blast from the strong, flapping wings tried to dislodge him from his precarious position, but he dared not look.

Concentrate on what you need to do, Gameknight thought. *Focus on what's important, focus on Crafter.*

Ignoring the sound, he continued moving upward.

Suddenly, a pain-filled, growling roar sounded; their arrows had found their target.

The flapping wings moved off.

Speeding up, Gameknight reached the peak. Before him hovered the ender crystal. It was a pink cube with cryptic letters scrawled in red on each face. The symbols were completely undecipherable, being written in the Standard Galactic Alphabet. Around the crystal, flames licked upward, bathing the intricate object in unquenchable flame. It bobbed up and down as if balanced atop a constantly moving spring.

A roar sounded from behind him. Without looking, Gameknight crossed to the opposite side of the pillar and faced the crystal. The dragon was approaching, heading straight for him. Its blazing eyes were filled with a violet rage, focused on him like two giant hateful lasers. Beating its massive wings, it accelerated. The User-that-is-not-a-user could see flaming arrows streak upward at the monster, striking the dragon in the stomach and wings, but it continued on, intent on destruction.

A purple healing beam of light shot out from the crystal, replenishing the dragon's HP.

It's the perfect time, Gameknight thought with a smile.

Stepping backward, he moved to the very edge of the towering structure, his heel feeling the boundary between obsidian and air. Drawing his bow, he aimed an arrow at the crystal and then took a step backward. He released the arrow as he fell from the impossible height.

CHAPTER 31

THE LAST ENDER CRYSTAL

As the User-that-is-not-a-user fell, he lost sight of his arrow, but he heard its effect. The ender crystal exploded in a shower of pink shards, the blast damage moving up its healing beam and injuring the dragon. The monster roared in pain and banked toward another obsidian tower, leaving his prey for the moment.

The wind whistled past Gameknight's ears as he fell. He hoped Digger and Herder were ready. If he'd jumped too soon, then there would be nothing to catch him other than hard End Stone—and that would likely not end well.

Gameknight laughed as he released his fear and just let things be what they would be.

Almost there . . .

The ground was rushing up to meet him, but he did not look down. There was nothing he could do to change his fate now. Normally, Gameknight would have been staring down, panicking about what would happen, but rather than give in to fear, he just looked about at the landscape around him and enjoyed the spectacular view of The End, and then ...

SPLASH!

Cool water sprayed all over his chest and face as he landed in a shallow pool of water. Next to him was Herder, standing knee deep with an empty bucket in his hand, the lanky boy smiling at his idol.

"Hi, Gameknight," Herder said, then gave him a nervous giggle.

"Hi, Herder," he answered with a smile. "What's going on? Anything new?"

Herder giggled again, then scooped up the water with the bucket and put it back into his inventory.

"ARE YOU CRAZY!" exclaimed his father. "That was terrifying!"

"I bet it was much scarier from Gameknight's point of view," Hunter added with a smile.

"Hunter, you're not helping," Stitcher chided.

"Tommy, these risky antics have to stop," his father lectured. "Maybe we were wrong to try this. You could have been—"

"I was doing what I had to do to take care of my friends," Gameknight snapped, anger and frustration sounding in his voice. "They need me here, now, and I'm going to help them. This is what I do, take care of my friends, just like you're doing what you need to do to take care of us at home. I know that it has been hard on you to travel so much; it's been hard on all of us. But right now, we need to take care of Crafter and my friends, and the only way we can do that is to get rid of this dragon."

Monkeypants looked at the ground, afraid for his son. Gameknight could tell his father was terrified and wanted to keep him safe, but being safe wouldn't save Crafter. They had to keep moving forward, or else ...

"Son, you know that I've been—"

"Dad, I understand why you've been traveling, really I do. I get that now. But sometimes I need you, and that time is NOW!" Gameknight shouted. "Are you going to be here for me, now, or are you going to give in to the *what if's*?"

DRAGON COMING! Jenny typed in the chat.

The dragon's roar pierced through The End.

"Here it comes!" Gameknight shouted.

Hunter and Stitcher ran off, their bows singing their deadly tune. Their arrows scored critical hits on the monster, and it banked away to get healed again. But as it roared, the User-that-is-not-a-user could tell the monster was getting angrier and more desperate—and that was not good.

Looking at his father, Gameknight could tell he wanted to talk, but the dragon made that difficult. Clearly, there was an internal struggle taking place within the monkey, but Gameknight could not help there. All he could do was be honest and brave and not let down his friends.

"OK, let's do this," Monkeypants said, a look of pride coming across his square face "We'll talk after." Turning, he looked at Digger and the sisters. "Come on, everyone, we have crystals that need destroying. I'll do whatever is necessary as long as I can keep my feet on the ground."

Hunter giggled, then stepped forward and patted the monkey on the shoulder.

"That's a good strategy," she said.

Pulling out her bow, she sprinted for the next obsidian pillar, Gameknight at her side.

They moved from pillar to pillar in this method. Those low enough were shot with arrows, and the taller were climbed by Gameknight999. Grassbrin and Treebrin moved out on their own, placing blocks of dirt on the End Stone and making patches of grass and trees sprout up out of the pale yellow landscape. This confused the dragon and at times drew him to the light-crafters and momentarily away from Gameknight and the others, but as the winged creature closed on the grass and trees, it just veered away and continue the hunt for its enemies.

As they approached the last ender crystal, Monkeypants moved next to his son's side.

"This next one is taller than all the rest," his father said.

"I know," Gameknight answered.

They had worked their way around The End

and were now near where they had started. Gameknight could see the pig staked out on the ground next to the tall oak tree Treebrin had planted, Crafter and Morgana sitting nearby.

"The dragon will know that you're heading for that one," Monkeypants said. "It looks like it's the last one."

"You're probably right," his son replied.

Gameknight looked up at the massive pillar of obsidian as they neared. It was the biggest he'd ever seen. It was easily the maximum height, thirty-seven blocks tall, but as they neared, Gameknight could see that it was actually three pillars right next to each other. They couldn't see the ender crystals on top, but by the look of the pillars, he knew there would be three crystals at the summit.

"How do you want to do this, Gameknight?" Hunter asked as she scanned the sky for the dragon.

"Behind us!" Stitcher yelled.

Gameknight spun around and looked for the monster. It wasn't hard to find. Two bright purple eyes were focused down on the party and getting closer.

"Everyone get ready to scatter!" Gameknight shouted.

"Can't we just stop and fight it?" Monkeypants asked.

"No, it's too strong," his son answered. "That would truly be dangerous because— EVERYONE SCATTER!"

The dragon swooped down on the party, its claws outstretched, a roar bursting from its fanged mouth.

Gameknight999 shoved his father to the ground, then dove to the side, trying to get as low as possible. Blasts of air hammered down upon him as the great wings flapped directly overhead, the claws lightly scratching his armor. If he'd been one block higher, the damage would have been much, much worse.

As the beast passed by, Gameknight stood, but too soon. The dragon's tail whipped about as it climbed into the air and smashed into the User-that-is-not-a-user's chest again, throwing him across the pale ground.

"Gameknight!" Stitcher yelled as she ran to his side.

Dazed, he looked up and watched the dragon climb into the air. Flaming missiles streaked up at the beast, chasing the monster, one of them finding their mark in its scaled back. The monster flashed red, then turned and headed for the last ender crystals.

"User-that-is-not-a-user, are you alright?" Digger asked as he and Stitcher help him to his feet.

"Yeah, I forgot about the tail," Gameknight said.

He rubbed his chest plate. His fingers found a new crack that ran across his diamond coat, marking where the thorny tail had struck him.

"I'd recommend you don't do that again," Hunter said with a grin.

"Ahh, thanks for the advice," Gameknight replied. "Let's get this done."

"What's the plan?" Digger asked.

"Digger, Herder, you need to prepare the water for our fall. We'll come down right along the center pillar."

"What do you mean 'we'?" Monkeypants asked.

Gameknight ignored the question.

"Hunter, Stitcher, you need to keep the dragon busy while we're taking out the crystals," he continued.

"'We'?" Monkeypants asked.

Gameknight turned to Digger. "Signal for the Grassbrin and Treebrin. We'll probably need them, as well."

The big NPC nodded, then moved to a hill of End Stone. Holding his pick up high, he waved it at the light-crafters, who were still moving about The End, planting clumps of grass and trees.

"You still haven't explained 'we,'" Monkeypants said.

"I'm going to need your help ... up there," Gameknight said.

Monkeypants looked up at the tall pillars then back down at his son, his monkey-face now white.

"You have to be kidding," his father said.

"Look, this is Crafter's only chance," Gameknight999 said. "If we don't destroy the dragon, then none of these NPCs ever get out of The End. Eventually Feyd and his army of

endermen will arrive. We may only have minutes before hundreds of those dark monsters
are here. These crystals have to be destroyed
so we can take on the dragon, and I can't do
it alone. With three crystals up there, I'll need
you watching for the dragon while I'm shooting
them."

"But why can't Hunter go up with you?"

"You know why," Gameknight replied. "She
has to stay down here and keep the dragon
away from us, same with Stitcher."

"But Digger could—"

"Digger and Herder need to be down here
with the water," Gameknight answered. "If
the water isn't in the right place at the right
time, then we'll hit the ground too hard—game
over."

"But . . ."

Gameknight stepped up to Monkeypants
and put a hand on his shoulder, staring him
straight in the eye.

"Dad, I need you, here and now. If we fail,
then Crafter is dead as well as the rest of my
friends. I couldn't bear that kind of failure."

Gameknight took a step closer.

"Dad," he said. "You told me that sometimes
we must reach a little farther than we can, be a
little stronger than we are, and do things that
we normally wouldn't be able to, because we
must, to take care of those we love. Well, I'm
asking the same of you. I need you up there
with me because—"

"DRAGON!" Digger yelled.

Not looking where it was, everyone scattered and dove for the ground. Gameknight and Monkeypants both dove to the right, tumbling down into a recession and far from the razor-sharp talons that streaked by.

Hunter yelled out in pain, then shouted curses at the dragon. Carefully standing, Gameknight saw Hunter running after the flying monster, her bow singing as she fired arrow after arrow toward the beast.

"Are you OK?" Gameknight asked as he moved to her side.

"That stupid dragon got me with a claw," she replied.

Looking down, Gameknight could see a deep gouge in her armored leggings. The claw had sliced through the metal pants and had found the tender flesh the armor was supposed to protect. Pulling out an apple, Hunter ate it quickly, then gobbled down a piece of bread, letting her HP slowly rejuvenate. Limping, she headed toward the obsidian pillars, each step causing her face to cringe in pain.

"Let's get this finished one way or the other," she growled.

Stitcher moved to her sister's side and put her arm around her shoulder, helping her walk. Digger took Hunter's other arm and helped Stitcher with her older sister; clearly she was in a lot of pain.

"Come on, Dad," Gameknight said, "are you in, or out?"

Monkeypants looked at his son, then to

Hunter as she struggled to walk, her face contorted in agony.

He sighed. "I'm in."

"Great," Gameknight said, slapping his father on the back. "Let's get this done!"

They ran toward the last ender crystals. As they approached the impossibly tall structures, Gameknight searched the sky for the dragon, but could not find it. This made him nervous. Normally, the dragon liked to line up with its prey from far away and fly in a straight line toward them, claws extended.

"What are you up to, dragon?" Gameknight muttered to himself as he scanned the sky.

An enemy that can be seen is one that can be avoided. Gameknight knew this, and that was why he was so concerned. The Ender Dragon had disappeared, and who knows where it would appear . . . and when.

CHAPTER 32

LEAP OF FAITH

Gameknight moved to the base of the pillar, his father at his side.

"Does everyone understand the plan?"

"We got it. Let's get started," Hunter complained.

Gameknight turned to Digger.

"Remember, we'll come down by the center pillar," Gameknight said.

"We'll be ready," Digger answered. "But remember, this pillar is big. If you come down somewhere else, we may not be able to run around the perimeter fast enough to get some water on the ground before you ... well ... you know."

"He means smashes into the ground," Hunter added.

"Hunter!" Stitcher chided.

"Just wanted to make sure we're all on the same page," she replied. "Now let's get going.

I don't like the fact that the dragon seems to have disappeared—it could be anywhere."

"OK. Come on, Dad," Gameknight said, "lets start climbing."

Jumping in the air, Gameknight placed a block under his feet, then jumped again and repeated the move. Looking down, he saw his father still on the ground, a look of fear on his goofy monkey-face.

"Dad, I know you can do this, I believe in you," Gameknight said. "Right now, I need your help. I need you *here* with me. Can you do this?"

Monkeypants looked up at his son, then gritted his teeth and looked up at the top of the pillar. Frowning, his face took on a look of grim determination as he jumped into the air and place a block of End Stone under his feet.

"Alright!" Stitcher exclaimed.

Way to go, Dad! Jenny typed.

Monkeypants jumped again, placing another block under his feet, then kept going, passing his son.

"Alright, Monkeypants!" Hunter shouted. "Herder, put some water down around them in case they need to jump."

The lanky boy pulled out a bucket and poured it on the ground around Monkeypants's stack of End Stone, then pulled out another bucket and poured it by Gameknight's.

Looking down at his friends, Gameknight gave them a smile, then started climbing.

Quickly, the User-that-is-not-a-user caught up with his father.

"Dad, you look to the left and I'll watch to the right. If we see the dragon, we can jump off our stacks and land in the water below."

"Are you kidding? Jump? From this height?"

"In Minecraft, any amount of water can keep you from taking damage when you fall," Gameknight explained. "It's not like in the physical world. Here, even the thinnest layer of water will protect you, no matter how high you were. We're perfectly safe."

"Yeah, OK, if you say so," his father replied, his voice shaking with fear.

"Just get into the pattern: jump, place a block, jump," Gameknight said. "We'll be to the top in no time."

The father and son moved quickly up the side of the obsidian structure. They watched for the dragon, but saw nothing, and it worried Gameknight even more.

The dragon knows that we're going after these last three crystals, Gameknight thought. *Where is it, and what's it up to?*

After a few minutes, they made it to the top. Monkeypants quickly moved away from the edge and near the bobbing crystal that sat in a sheath of flame.

"Don't get too close, Dad," Gameknight said. "You'll get burned."

"You sound like a parent talking to a child," Monkeypants replied with a nervous smile.

"Well, in Minecraft, I *am* the parent and *you*

are the child," Gameknight said. "Now when I shoot these crystals, they're going to explode. Don't let the blast knock you off the edge."

"That is excellent advice," Monkeypants said as he looked for something to grab.

Pulling out his bow, Gameknight aimed for the far crystal.

"Dad, watch for the dragon," Gameknight said as he released his arrow.

The projectile streaked to the far crystal and hit the cube in the side. It instantly exploded, showering the pair with tiny crystal shards that stung when they reached exposed skin.

"Go to the far side, Dad, and watch for the dragon. I don't know where it is and it makes me nervous. It's out there somewhere, watching. I can feel it."

Monkeypants carefully wove his way around the remaining two crystals and stood on the far pillar, the flames there now extinguished.

"Get ready for the next one," Gameknight yelled as he drew back another arrow.

Releasing it, the projectile struck the crystal on the center pillar. The explosion rocked the pillars, making them sway back and forth a bit.

"Son," Monkeypants said as he looked straight up into the sky.

"Dad, what are you doing?" Gameknight asked.

"Gameknight," his father said, this time louder.

"Dad, what are you—"

"TOMMY! DRAGON!" Monkeypants yelled, pointing straight up into the air.

Gameknight looked up and saw the dragon coming straight down at them, its purple eyes blazing with anger and hatred. It had its massive wings fully extended as it plummeted; the scaly beast was like a bolt of black lightning. With its wings out, the monster would hit them both and send them falling to the ground. Drawing back another arrow, Gameknight got ready to fire. Glancing at his father, he could tell that his dad was petrified with fear.

I can't just leave him there; the dragon will get him. But he's too far from the center.

"Dad, go to the center and jump!" Gameknight yelled.

His father didn't move, his mind overwhelmed with fear.

I have to save him! But can I make it to him in time?

The roar of the dragon started to fill his ears. It was getting closer, and fast.

Dropping his bow, Gameknight sprinted for his father. As he ran, he pulled out his iron shovel.

If this doesn't work, then we're both dead, Gameknight thought.

Just before he slammed into Monkeypants, Gameknight spun around and threw his shovel at the last ender crystal. The iron tool tumbled end over end toward the bobbing cube, and then the father and son fell off the edge, the *whoosh* of the dragon's wings blowing air into their faces as they plummeted.

Grabbing his father firmly by the wrist, the User-that-is-not-a-user pulled out his iron pick. Reaching out, he slammed the sharp tip into the side of the obsidian pillar. The metal tool dug into the stone, not doing any damage, but still dragging against the dark cubes.

An explosion sounded from the top of the pillars; his shovel had found its target. The dragon screamed in rage.

"HERDER, DIGGER, HELP!" Gameknight screamed as they fell.

Pulling hard on the handle of his pick, he tried to dig the tip into the obsidian even deeper. Fragments of iron broke away from the pick as the hard stone wore done the metal, the tip beginning to heat up and glow red.

He could feel Monkeypants grow heavy in his grip—they were slowing.

"HANG ON, DAD ... WE'LL BE FINE!" Gameknight screamed, but his father didn't reply.

He looked down into his dad's face. It was white with fear, his mouth frozen open in mid-scream. His monkey-eyes darted about, looking for some kind of salvation. Far below, Gameknight could see Herder sprinting around the pillar, a bucket of water sloshing in one hand, Digger too far behind to be of any help. If they didn't make it to them in time ...

Glancing at Herder, Gameknight saw the lanky boy stumble for a moment, then sprint again. Suddenly, the boy jumped high up into the air and threw his bucket with all his strength. Digging his pickaxe deeper into the obsidian, Gameknight tried to slow their descent a little more. Looking down, he saw the brown pail fly through the air as they neared the ground. Gameknight could see the End Stone rushing up to meet them, but just before they hit, Herder's pail landed on the ground and split open, spilling its contents. The water flowed outward just as Gameknight and Monkeypants landed with a splash.

Sitting up, Gameknight looked at his father. Monkeypants stared back at him.

"I guess that could have been worse," his father said.

Gameknight laughed, then reached out and gave his father a huge hug.

Herder and Digger reached them and helped both of them to their feet.

"That was kinda close," Herder said. "Sorry I broke the bucket. I'll make a new one when we get back to the village."

"I don't think anyone is upset about the bucket," Digger said as he slapped the boy on the back. "That was a great throw."

"Thanks," Herder replied, beaming with pride.

Hunter and Stitcher arrived with arrows notched.

"What now?" Hunter asked.

"Now we lure the dragon to the ground," Gameknight said.

"How are we going to do that?" Stitcher asked.

"We're going to use some bait," the User-that-is-not-a-user replied.

"I don't think I'm going to like what you have in mind," Monkeypants said.

"Probably not," Gameknight agreed.

CHAPTER 33

RIDE OF HIS LIFE

They moved out into the open, all eyes scanning the dark sky for their adversary. Gameknight shot a glance to Crafter, Morgana, and the pig that sat nearby. Crafter looked weak, and the witch was giving him some kind of pinkish potion to drink. His friend cast him a thin smile, then pointed up into the air. Looking in the direction Crafter pointed, Gameknight saw a pair of purple eyes descending down at him from the darkness.

Sheathing his swords, Gameknight drew his bow.

"Everyone, ARROWS!"

Digger and Monkeypants pulled out their bows and started firing at the beast, Hunter's and Stitcher's flaming projectiles streaking out ahead of the others. The arrows should have kept the dragon at bay, but the monster kept flying straight ahead, its purple eyes focused on the User-that-is-not-a-user.

"Look out," Stitcher yelled, "HERE IT COMES!"

The dragon dove straight at Gameknight999, its razor-sharp talons extended. Looking about, the User-that-is-not-a-user found that there was nothing nearby, no cover behind which he could hide. He was out in the open.

"Well, if you can't retreat," he said, thinking of his friends Impafra and Kuwagata498, "then ATTACK!"

Drawing his two swords, Gameknight charged straight at the winged beast. Yelling at the top of his lungs, he swung his sword before him, hoping to distract the dragon, but it did not swerve or alter its course; it was still heading directly for him.

Suddenly, Treebrin streaked past him with lightning speed. Quickly, he placed a block of dirt between Gameknight and the dragon, then planted a tree and made it sprout to full size using his crafting powers. The tall spruce shot upward like a giant wooden missile, smashing into the dragon's belly and making it flash red.

Roaring out in pain, the Ender Dragon pivoted in the air, then beat its leathery wings as it climbed up into the sky, seeking the healing crystals that were no longer there.

Moving next to the light-crafter, Gameknight patted Treebrin on the shoulder.

"Thanks," the User-that-is-not-a-user said.

"Grrblrraa," the light-crafter mumbled.

Just then, Gameknight heard a wooshing sound behind him.

"Drraglarr!" Treebrin shouted.

Gameknight spun around just as the dragons claws raked across his armor, tearing into the diamond as if it were paper. Pain erupted through his nerves as if they were aflame, his head spinning. Stumbling, Gameknight999 fell to the ground.

"TOMMY!" Monkeypants shouted as he ran to his son. "Are you OK?"

"Just perfect," Gameknight growled, anger now starting to boil over in his mind. "I've had just about enough of this!"

Standing, he pulled out an apple and ate it quickly, then munched on a piece of pork. This let his HP start to rejuvenate. Gameknight knew his health would not come back instantly, but he couldn't wait. Nearby, Crafter was sitting on a piece of End Stone looking exhausted, Morgana giving him a sip from another potion. The ancient witch turned and looked at the User-that-is-not-a-user and shook her head.

Gameknight knew exactly what the look meant—he had to hurry or Crafter would die.

"Where's the dragon?" Gameknight shouted.

"Off that way," Herder said, pointing out into the darkness. "I saw it go in that direction after it hit you."

"It won't be out that way when it comes back," Gameknight explained. "Dragons always fly away into the darkness, then curve in a large arc so that they can come at their prey from a different direction."

Running to a small nearby hill, Gameknight

climbed to the crest and looked across The End.

"Everyone look for the purple eyes," the User-that-is-not-a-user said. "They'll show up first."

The NPCs scanned the surroundings, looking for their enemy, but all they saw was the dark starless sky.

"He's out there somewhere," Hunter said. "I can feel him watching us."

Suddenly, an ear-splitting roar crashed down upon them from directly above. Looking straight up, Gameknight could see the dragon diving straight down at them, its wings tucked, making the monster look like a dark missile.

"LOOK OUT!" Digger shouted.

Suddenly, the dragon spread its wings, slowing down right before it hit the ground. Pulling up, it swooped across the ground, flinging its long tail about like a whip as it climbed again. The pointed tail smashed into Gameknight999, crushing his chest plate and throwing him off the hill. He flashed red when he hit the ground, his body and mind stunned by the pain.

The Ender Dragon sensed the helplessness of his prey. Pivoting in mid-air, the monster dove toward the User-that-is-not-a-user. Its razor-sharp claws sparkled as it opened its mouth, the jagged white teeth that lined its jaws shining with ominous intent. Drawing in a huge breath, the monster bellowed an angry scream.

Gameknight struggled to stand, but the wind was knocked out of him and his head was ringing; he was confused and disoriented.

Looking toward his friends, Gameknight saw the strangest sight: Herder running straight toward him with a block of TNT in his hands. As he passed, the lanky boy gave Gameknight a quirky smile.

"Hi, Gameknight," Herder said as he sprinted straight toward the dragon.

When he was directly between Gameknight and the beast, he placed the explosive block on the ground, then darted to the right. The dragon, seeing the harmless block on the ground, ignored it and flew toward his defense-less victim. That was when Gameknight saw the flaming arrow streak through the air and hit the TNT.

BOOM!

The whole of The End shook with the blast as the TNT exploded. Screaming out in pain, the dragon tried to climb away from the fiery grip of the explosive, but it was too close. The explosion tore into the monster, making it flash red again and again as it broke a massive hole into the End Stone covered ground.

Roaring, the Ender Dragon climbed high into the air as more arrows streaked toward its body. Flapping its wings with all its strength, the monster disappeared into the darkness before Hunter or Stitcher could hit it with more of their barbed shots.

Standing, Gameknight shook his head as

the ringing slowly subsided. He reached up and rubbed his sore chest where the tail had struck him. A deep crack now ran across this chest plate, the armor nearly destroyed. The dragon's tail had hit him hard.

I don't think I can survive another hit like that, Gameknight thought.

Shaking his head again, he turned and found Herder. The skinny NPC was looking at his idol, a huge grin on his face.

"Thank you," Gameknight said to the boy, then turned and said the same to Hunter.

"No big deal," Hunter said. "Besides, it was fun, right Herder?"

The boy nodded his head, his long dark hair flinging about.

Gameknight laughed.

"OK everyone, keep your eyes sharp," Gameknight said. "The dragon will be back, and I bet it's really mad now."

I see it, Jenny typed. *It's coming at you from the right.*

Looking to the right, Gameknight could see tiny points of purple light sliding noiselessly over the landscape, low and fast.

"Here it comes," Gameknight said, pointing with a boxy finger.

In the distance, they could see two bright purple specs moving a hair's width above the pale landscape. But now, the eyes were burning with an overwhelming hatred for the NPCs, the blazing purple light from the dragon lighting the ground as it sped toward them.

"This is it," Gameknight999 said. "It's all or nothing, him or us. You can tell the monster is enraged beyond the point of rational thought— it will be more dangerous now than it ever has been, so everyone stay sharp."

"Great pep talk," Hunter said with a smile.

The User-that-is-not-a-user ignored her. He was focused on the flying demon that was about to crash down upon them.

Can I save my friends? Am I strong enough for this? Gameknight thought. *I have to stop the dragon before any of them get hurt.*

Charging forward with both swords in his hand, Gameknight ran toward the beast. They met next to the gigantic hole formed by the exploded TNT. The dragon's claws swiped out at him with incredible speed. Rolling across the ground, Gameknight evaded most of the pointed talons, but not all. One of the sharp claws tore into his arm, tearing his blue shirt and causing him to cry out in pain.

Hunter and Stitcher ran forward, but they were too far away to help Gameknight.

The dragon brought a deadly paw down upon the User-that-is-not-a-user. Jumping to the side, Gameknight could feel the talons just miss his head as the monster's fist smashed down upon the ground.

Digger was now running toward the pair, but he was also too far away. Only Monkeypants was close enough to help his son, but he was terrified, his body unable to respond to any commands.

Spinning on one of its gigantic rear feet, the dragon whipped its tail around, taking Gameknight's legs out from under him. He smashed to the ground, his swords slipping from his grasp—he was completely defenseless.

"No . . . NO!" Monkeypants yelled, his anger overpowering his fear. "THAT'S ENOUGH!"

Dropping his sword, Gameknight's father stormed straight toward the dragon, his blocky hand out before him, his index finger extended.

"NO MORE VIOLENCE OUT OF YOU!" Monkeypants yelled, overcome with rage. "THAT'S MY SON AND YOU AREN'T GOING TO HURT HIM ANYMORE."

As Gameknight's vision cleared, he shook his head and took in the scene. The dragon was hovering in place. The dragon looked confused while an apparently unarmed monkey approached him. As the monster stared at Monkeypants271, the User-that-is-not-a-user realized that this was his chance. Standing, he picked up his swords and stuffed them into his inventory. He then pulled out a slime block and sprinted for the small hill next to the dragon. Reaching the crest, Gameknight jumped high into the air. When he was about to hit the ground, he placed the slime block and then bounced high into the air, straight toward the dragon.

Soaring through the dark sky, Gameknight999 landed on the monster's scaly back. Wrapping one arm around the creature's long neck, he pulled out his diamond sword and struck at the beast, his father watching from the ground in shock.

His friends all stood far to one side. They fired arrows at the beast, trying to avoid hitting Gameknight, but they dared not get any closer; the dragon's tail was whipping about in all directions. To be too close could be fatal.

The Ender Dragon roared out in pain as the User-that-is-not-a-user hit him over and over again. Whipping his tail about, the dragon tried to strike at Gameknight999, but the pointed appendage just could not reach.

Attacking again and again, Gameknight drove his sword into the beast, making it flash red over and over again. The creature screamed out, more in fear than in pain, as its HP slowly ebbed from its body. The User-that-is-not-a-user continued the attack, tearing the HP from the monster. Finally, as its strength waned, it crashed to the ground in a heap right near Crafter and Morgana, throwing Gameknight from its back. Bright shafts of purple light shot out of the dark creature's body as it expired, the light illuminating The End and casting strange shadows on the ground. The monster roared and flung its tail about as the rays of light grew brighter and brighter. No one but Crafter noticed the tail strike the fence post to which Herobrine was tied. The wooden post suddenly shattered into splinters as it was destroyed by the last act of the Ender Dragon. The dark creature then exploded and disappeared, leaving behind a bedrock portal and a dragon's egg in its place.

Everyone cheered, except Crafter.

The infirmed NPC was chasing Herobrine. The pig was sprinting for the exit portal, the long rope trailing behind its soft pink body. The tiny creature worked loose the ropes around its snout and oinked loudly as it approached the exit portal, its eyes white hot.

"He's getting away!" Crafter yelled, but his feeble voice was barely audible.

"What?" Gameknight shouted, then turned to his friend. He was shocked at what he saw: Herobrine loose and trying to escape. "Quick, everyone get him!"

But no one was close enough except Crafter.

Gameknight ran toward his friend, but was still too far away to help. He watched as the young NPC used every bit of his strength to sprint forward, then dive into the air. Landing on the ground with a thump, Crafter was able to get one hand on the rope. Holding it tight, he pulled on the animal's leash, yanking the pink creature backward. Herobrine stopped suddenly and let out a wail of shock and despair.

Standing, Crafter carefully pulled in on the rope and brought the evil pig closer. Lifting the animal off the ground, he held Herobrine in his arms, careful to avoid his snapping teeth. Crafter walked to the massive hole that had been created by the exploding TNT. The explosive had carved a hole all the way through The End, revealing the dark void beneath the floating island of End Stone.

"This is where you go away, Herobrine,"

Crafter said as the terrified little pig stared up at his captor, its eyes glowing bright white. "I'm dropping you into the void where your evil will finally perish, for nothing survives the void." Crafter then glared at the pig and frowned. "You aren't going to hurt my friends anymore!"

And with that, Crafter dropped Herobrine into the gaping hole. But as the animal fell, it reached out with its blunt teeth and grabbed hold of the hem of Crafter's pants. The sudden jerk pulled Crafter off his feet and pulled him into the hole with Herobrine, disappearing from sight.

"Crafter!" Gameknight999 screamed. "CRAFTER!"

CHAPTER 34

THE PREY ESCAPES

Xa-Tul climbed out of the stronghold entrance, carving steps into the destroyed stairway as he ascended. When he finally reached the surface, he found a sea of endermen glaring down at him, hands balled into fists as a purple mist of teleportation particles surround each of the dark monsters.

"Hold!" screeched Feyd. "It's only a zombie."

Teleporting next to the newly formed stairs, the king of the endermen glared down at Xa-Tul, a look of excited expectation on his dark red face.

"Are you returning because the user and all his NPC friends are destroyed?" Feyd asked.

Xa-Tul looked up at the dark creature, then finished stepping out of the makeshift stairway.

"Well?" Feyd screeched.

"The User-that-is-not-a-user is gone,"

Xa-tul growled. "The zombies cannot find him anywhere in the stronghold."

"What? YOU LET HIM ESCAPE?!"

"It was the endermen's job to keep them from escaping, not the zombies'," the zombie king growled back.

"You are as stupid as you are incompetent," Feyd said, his eyes glowing bright white.

Xa-Tul gripped his sword firmly and raised it, ready for battle. "Be careful what is said to Xa-Tul," the zombie growled, his red eyes filled with rage.

Two endermen teleported next to Feyd, ready to defend their king.

"Everyone be calm," Feyd said, raising his long arms in the air and glancing around at his army. He faced Xa-Tul. "Tell me what happened in the stronghold."

Slowly, Xa-Tul lowered his sword, but did not put it back into his inventory.

"The zombies followed the enemy through the stronghold. They were pursued to the portal chamber where they sealed themselves in," Xa-Tul said. "The zombies spread out around the chamber to make sure the enemy did not tunnel through the walls and escape." The zombie king looked about at the endermen, then brought his gaze to their leader. "Escape from the chamber was impossible, but when Xa-Tul broke through and went into the portal chamber, silverfish burst from the blocks and attacked the zombies. Xa-Tul glanced into the chamber while fighting the filthy little creatures and could see the enemies were gone."

"Was the portal activated?" Feyd asked.

"What?" the zombie replied.

"The portal—was it working?" Feyd asked again. "Did they put Eyes of Ender in all the portal blocks?"

"Xa-Tul doesn't know anything about these Eyes of . . . whatever they are called," the king of the zombies replied.

"You FOOL!" Fey'd screamed. "They did not get out of the portal chamber. They went to The End."

"Why would the enemy do that?"

"Who knows why Gameknight999 does anything!" Feyd screeched. "We must get to The End before he accomplishes whatever he is planning. Quickly, get your zombies out of the stronghold. We're going to The End."

Xa-Tul looked up at the enderman, confused.

"Get your warriors up here!" Feyd commanded. "My endermen will take them to The End, NOW!"

The king of the zombies snarled, then went back down the steps. Feyd could hear the monster release a loud, angry growl that made the ground on which he stood vibrate and shake with fear.

"You won't escape me, Gameknight999," Feyd said. "Let's see what you do when you have the Ender Dragon on one side, and my army of endermen and zombies on the other."

The dark creature gave a maniacal, ender-man chuckle as his body became enveloped in a mist of purple particles.

"I'll see you soon, User-that-is-not-a-user. Very soon!"

CHAPTER 35

THE VOID

"**N**ooo!" Gameknight screamed as he sprinted for the hole.

Reaching the place where Crafter fell, Gameknight looked down into the gaping cavity. The TNT had torn an opening completely through The End, revealing the great endless void beneath the floating island of End Stone. On the edge of the hole, Crafter hung by one hand, his square fingers barely holding onto a block of End Stone. Dangling from his leg was Herobrine, the pig holding onto the end of Crafter's pant leg with his little teeth, his eyes glowing white.

"Crafter, are you alright?" Gameknight said as he knelt next to the edge.

"I'm not sure I can hang on for very long," his friend replied.

"Hold on, I'm coming."

The edge of the hole was sheer; Gameknight could not climb down to reach his friend.

Instead, he laid down on his stomach and reached down, extending his hand to the NPC.

"Grab my hand," the User-that-is-not-a-user said.

Crafter pulled up on his free hand and tried to reach but quickly gave up.

"I can't," the NPC said. "I'm so weak and Herobrine is too heavy. I don't think I can raise my hand up to reach you; it's hopeless."

"No it isn't!" Gameknight snapped. "You can do this. Try again."

Crafter gritted his teeth, then lifted his hand upward. Slowly, he raised his arm, grabbing up to the next block, but he couldn't quite get to it. Leaning farther into the pit, Gameknight reached down for his friend, trying to grasp his hand. Their fingers brushed against each other, then Crafter's hand fell back to his side.

"I can't do it. I can't," Crafter said, his voice sounding weak.

Gameknight could see the color in his friend's face starting to fade, his skin slowly becoming pale.

Morgana's potion is wearing off! Gameknight thought. *I need help.*

Gameknight could hear the shouts of his friends as the ran toward him, but he knew they were too far away to be of any help in time. He had to save Crafter on his own, right here and right now!

"I can see the worry on your face," Crafter said. "The potion is wearing off. I can feel it. This is hopeless."

"NO, IT'S NOT!" Gameknight shouted. "You have to try. If I crawl out of this hole without you, think about how mad Hunter is going to be. I'll never hear the end of it!"

The User-that-is-not-a-user smiled at his friend, then reached farther into the pit, trying to get his hand on his friend's wrist. But now, Gameknight realized that he'd gone too far and was starting to slide in. Ever so slowly, his body inched its way into the hole, moving farther and farther into the abyss that led to the void. Gameknight couldn't stop it. He tried to dig his square toes into the End Stone, but they could not find purchase to stop his slow descent.

He was going to fall!

Panic bubbled up from within the back of his mind.

If I fall, then Crafter will die! he thought. *What am I going to do?*

Fear ruled his thoughts to the point that he couldn't even speak. All he could do was stare down into Crafter's blue eyes. He felt so alone. Both of them wore looks of panic and terror as they slowly crept a little farther over the precipice.

"Gameknight, I see you slipping over the edge," Crafter said, his voice barely a whisper. "Just go back; it will be OK. It makes no sense for both of us to die. The others still need your help. If the User-that-is-not-a-user were to die, it would crush the spirit of NPCs everywhere. The monsters would win—you can't let that happen."

Gameknight could tell that Crafter was about to let go of the End Stone so that Gameknight would not risk himself.

Am I finally defeated? Gameknight thought. *Is this the end of my best friend?*

"Crafter, I never thought—"

"DON'T YOU DARE STOP TRYING!" sounded a loud voice from behind.

Suddenly, a pair of strong hands grabbed his legs and held them firm, stopping his slow crawl over the edge of the hole. Glancing over his shoulder, Gameknight could see a ridiculous looking monkey dressed in a Superman outfit holding onto his feet.

"You reach down there and save him, Gameknight999. That's your responsibility," Monkeypants said, a look of grim determination on his ridiculous monkey-face. "I don't care if you are getting tired or your muscles hurt. You do what you do best, and that is taking care of your friends.

"Thanks, Dad," Gameknight said.

"Don't worry son, I'm *here*—really here," Monkeypants said. "You do what you need to do. I have faith that you can save Crafter. Just get it done."

His father's faith in him filled the User-that-is-not-a-user with renewed strength. Looking back at Crafter, he reached farther into the pit, his dad anchoring him firmly to the ground. Stretching forward, Gameknight extended into the hole further than he ever could on his own.

"Come on, Crafter, try one more time!"

The young NPC looked even more pale now, his face looking sickly and strained. Gritting his teeth, Crafter used all his strength to reach up with his free hand. Leaning even farther into the hole, Gameknight extended his arm as far as he could. Their fingers brushed against each other again for just a moment and then the User-that-is-not-a-user lunged. Feeling something, he grabbed it—it was Crafter's sleeve.

"I've got you, Crafter," Gameknight said. "Now get rid of that thing on your leg."

Crafter looked down at their enemy. The pig's eyes were blazing with a harsh white glow, making it difficult to look at the beast. Herobrine slowly closed his eyes.

It's coming—the shadow of evil, Jenny typed in the chat. *It's heading straight for you!*

"The shadow is coming!" Stitcher yelled.

Gameknight could her the hum of her bow, but he knew that it would not slow the ghostly shade.

"Crafter, hurry," Gameknight said, looking deep into his friend's pale eyes. "If the shadow gets here and attacks . . ."

Gameknight didn't finish his sentence. He knew that the shadow would attack them all. If Monkeypants released his grip, then Gameknight and Crafter would fall into the void. If it attacked Crafter, surely he would die.

They had to hurry!

"Crafter, kick Herobrine, get him off your

leg, quick! Gameknight said. "But don't kick him hard enough to kill the little monster. You don't want to get infected with his XP. Just knock him loose!'"

Looking down at the little pink creature, it almost looked harmless with its eyes closed, but they all knew different. Pulling up his free leg, Crafter kicked Herobrine hard, then did it again and again.

"The shadow is almost there, hurry!"

"Gameknight, just let me fall," Crafter said. "The potion is wearing off and the shadow of evil is coming for me. I don't think I can survive another of Herobrine's attacks." Crafter looked up into his friend's eyes and a solemn peace came across his face. "It's my time, Gameknight, just let me go."

"NO!" the User-that-is-not-a-user shouted. "I will never let go—no matter how hard it is or how terrifying, I'm always going to be here for you. Ages ago, you taught me to be strong and never give up. 'Deeds do not make the hero, the fears they overcome defines them'— you taught me that. Now it's my turn to teach you something my father taught me: 'Sometimes you have to reach a little farther than you can and be stronger than you are because people are relying on you.'"

"But I'm getting so tired," his friend said, the color in his face slowly fading to bone white.

"I don't care if you're tired!" Gameknight shouted. "Your villagers are relying on you. Are you just going to give up and let your community suffer? What kind of crafter would that make you? Huh?"

Crafter scowled as this thought percolated through his head.

"It's getting closer," Hunter screamed. "HURRY!"

"Your villagers need you," Gameknight said in a soft voice. "We all need you. I need you."

"My villagers . . ." Crafter mumbled, then his face took on a visage of anger and determination.

Glancing down at the pig, Crafter scowled at the creature, then an animal-like growl came from the NPC.

"You've hurt too many of my villagers, and I won't allow you to hurt any more," Crafter said, his voice filled with strength and rage. "It's time for you to go!"

The fabric in Crafter's sleeve tore, causing the NPC to start slipping from Gameknight's tenuous grip.

"Dad, get me farther down!" Gameknight yelled over his shoulder.

Monkeypants held onto his son's legs with an iron grip, then pushed him farther into the hole. If the shadow of evil hit him, he'd likely lose his grip on his son.

"Herder, grab my waist and help me!" Monkeypants yelled.

Suddenly, a thin pair of arms wrapped around Monkeypant's waist, then a pair of stocky arms grabbed hold of the lanky boy's legs.

Moving forward, Monkeypants lowered his son farther down into the hole.

Gameknight smiled at Crafter, and with lightning speed, grabbed his wrist, holding on with all his might. Crafter looked up at Gameknight, and a look of determination came over his face.

Out of the corner of his eye, Gameknight could see the shadow of evil reach the far side of the hole and move quickly along its perimeter. Crafter glanced at the dark stain of hatred, then looked back at Gameknight999. Without losing eye contact with his friend, Crafter kicked with all his might, smashing into Herobrine with his iron-covered boot, then kicked again and again until the hem of his pants tore away just as the shadow of evil reached them.

Herobrine squealed, his piggy voice filled with terror. Instantly, the shadow of evil disappeared as the monster lost its concentration while it fell into the void. Gameknight watched as the vile creature plummeted into the darkness, its eyes blazing bright white. The two eyes grew smaller ... and smaller ... and smaller until they finally blinked out, their glowing hatred extinguished by the void.

Herobrine was gone.

CHAPTER 36

ESCAPING THE END

Monkeypants pulled his son up out of the gaping hole, Crafter dangling from Gameknight's grasp. They landed in a heap, bodies tumbling on top of each other. Struggling to get out of the pile, Gameknight looked down at his friend. Gameknight breathed a sigh of relief when he saw color had returned to Crafter's face; the taint of evil that had resided in the NPC's body now gone after its master's demise. He then looked down at Monkeypants, Herder, and Digger. They all had cubes of sweat across their faces; each looked exhausted from keeping Gameknight and Crafter from falling to their deaths.

"Thank you, all of you," Gameknight said, and then a smile slowly grew on his boxy face. "We saved Crafter and destroyed Herobrine. Minecraft is safe!"

"Minecraft is safe!" Herder echoed as he stood and wrapped his arms around Crafter.

"We aren't safe yet!" Hunter said from the top of a small End Stone hill.

"What are you talking about?" Digger asked. "We destroyed the dragon, sent Herobrine into the void, and saved Crafter. What else is there to worry about?"

"Ummm . . . how about an army of zombies and endermen?" she replied.

"What are you talking about?" Gameknight asked.

"Get up here and see," Hunter replied, "but stay low. We don't want them to see us, yet."

Gameknight climbed the hill, then laid down on his stomach next to Hunter. Across The End, endermen were materializing in clouds of purple mist, a zombie held in each of their long, dark arms. As soon as they appeared, the monsters spread out in all directions.

"Are you kidding me!" Gameknight exclaimed. "Can't we ever get a break!"

"It looks like they're looking for something," Stitcher said.

"Yeah, us," Hunter replied. "We need to get out of here. There are too many of them for us to fight."

"Agreed," the User-that-is-not-a-user replied.

Looking to where the dragon had finally died, Gameknight saw an exit portal that had popped into existence. It was made of bedrock and floated two blocks off the ground. Torches were placed on the faces of the central pillar, lighting the structure and showing the delicate dragon's egg, which set precariously on top.

"If we run straight for the exit portal, they will see us and teleport to our position," Stitcher said. She had climbed up the hill and now lay right next to Gameknight. "But if we follow that recession to the left for a little while, then we can run out and go straight to the portal. That will reduce the time we can be seen."

"That's perfect," Gameknight said as he tussled her red curls. "Come on, let's get out of here."

They slid back down the hill, then stood and walked to the others.

"Everyone, Stitcher has a plan," Gameknight said. "Listen to her, for she is going to lead us out of here."

"Lead, me? No, no, no—I just had the idea, but you're the leader—"

"We don't have time for your complaining. Just lead us out of here," said the User-that-is-not-a-user.

Stitcher smiled up at Gameknight999, then put away her bow and adjusted her armor.

"OK, here's the plan," she explained. "We're going to follow the edge of that rise, staying low so we won't be seen. When I tell you, we'll run up the hill and sprint for the exit portal. Everyone put away your weapons and get out buckets of water. If an endermen gets close, douse them and keep running. Got it?"

They all nodded.

Casting them a nervous smile, Stitcher led

them along the gentle recession, keeping their heads low so as to not be seen. Gameknight stayed right on Crafter's shoulder in case he was still weakened from his battle with Herobrine. Morgana followed right behind, a healing splash potion in her hand in case someone needed it.

When they reached the right spot, Stitcher stopped and turned to look at everyone.

"This is it. Everyone ready?" the young girl asked.

Gameknight looked at everyone and saw heads nodding.

"Let's do this, quick and quiet," Stitcher said. "Now!"

They ran up the gentle rise and bolted for the exit portal. Instantly, a shriek filled the air as an endermen saw them sprinting across the pale landscape. This was followed by more screeches as the dark monsters teleported nearby.

"Throw your water on the ground around us!" Gameknight yelled.

They tossed their pales of water on the ground, creating a watery shield that would keep the endermen back, but it had little effect on the zombies they had brought with them. The decaying green monsters waded through the water, their arms outstretched, claws reaching for new victims. Thankfully the water slowed their progress; the monsters couldn't get to them in time.

Stitcher was the first to reach the exit

portal. She placed a block on the ground, then jumped up and fell into the dark, star-filled depths. When Hunter reached the portal, she carefully stood on the bedrock rim and waited for the others, her bow singing its deadly song as she fired at the approaching monsters. Monkeypants climbed to the makeshift steps but froze when he saw the endless depth of the portal. Rather than waiting for him to complain, Hunter kicked him in the behind, sending him falling into the portal, his monkey-like scream filling the air. Crafter climbed the stairs and leapt into the portal with Morgana and Digger, the light-crafters following close behind, leaving just Gameknight999 and Hunter.

Suddenly, a screeching cackle filled the air as Feyd materialized next to the exit portal. Quickly, Gameknight and Hunter threw the last of the buckets to the ground, surrounding the portal with a wide pool of water. It would keep the endermen away, but would do little for the zombies that were now closing in on them from all sides. In the distance, the hulking form of Xa-Tul stormed toward them, his massive broadsword in his hand.

"So we meet again, User-that-is-not-a-user," Feyd said in a high-pitched voice. "I see you have murdered our dragon."

"Murdered? It attacked us, as it always does," Gameknight replied.

"The Ender Dragon responded to your invasion," the enderman said. "But I can see that you really came here to steal the dragon's egg.

You are nothing but a common thief and a coward. Come down here and face me in battle; it is inevitable."

"I don't want to fight you, Feyd," Gameknight replied. "I just want to leave. We came here to finally rid Minecraft of the virus, Herobrine, and that is done. Now it is time for us to leave."

"Herobrine?" Xa-Tul growled as he approached.

Hunter laughed.

"You thought he was dead after the Last Battle," she said. "You are as stupid as you are foul-smelling. That monster wasn't dead; we had only captured him. But now he's gone, for we threw him into the void. Herobrine is now truly dead."

Xa-Tul growled up at her and took a step forward, but Feyd extended a long arm and restrained the zombie.

"This is not the time to destroy them, my green brother," Feyd said. "Their time will come soon enough."

"Xa-Tul will follow them with the zombie army," the king of the zombies growled.

"Ha!" Hunter laughed. "Now who is the Fool? The exit portal only works for NPCs and users. You'll have to chase us some other way, zombie!"

Xa-Tul growled, but Feyd put a calming hand on the monster's shoulder, then looked up at Gameknight999, his eyes glowing bright. This time, the User-that-is-not-a-user refused to look away.

"You can run from me for only so long," Feyd screeched, "but eventually, we will find you again and you will face me in battle. I will have my revenge while I watch you suffer."

"We'll see, enderman," Gameknight growled, "we'll see."

And with that, Hunter and Gameknight999 stepped back and fell into the exit portal, disappearing from The End.

CHAPTER 37

PAYMENT

The bright square face of the sun filled Gameknight's vision as he slowly opened his eyes. Above him was a clear blue sky, boxy white clouds drifting off toward the horizon.

Reaching out, he could feel blades of grass between his blocky fingers. They felt warm, and peaceful, and alive. The mooing of a cow made Gameknight look to the left. In the distance, the brown spotted animal meandered about, its head buried in the grass, munching its fill. A pig oinked on the other side of him. Standing quickly, he drew his sword and faced the beast.

"It's just a pig," Hunter said from behind.

Turning, he found his friend standing there with no weapon in her hands. Sadly, it looked strange not seeing her bow at the ready, an arrow pointed at some kind of monster. How accustomed he'd become to violence.

"Where is everyone else?" Gameknight asked as he looked around.

They were on a grassy plain, a forest off to their left and right. Suddenly, a cheer erupted as a hundred voices rose up in celebration, their jubilant cries coming from behind a nearby hill.

"I think that's them," Hunter said. "Come on, let's catch up."

She ran toward the cheering, her crimson hair bouncing about with each step like so many coiled scarlet springs. Gameknight looked around one more time. Seeing that there were no monsters chasing them for the first time in a long while, he followed his friend, a smile creeping across his face.

Running to the peak of the hill, Gameknight stopped and looked down on the celebration. The exit portal had transported them to Crafter's village. From the crest of the hill, he could see the stone wall that ringed the village, a deep moat surrounding the community. The iron doors in the wall were wide open and NPCs were streaming out of the village, choking the narrow bridge that spanned the watery channel. Standing out on the grassy plain were his friends, with Crafter standing at the front of their party. The villagers were all running toward him, each wanting to hug their now-healed leader.

As he stood there, looking down upon the celebration, Hunter reached Crafter's side and said something to him. The young NPC looked up at the hill and smiled at him, then waved for Gameknight to join them.

Nodding his head, Gameknight sprinted down the hill and ran toward the massive party. Instantly, he was mobbed by villagers. When he reached Crafter's side, he found Digger's children, Topper and Filler, clinging to their father's blocky form. Turning, they ran toward Gameknight999 and jumped into his arms, hugging him with all their strength.

"You did it," Topper said. "You saved Crafter!"

"We knew you could," Filler added.

"It wasn't just me," Gameknight objected. "It was *us!*"

Crafter moved to the User-that-is-not-a-user's side and placed a hand on his shoulder. Gameknight turned and looked into his friend's now bright blue eyes.

"Thank you," Crafter said. "I know you risked a lot to save me."

"I only did what you would have done for me," Gameknight answered.

Crafter nodded, then reached over to Monkeypants. Pulling on his armor, he brought the father to his son's side.

"Your son has helped me and my people so many times that we don't have the words to properly thank him," Crafter said. "And now you are a part of that problem, as well. Monkeypants, you too risked yourself to help us, and for that we are all grateful. Forever, Monkeypants271 will be a part of this community—no, this family."

"I am honored, Crafter," Monkeypants replied. "Thank you, but I only came here because I knew I couldn't stop my son from helping you. And I needed to accompany him so that he would know that I was here, really here."

Monkeypants turned and faced his son.

"And I'm going to be here more and more, son."

"What do you mean?" Gameknight asked.

"I finally sold one of my inventions for *a lot* of money," Monkeypants said. "On my last trip, I sold the digitizer."

"The digitizer?" Gameknight asked.

Monkeypants nodded his head.

"I can't say who the company is until the sale is complete," his father explained, "but I won't need to be traveling as much. We'll be spending so much time together that you'll get sick of me."

"Will we be able to keep our digitizer?" Gameknight asked.

Monkeypants smiled, knowing what his son was really asking.

"Yes, you can come visit your friends, but only if I'm with you to make sure you're safe."

"Monkeypants271 is going to make sure Gameknight999 is safe?" Hunter asked, then laughed. "He's the one saving everyone else, including you, and you're going to keep him safe?" She laughed again, but this time it was echoed by many of the villagers.

Morgana then stepped forward and faced Crafter.

"You have a debt to pay, and it's time that I collected," the witch said.

Many of the villagers looked at the old sorceress and frowned, their distrust for her evident on their faces. Digger moved forward and scowled at the villagers, daring them to say something negative to Morgana. Seeing his gaze, the NPCs stepped back and looked to the ground.

"Morgana, we made a bargain with you so that you would help Crafter, and now we will meet our end of the bargain," Gameknight said. "What is it you ask of us? Name your price."

"I used my rarest potion to help save your crafter," Morgana explained. "And I risked my life on this insane adventure, even helping to destroy the evil Herobrine. I deserve payment, and you agreed to give it, no matter how much I ask!"

"Just name your price, witch," Digger said.

The witch frowned as she looked up at the stocky NPC.

"We agreed," the User-that-is-not-a-user said. "Just tell us what you want."

"You must pay what I ask," Morgan reminded.

Gameknight nodded his head, then looked at Digger and Crafter. They, too, nodded their heads. "State your price, Morgana."

She looked about at the villagers who sur-rounded them. Many were still frowning at her, but most had released their distrust, at least for now.

"What I ask is big—the most valuable thing that I crave," she said.

"Morgana, just tell us what you need and it will be freely given," Crafter said, placing a hand on her arm.

She nodded as she gazed into Crafter's bright blue eyes.

"Fine. I want ..." She looked nervously around at the villagers. "I want ... to be a part of this village."

The NPCs gasped in surprise.

"I want to be part of a community again," Morgana said. "You said that I could have anything for my help. Well, that is what I require."

Gameknight looked to Crafter, then Digger, then turned his gaze on the villagers. Some of them were frowning, but many were nodding their heads.

"Well," the User-that-is-not-a-user said as he looked at Crafter. "It's your village."

"This is the easiest thing for us to give," Crafter said in a loud voice. "You are always welcome amongst us. This will be your new home, Morgana, if you choose."

For the first time since meeting the witch, Gameknight saw a smile appear on the wrinkled face. In that moment, things finally seemed complete. But as he was about to say something, the music of Minecraft swelled in volume. He could tell that everyone heard the music, for the villagers stopped their celebration and just listened to the beautiful tune. Even the Oracle approved.

Gameknight turned to his father.

"Dad, are you ready to go home?" Gameknight asked.

Monkeypants looked at their surroundings, then back to the village, its stone wall standing tall. He brought his gaze back to his son and smiled.

"I was thinking maybe we'd first build Castle Gameknight, right over there," his father said, pointing off to the side of the village. "I was thinking of a concentric castle with a stone keep at the center. Perhaps with an outer wall rigged with redstone and an inner wall holding a few surprises. Maybe we could build some laboratories for Morgana, so that she can make her potions and experiment with them."

Morgana nodded her head, her smile growing.

"Well, what do you think?" Monkeypants271 asked. "You wanna build?"

Gameknight999 nodded and smiled. He had his father—*here*, with him, in Minecraft. And for the first time in a long time, things felt right.

EPILOGUE

Feyd walked nervously about through The End. He didn't like being without an Ender Dragon. He could feel the healing powers of their teleportation particles growing weaker in the absence of the dragon. Somehow, the HP they derived from their teleportation was linked to the dragon, and without the flying creature, they were dying.

But they still had the egg.

The king of the endermen could tell that it would hatch soon, and with that a new Ender Dragon would be born and they would be saved. But when would it hatch? He was getting impatient.

"Maybe we could crack it a little and let the dragon out," one of the endermen had suggested.

Feyd had pummeled the idiotic endermen with his fists, bringing him to within a hair's breadth of nonexistence, then stopped and let him live so that he could be an example to the others.

But now, the moment was near. The egg had begun rocking back and forth as tiny cracks snaked their way across the dark shell. Bright light seeped through the opening, lighting the area around the egg.

"Shouldn't the light be purple?" one of Feyd's generals asked. "The light coming out of the egg is white instead. Why would that be?"

"Who knows," the endermen king answered. "And who cares? As long as we have a dragon again, then everything will be alright."

The egg moved again. A crack widened, allowing more harsh light to escape from its interior. It was so bright that Feyd had to look away.

Why is the light so harsh and intense? Feyd thought. *Something is not right.*

The egg rocked back and forth as the fissure grew wider and wider until finally—

CRACK!

The egg split open, revealing a tiny little dragon, its wings tucked in close to its sides. The creature's long neck was wrapped around its body, its beautiful head nestled on its back. Slowly, the creature opened its mouth, and Feyd could see rows of white razor-sharp teeth. Each would be able to pierce armor when the creature was full grown.

Kneeling, Feyd reached out for the creature, but it snapped at his hands with its sharp, jagged teeth and gave a tiny roar of annoyance.

"That's peculiar; they always want to be carried through their first teleportation," Feyd said.

"Why hasn't it opened its eyes yet?" the general asked.

Feyd looked down at the creature and noticed that it still had its eyes shut. Normally, the creature would be taking in its surroundings, its purple eyes looking at everything, but this dragon still had its eyes closed as if it were hiding something.

"Ender Dragon, what is wrong?" the king of the endermen asked.

The monster turned its head up toward him but kept its mysterious eyes closed, instead spreading its leathery wings. Flapping them once, the tiny dragon leapt up into the air. It flew in a tight circle, then landed on a block of End Stone, eyes still shut.

"You see that?" the general asked. "It flew—they never fly this young. And it still has its eyes closed. Our Ender Dragon didn't even need to look to see where it was going."

"Be quiet!" Feyd snapped.

Moving close to the dragon, Feyd knelt again, looking straight into the face of the flying beast.

"What is wrong with your eyes?" the enderman asked. "Open them so that we can see their color and be assured that you are well."

The dragon pointed its head directly at the king of the endermen, then slowly opened its eyelids. A harsh white glow came from eyes that were filled with such malice and hatred, it almost hurt to look upon the creature. Instantly, Feyd recognized the glow and bowed his head low to the ground. Glancing to his side, he looked at the other endermen and motioned them to also bow or suffer his wrath. The creatures of The End all knelt and bowed before the tiny dragon, many of them not sure why.

"Endermen, this is a special day," Feyd shouted, his head still down. "For behold . . . the return of the Maker!"

playing PvP against me, probably because I'm terrible at PvP and always seem to lose. Oh well!

Keep those stories coming in, I love posting them on my website.

Keep reading and watch out for creepers.

– Mark

me every time I start a new book. But a quote from my favorite author, Ray Bradbury, says it all: "You only fail if you stop writing."

If you get stuck in your writing, look at the Story Fun section of my website to get ideas. There are some great story beginnings that will jump-start your imagination.

I've started going on to Minecraft servers again with my son and have found some really interesting ones. In fact, Gameknight999 and I have also started our own server called SuperCraft. Pictures of the server and the IP address are on my website. Come onto SuperCraft and say hello! But I also like going on to other servers as well. Of course there are the classics, like Mineplex and Hypixel, but I've found some new ones like Vortex and Mythcraft. I've been especially enjoying many of the new skyblocks servers out there as well. We've been looking at the fantastic server tutorial videos from LBEGaming on YouTube, and he has been kind enough to help us set up our server. He clearly knows a lot about Minecraft servers, and his help in setting up our server has been greatly appreciated. Check out his YouTube channel and see if you can learn something new. If you see quadbamber (LBEGaming) out there on our server, be sure to say hello, and look for me, Monkeypants271 and Gameknight999, as well. Maybe we can play one of the many minigames together that we have on our server if I'm not building Gameknight's castle. Readers seem to like

NOTE FROM
THE AUTHOR

I am deeply touched by all the kind emails I get through my website, www.markcheverton.com. I try to reply to them all, but if you type your email address incorrectly, then I cannot reply. Sorry!

It is incredibly gratifying to hear that so many of you are reading more and more. That is wonderful, but I am especially excited to hear that many of you are starting your own Minecraft stories. Writing is a fantastic thing; you can create your own characters and the world they live in and take them on incredible adventures, like I have done with Gameknight999 and his friends. I recently read a quote from Ben Franklin that I think is appropriate here: "Either write something work reading, or do something worth writing." I love that quote and try to keep it in mind every day. You should, too. Maybe helping out a friend is something worth writing about; helping someone in Minecraft, or at school—anything and everything is worth writing about. I know it can be scary starting your story; it's terrifying for

EXCERPT FROM DESTRUCTION OF THE OVERWORLD

Gameknight999 leapt out of the minecart when it emerged from the tunnel and into the new crafting chamber. Instantly, his heart sank when he saw the items strewn about on the sandy cavern floor.

They were too late. The endermen had already been here and had wreaked terrible destruction on this village. Not waiting for anyone else, Gameknight charged up the sandstone steps that led to the tunnels and the surface, his mind blinded with rage.

"Gameknight, wait for the others!" Crafter shouted, but was ignored.

Pushing open the iron doors, he bolted through the round chamber and sprinted through the tunnel that would take him to the vertical ladder. As he ran, he could hear footsteps echoing behind him. Gameknight999 readied himself for battle. Stitcher emerged from the darkness and skidded to a halt.

"Come on, let's go," she said, then streaked past him.

He sprinted after her. More footsteps sounded behind him, but he ignored them and just ran, hoping to get to the surface and save someone, anyone. Scaling the tall ladder, he moved his hands and feet in a constant rhythm, climbing as fast as he could. When he reached the top, he saw Stitcher's lithe form climbing the ladder that would take her to the topmost level of the watchtower.

Leaping high into the air, he grabbed the third rung and climbed after her. In seconds, he was at the top of the tower. All around, the village, more items sat discarded on the ground, the tools and food left to decay in the sun. All the villagers were gone, destroyed by Feyd and his army of monsters.

Gameknight growled.

"We're too late!" he snapped.

"But just barely," Stitcher said as she pointed out across the desert dunes.

In the distance, Gameknight999 could see the army of endermen moving away from the village, the dragon flying high above, carving out lazy circles above the dark nightmares. He could just barely make out a dark red ender-man at the head of the formation; it was his enemy, Feyd.

Drawing his sword, Gameknight turned toward the ladder, but Stitcher's hand grabbed the back of his armor.

"You can't go out there," she said. "There

are too many of them and too few of us. It would be suicide."

Gameknight turned his head and glared at his friend, but knew she was right. Sheathing his sword, he moved back to the tower's edge and stared out at the enemy forces. Below, he could hear his friends moving out into the village, looking for survivors; he knew they would find none.

Just then, the dragon turned and stared back at the village.

"Quick, HIDE!" Gameknight shouted to Stitcher and those below.

Gameknight ducked behind one of the stone crenellations that ringed that tower's peak. Looking to Stitcher, he could see that she had done the same, hiding behind a stone cube. Somehow, Gameknight could feel the monster through the fabric of Minecraft. He didn't understand it, but he could sense the monster in the distance—and there was something familiar there, a feeling he'd felt before. Chancing a glance, Gameknight peeked around the block's edge. In the distance the dragon hovered in the air, staring back at the village. It was surrounded by sparkling purple teleportation particles, but also intermixed was a cloud of sickly yellow particles that gave the monster a sinister and diseased look. When the creature turned its head, Gameknight expected to see the purple eyes staring back at him, but to his surprise, they were absent. In their place blazed two intense white rectangles, the hatred of a thousand suffering lives held within those eyes.

And at that moment, Gameknight recognized his enemy—Herobrine.

Somehow, the terrible virus had survived the void and now infected the Ender Dragon. Gameknight pulled his head back and sat on the ground, his back against the stone block, his mind reeling.

"Gameknight, what's wrong?" Stitcher asked. "You're as pale as a skeleton."

"Look at the eyes of the dragon, but be careful so that it doesn't see you."

Stitcher leaned out just enough to move one eye past the block. A gasp escaped her mouth as she pulled back and sat down, her face as white as Gameknight's.

"It's Herobrine," she whispered as though she did not want the distant dragon to hear her.

Gameknight nodded his head.

"But how can that be?" she asked.

He shook his head as thoughts exploded in his mind.

We threw him into the void, he thought. I saw him fall, saw his terrible eyes blink and go out. How can he still be alive?

Memories of every battle with the terrible monster replayed themselves as he sat there, shaking with fear.

How am I going to stop him now? He's a dragon!